Briana

DARK EDITION

Also by Carmen Rosales

Hillside Kings Series

Hidden Scars

Hidden Lies

Hidden Secrets

Hidden Truths

Cartel Kings

Cartel Kings Book One

Steamy Romance Standalone's

The Sweat Box

Until Us

Love or Honor

The Prey Series

Thirst

Lust

Appetite

Forgive Me For I Have Sinned

Forbidden Flesh

Dark Romance

Dirty little Secrets

Sugar Coated Secrets

Like A Moth To A Flame

Giselle

To my husband and children thank you for all your support.

"Our lives begin to end the day we become silent
about things that matter."

MARTIN LUTHER KING, JR.

Trigger Warning

This story contains content that might be troubling to some readers, including, but not limited to, rape, death, references of death, suicide, vivid nightmares, bad language, abuse, child hood trauma, and PTSD. Please be mindful of these and other possible triggers. Seek help if needed and do not read. This is a dark romance and if these types of scenes or references trouble you **please do not read**.

All she wanted was his love.
All he gave her was his pain.

Briana knew Jaden Cyprus was broken. Even with her dark past, it didn't stop her from falling in love with him. She thought he wanted her. She thought he cared about her. He promised to protect her, but girls like her aren't so lucky. He didn't break her heart; he obliterated what was left. Now, her time is spent picking up the pieces of her shattered life and starting over.

The Destroyer) Cyprus Pro MMA fighter is living his dream undefeated. His regret...letting the girl of his dreams go for selfish reasons. One night, he sees Briana in the last place he never thought she would end up.
He thinks she is the same girl he first met.

But he's wrong...

Author's Note

Please note, Briana is part of my Dark Room. On my website I have two categories in the book section listing steamy romances and dark romances. This is dark and may touch on topics that are sensitive to some. Although it will not be my darkest to date, it is still dark.

It is for mature audiences only. Please be mindful of triggers. Please have patience for Nate, Giselle, Jaden and Briana. They come from a really dark place.

Briana
DARK EDITION

CARMEN ROSALES

Briana

"Brie, did you know?" Giselle asks, coming into the private dance room at the dance studio. We keep a private dance room for pole dancing out of sight from the younger children enrolled in ballet classes. Pole dancing is something I have perfected from dancing at the Doll House since I was eighteen when I moved out of my mother's trailer.

The Doll House is a dance club Giselle and I worked at before moving to Las Vegas with Jaden and Nate.

Giselle lives with Nate and I live in one of Jaden's apartments. According to Nate, Jaden has a troubled past and dislikes talking about it. He refuses to allow anyone in his house except for Nate.

We all have a way to hide our demons.

Holding the metal pole with both hands and steadying myself in my six-inch heels, I ask Giselle, "Hear what?"

Even if I'm not dancing at the club anymore in our hometown, I give lessons to those who want to learn the art of pole dancing. I also help market the dance studio for Giselle and help her with signing her students up for classes.

Instead of dancing for money, I instruct people while attending college. As a Juilliard graduate, Giselle teaches ballet and performs monthly at the Las Vegas Center of Performing Arts.

Nate loved her so much he bought her the dance studio so she could live her dream and keep dancing and teaching the art of ballet. I'm happy for them both and for finding each other. I'm also lucky to have found Jaden. Other than Giselle, he is the only other person I love.

"I was talking to Nate at the gym, and he broke the news that Jaden is going pro." Her eyes light up. "He's going to fight." She closes the door so no one can hear our conversation. "Didn't he tell you?"

Shaking my head with worry, I want to feel excited but a sense of unease washed over me. "He didn't mention anything to me this morning or last night."

Why didn't he tell me? I thought we didn't keep secrets about our plans, but maybe he didn't know how I would react. He is passionate about fighting and managing the gym.

For Jaden, failure is not an option.

It is why he is the most sought-after manager in MMA. Any fighter would do anything to have Jaden Cyprus manage them.

Jaden was brought up in the foster system with Nate. They both have made a fortune and quite the name for themselves. A rag to riches story. The underdogs gone pro.

"Well...knowing Jaden and how private he is, I'm not surprised. Has he taken you to his house yet?" she asks, lowering her voice on the last part, not wanting anyone to overhear our conversation if they eavesdrop outside the door.

Giving her a deflated look. Giselle senses something is off.

It was one of the things I had been secretly hoping for when he would finally let me in. Literally.

"No," I tell her.

Even as I say the two-letter word, it's also because I

haven't pressed the issue with him letting me stay at his house. His main home is like a panic room; only Nate is allowed inside. Jaden landed in the foster care system because his parents were inhumane and abused him, but no one, not even Nate, knows the details.

It's probably why he insisted on having me live in the apartment. He stays with me most nights unless he has a fight to attend with Nate or another engagement or he is training late, which has been the norm for the last six months. Now, thinking about it, he has been planning to go pro sooner than I thought.

Giselle places her hands on her hips, clearly annoyed that he hasn't taken me to his house or even discussed his plans with me. It's obvious Jaden is comfortable with the arrangement of me living in the apartment and not allowing me inside his personal living space, and personally, I can understand.

I also come from a horrible past of neglect and abuse. Except mine was the sexual kind. An upbringing of no food or acceptable clothing and always being threatened with eviction. The kind of abuse that involves your mother being so high she can't speak coherently or remember a single thing the next day. Sometimes, I had to use a neighbor's garden hose to shower in the middle of the night because she was too high to work and didn't have enough money to pay the utilities.

My mother is a heroin addict and would sell me for her next hit if she could. She doesn't remember who my father is. He could have been anyone. A drug dealer. The neighbor living in the trailer next door. My father could have been *anyone* from my neighborhood. Luckily, her drug use and her involvement with Jack landed her in jail for some time.

"That's fucked up, Brie. Are you serious?"

My hands slide down the metal pole in defeat. "Yeah, but it doesn't matter, Giselle. He said someday, but that day hasn't come. And I'm not going to pressure him. I understand. If he doesn't feel comfortable letting me in that part of his life. Then, I have to accept it. It goes both ways."

"You mean it's convenient for you because you don't have to tell him everything you have been through. Things you never told me. The only way I found out—"

"Please don't say it," I whisper, my eyes pleading.

Her being raped by Jack, my mother's drug dealer, because I asked her to come with me to help my mother was all my fault. It's a knife twisted inside my heart because I know I'm to blame. She was never supposed to be there, and I almost lost her.

I wonder where we would have ended up if it hadn't been for Nate and Jaden. They got us out of South Dakota and vowed to protect us like our guardian angels. Well, maybe like gatekeepers of hell.

I was getting beat up while they made me watch. I wake up in cold sweats, reliving that moment and every other dark moment from my past. No one knows I still have flashbacks when I sleep or that sometimes I like it when Jaden doesn't come home late at night to have him see me go through the aftermath of my nightmares.

She is right. It is convenient to not have him invite me to live with him inside his home or sleepover. What if he found out what happened?

Her eyes soften because I have repeatedly expressed my regret about what happened, asking her to get involved in helping me clean up my mess with my mother. Giselle was trying to help me out when my mother asked me to give her money or Jack and his miscreants would hurt her. All that did was channel their attention on us.

"I'm sorry, Brie. I didn't mean to bring it up. I…"

My eyes fill with tears, and one escapes, running down my cheek as my hand begins to shake, holding the shiny silver pole. The memories of that fateful day replaying in my mind.

The tears only come when we're alone or when I'm in the apartment, where I try to shed my sorrow.

When the nightmares come, I lie crying in the dark, hoping the demons stop reminding me of the pain. Hoping they have mercy on me.

She hugs me. My arms wrap around her while I try to keep my tears at bay. "It still hurts, Giselle. I'm so sorry. A part of me died that night," I say, whispering into her embrace.

"I know, Brie. I know." She steps back, wiping my cheeks, and I give her a watery smile, trying to compose myself to face Jaden and congratulate him. He needs my support, not my whining about him not telling me.

Taking off my heels and pulling sweats over my dance outfit, I slide my feet into a pair of pool slides and open the door. "Let's go and congratulate him. He must be so excited. I remember him telling me he would fight when Nate was ready for a break."

"Yeah, Nate said he was taking time off, switching roles with Jaden. He needs it. Jaden is going into the heavyweight class." My eyes widen while she locks the dance studio door.

"Heavyweight?" I lift my blonde locks and wrap them in a bun. "He will have to gain weight, which means he will get bigger."

"That's what I said. It adds more pressure to the training."

"Shit. I can't believe he is actually doing it. It has been his dream to go pro. He can fight. I have seen him sparring with Nate and the other fighters." My brows pinch in worry, and I sigh. "I just worry about him getting hurt."

Giselle snakes her arm through mine as we walk across the plaza toward the freestanding MMA gym. "It's something I have gotten used to. I'm the one cleaning the blood off the bedroom sheets."

"Maybe Jaden will want me to help him if I'm patient and supportive. I love him, Giselle."

I am halfway done with becoming a physical therapist for

combat fighters. It is what I've wanted to do since meeting Jaden. I have been working toward a degree, and physical therapy would fit well in helping him out with the gym and even the dancers at Giselle's studio.

"Does he know? Have you told him how you feel?"

"Not really. We just take it a day at a time. No pressure."

The sex is great, but it's not vanilla sex. With Jaden, it's hard sex. He's never hinted at a marriage proposal or that we are in a serious relationship; he has said none of those words, and we both respect our boundaries. We also don't see other people, and I understand him. All these things pop in my head, but I don't say them out loud to Giselle.

"Brie, you need to talk to him. You should be honest with him and let him know how you feel. One thing I've learned from being with Nate is that you have to communicate with each other. If you don't, things get mixed up. Then the worst happens. You assume."

My steps falter as we approach the entrance to the massive gym. Before I open the door, I answer, "We'll see."

Inside the gym, the smell of musk and sweat hits my senses. We walk side by side, passing the desk where Charlie greets us with a smile. "Hello, ladies."

"Hey, Charlie. Do you know where Brie can find Jaden?" He points at the door to his office, but his eyes look at me with a frown.

"He is having a meeting with his massage therapist."

Massage therapist? When did Jaden hire a massage therapist?

Looking at Charlie with a confused expression, I pinch my brows and head toward his office. What is so important is that he needs a meeting with his massage therapist that involves having the door closed.

Leaving Giselle with her eyebrows raised next to Charlie, I march toward the door to Jaden's office. I open the door without knocking. Because why the fuck not? I am his girlfriend and don't deserve to be shut out. I obviously have yet to be included in his plans. I'm the last to know he is going pro, and now I'm the last to know he has a massage therapist.

Barging in, I stop in my tracks. "What the fuck?" My eyes widen, and my heart sinks. A petite blonde has her hands all over Jaden's broad shoulders while his shirt is off. She glances in my direction, leaving both hands on his shoulders, caressing his skin. My eyes stare at them both, hiding the emotion burning inside me. My stomach clenches when the petite blonde smirks while I cross my hands over my chest.

"What the fuck are you doing?" I ask, seething. Massage therapist, my ass.

He quirks a brow. "Have you heard of knocking? I'm having a session with my therapist, Janine."

"I didn't know your girlfriend had to knock," I say sarcastically. "I also wasn't aware that you even hired a massage therapist, and I also didn't know that you were going to begin fighting."

The blonde continues to rub her hands all over his muscles, and I'm about to go Chun Li on her ass.

"Does this hurt?" she says softly, like I'm not here. My eyes zero in on his hand as he places it over hers gently.

"Give me a second, sweetheart," he tells her. My stomach plummets at how soft his voice is with her compared to how he greeted me when I opened the door.

"If you are sore or in pain, a physical therapist is what you need. Not a massage."

He lifts his head, and a side of Jaden I only see when he talks with his fighters makes an appearance. "Brie, that is why I have a rule about women in my gym unless they are training." I flinch like I have been struck. "It's a distraction and, right now, one I can't afford. I appreciate your concern, but Janine is handling my needs just fine. Just because you're attending school to be a physical therapist doesn't mean you know what is best for me. You have barely just finished your undergrad degree and have not begun the main program."

He doesn't even realize that I am way past that. I am in the first year of the doctorate part of the program.

I tilt my head and lean my back against the door jamb. "What kind of needs?" I ask.

He scoffs. "Needs you can't help me with. Does that answer your question?" He sighs. "Look, I'm sorry. But I can't have you interfering with my training or any fighting session. It's not going to work."

The tears behind my eyes burn the back of my eyelids like acid. Is he for real? Is he fucking her? Is he trying to break it off with me because he feels like I'm a distraction? Glancing at Janine, she gives me a predatory smile he can't see because she is standing behind him.

"Are you two fucking?" I blurt. Janine gasps, but she looks guilty.

His head snaps in my direction. "No. We are not fucking."

"We used to date."

"That was before I got my license," she chimes in.

I purse my lips, and all the air feels like it has escaped my lungs. It is like I can't breathe. They used to be together, and he called her. Hired an ex-girlfriend or whatever she was to him.

"Is that right? I wasn't even talking to you," I snarl, giving her a hard glare. My gaze falls back on Jaden's annoyed expression. "So, I'm supposed to sit here and accept this? I have no say?" I point my finger back and forth between them. "Do you think this is funny, Jaden?"

He rises out of his chair in a flash and gets in my face. My heart constricts because I'm madly in love with him, and he is acting like I'm being unreasonable. Deep down, I know he is shutting me out because it's what I do when I want someone to leave. It suddenly dawns on me that he wants me to go. Not the gym. He wants me out of his life. He doesn't love me. My hands begin to shake because I sense it in the pit of my stomach. He wants me to get mad and act rashly so he won't feel guilty when he ends it.

Some fighters approach from training near the cage but keep their distance. The door is wide open, and they see him cornering me. I'm about to cower, but my pride won't allow it. Memories from my past flash in my mind when I would be cornered in my room from being dragged from my small bed, but I keep them at bay. This is Jaden. I'm not supposed to fear him. He promised to always protect me.

"No, this is not funny. This is me telling you that you can't come inside the gym. This is me telling you I don't need you accusing me and embarrassing yourself."

"You want me to leave," I whisper. The tears that have pooled on my lower eyelids threaten to spill as my vision blurs.

His nostrils flare, and two stubborn tears burn down my cheeks. When my vision clears, his gray eyes are hard as steel.

His teeth are clenched when he says, "Yeah, I want you to get the fuck out."

Looking around, everyone is looking at me like I'm an intruder. My hands tremble, but I squeeze them together and swallow the lump that has formed in my throat.

"Come on, man. Don't do her like that," Jake, one fighter, says.

Jaden points while still staring at me with a tight expression. "Stay out of it, Jake," he warns.

"Bastard," Giselle says with a hard edge to her voice. My eyes find hers, and a secret message passes between us in a language made for us– created by us. What is left of me is breaking. My heart and every feeling I had inside diminished into the darkness that lives inside of me. A suit of impenetrable armor is taking over.

"Brie," Giselle calls out.

My eyes are still trained on hers, and she knows. She knows I'm slipping. Every man I have encountered hurts me in some way. I thought the exception was Jaden. *He promised to protect me.* He would whisper it every time we were together in bed. But he wants to be free of me. There is no use or need for me in his life. No girl wants to find the man she loves and trusts in a closed room getting a massage from one of his ex-flames. Out of all the massage therapists he could have hired, why her? The answer is staring right in my face. He doesn't care about me or how I would feel because he doesn't love me.

"Crying over dumb shit is what will get me hurt inside the cage. I can't risk it."

Nate walks up behind Giselle, and maybe he sees the look on my face even if he can't figure out what's happening inside my head when he says, "Jaden, don't."

Jaden's eyes turn cold like molten steel before he delivers the final blow to my heart.

"Janine, get my shirt. Let's go to lunch."

She walks over and hands him the shirt with a coy smile.

Pushing myself off the door's molding, I wall out of his life without another word.

Like every man that is done using me, all I take with me is the pain.

CHAPTER ONE
Briana

"Are you ready?" Marcus, the private club manager of Equinox, asks.

Taking a deep breath, I glance up at the monstrous man in front of me.

"Yeah."

After working here for almost three years, tonight is the first night being placed on the VIP list. I have avoided giving private dances to special VIP clients.

All dancers must be available if there is a request, and only select members are allowed special VIP status.

After I left Jaden, or rather when he kicked me out of his life. I knew I couldn't keep working at the dance studio or living in his apartment. Whatever we had was officially over.

Giselle knew I would leave quietly. She knew I couldn't continue to work at the dance studio with Jaden so close, live in an apartment he pays for, or drive a car he bought me. I left everything behind except what I came with. Basically, the clothes on my back.

I needed to find work, and pole dancing was the only skill I had that could earn me cash fast. I was officially back where I started after leaving my mother's trailer. She warned me I would end up being a whore and that I was damaged, like her.

No man would want a stripper raised in a trailer park. I

guess she was right. The rumors I hated, spread by Jace in high school, were right. This is where I ended up. This was my future.

A friend at the Porcelain Dollhouse, where Giselle and I worked, put a good word in for me at an underground club for elite members only. Basically, the super-rich. Men who wanted to enjoy the company of a dancer with no one being privy to it. That includes paparazzi, wives, children, or the media.

Every member is screened medically and financially.

"You know the rules," Marcus says, and I answer with a nod, taking a deep breath.

"I'm just nervous. This is my first time alone with a man in the VIP room."

"Remember, all you have to do is say no. You don't have to do anything you feel uncomfortable with."

One night in the VIP room pays for two of my courses in the physical therapy program. I never intended to allow myself to take strange men in the VIP room, but it was also a requirement to at least have one when I was hired. It is outlined in the job description at Equinox, and it was also highlighted in the contract they had me sign.

Marcus has been making excuses for me since I started. The other girls have said nothing, or they haven't noticed. Every time men have asked for me, I have made excuses. I need this job. It lets me attend school during the day and pay for all my basic expenses. I have six months left to finish the program, and then I'll be officially a physical therapist.

I took loans when I started six and a half years ago, but I'm tapped out. Even with Jaden, I never asked for a dime to pay for school. He offered to help me once, but I quickly turned him down. School was something I wanted to accomplish on my own. It was a way to prove to myself that I could do it. That I wouldn't end up like my mother said I would, a whore no one wanted.

My luck with student loans had run out when the financial

aid adviser called me into his office and told me I couldn't take out any more loans. My face fell, and my stomach bottomed out. The only option I could think of was the VIP room.

Something I told myself I would avoid until I finished school if I could. But my luck had run out.

I keep telling myself it doesn't matter anyway. I'm a shell to be used. Nothing more. Nothing less. Most of them just look at my body, palm their cocks, and throw money at me when I'm dancing on the floor.

"Got it, Marcus."

"You'll do great. You know where the panic button is, and I'm right outside the door."

Easy for you to say. You don't have some creep getting off with the image of you or touching your skin. The thought of what awaits me behind the door has my skin crawling.

"I know. Thank you."

I could do this, I tell myself.

I adjust my corset with the expensive lace bra, garters, and tights.

Marcus opens the door when I give him the signal.

Walking slowly in patent leather six-inch heels, a man is seated on a blue velvet chaise. His suit is impeccably tailored, and as I inch closer, his gaze travels over my body until it reaches my face. His eyes are dark, like pitch-black orbs trying to see inside me. They say your eyes are a window to your soul. Too bad my soul can't be seen.

My eyes caress his strong jaw and handsome face.

When he sits up, my gaze meets his head-on for a beat.

He opens his legs, clearly an invitation for me to stand between them. He unbuttons his suit jacket and removes it, folding it neatly beside him.

"Hi, handsome."

"I'm glad you accepted my request, Coco." I smile, but he sees it doesn't reach my eyes.

I recognize him from dancing on the floor. He sits quietly at a table, nursing a glass of Macallan 18.

"Of course. May I?" I ask, motioning with my hand to straddle him.

"By all means. Please."

My legs straddle him, and I feel the muscles of his thighs through his trousers. My hands rest on his strong shoulders to maintain my balance, and his hands slowly find my waist.

"What would you like to do while I'm here?" His gaze travels down my body to the short lace shorts hovering over his cock that is now hard as a rock.

"I want you to dance for me or rather... dance on me. Next time, I will tell you what I want and like." He pauses. "If you agree, of course." His voice is stern and assertive.

This man likes control. He slowly rubs his thumb on my skin near my rib cage.

He thinks it will turn me on. How interesting. He wants me to want him.

It is too bad I don't feel a thing for anyone. He is undoubtedly attractive and gives me a feeling that he expects women to be flattered or lucky to be in his presence. I'm just not one of those women.

"Can You Hear Me" by Fleurie plays softly through the speakers, and her sultry voice sets the mood in the room.

When I rock my hips and arch my back to the tempo of the music, his cock digs into my pussy.

His breathing becomes harder with each breath, and I know he's trying to hold back. I'm screaming inside of my head that I want to jump off his lap and run out of this room, but I can't. I need this job, and if I plan on never doing this again, I have to set my eyes on the prize. Finish my education and get the fuck out of here.

When I roll my hips, causing me to rise, I slide my legs down and turn around. I bend over to give him a better view of my pussy trapped in lace and slowly... straightened.

I turn around. My fingers run through the strands of his silky black hair. He looks up. The masculine scent of his exotic cologne hits my senses. He smells of sin and bad judgment. Everything about this man screams danger and should come with a disclaimer.

He guides me down so I can straddle him again. He grinds his erect cock, now tenting his pants against my pussy, and a drop of sweat appears on his forehead.

Wanting to get this over with, I wrap my hand around his neck and dry hump his cock, hard and fast. He grunts and groans while I have a strong grip on the back of his neck as I rub myself on his dick.

Our eyes are locked, and his breathing picks up while I grind faster over his cock like I'm possessed, but I'm controlled.

The faster I rub myself, the more sweat drips from his forehead. This is what men want from me. But here, the quicker I get him off, the faster he leaves.

After a few minutes, he can't take it anymore. He grips my ass, holding me still, he comes hard in his trousers.

"Fuck," he cries, but he never breaks eye contact as I watch him come undone.

I lean in, my eyes hard, my mouth inches from his, and say, "Time's up."

His eyes are hard slits as he watches me climb off his lap and without a backward glance I exit the room.

Jaden

The sweat drips down my face, and I swipe my arm over my eyes to avoid the sweat from stinging them.

I strike the punching bag, each punch stronger than the next. The demons in my head from my past, mocking me to hit the bag harder and harder. The pain I suffered as a child play in my dreams, suffocating me in my sleep. My mother and father beat me because I asked for food. The pain of hunger blinded me as a child with each forceful blow.

My mother was a crack addict, and my father, an abusive alcoholic, would either hit my mother after downing a bottle of vodka or take his anger out on me because I wanted to go to school or was hungry.

Social services took me at age five because the school reported them when the teachers noticed my clothes smelled because they hadn't been washed for days. I was scared when they came to the school and took me. They gave me food and a fresh pair of clothes. It was better than being at home; I thought it was a better place.

When I thought I was free of my parents, the flawed system gave me right back when they sobered up for a few weeks because the government checks weren't coming in, and I was an only child. I dreaded when they gave me back. The social worker dropped me off at the small house that was a pit of hell. An endless hell I could never crawl out of.

Every day, I would be starved, and some days, I would be given only bread and water. There was plenty of crack and alcohol, though. One night, I was so thirsty I had no choice but to drink a beer because the water was shut off for nonpayment. The food the school provided was the only sustenance I received. It was the only meal I sometimes had in a day.

When their addictions got worse, they began selling me to sick people who would watch me take my clothes off for drugs. Most were men with little boy fetishes. I blanked out most details from my memory, but the bits and pieces would haunt me in my dreams. All I would remember the next morning was pain, mental and physical pain. Like I was still there, stuck in that time, waking up thrashing and screaming. That is why I invite no one into my home except Nate. He is the only one I trust in my life. He is the only one who understands.

"You still at it, bro?" Nate asks, coming up behind me.

I stop punching the bag and lower my arms, burning with exhaustion. When my mind goes back to what awaits me at night alone in my almost empty ten-bedroom house. I train until my body can't take it, or Nate tells me I have had enough.

"Yeah," I tell him, taking slow, even breaths. I turn to look in his direction when he comes into view from the shadows of the gym. The only light on is at the back end of the gym, where the punching bags are located.

"You have been training for the past six hours. You're the champ and want to keep your title, but you can't burn yourself out. How's the shoulder?"

The tinge of pain is like an annoying sting that won't go away. I just pull through it during a fight and training. "Still bothering me like an annoying bitch," I say, rolling my left shoulder to ease the sting. "I thought the massage sessions would help, but it only relaxes me so far. The pain is still there."

He quirks a brow. "Relaxing, huh? For you or for her."

"Come on, Nate. You know I haven't slept with Janine since she started. The only slip-up was when she came on to me, kissing me, and I shut her down real quick. I have no interest in her whatsoever. Whatever we had in the past was a short fling, and I ended it."

With a stern voice, Nate says, "Letting her move into the apartment after Brie left didn't help the situation either. I also think she got the wrong message when you ended things with Brie, and she took off."

Wiping the sweat off my face and undoing the Velcro from my gloves, the sound echoing in the gym, I slide them off, clearly annoyed by him mentioning something I regretted doing. Not the apartment. Well, maybe letting her move into the condo after I removed Brie's things, hoping her vanilla smell lingered, was a huge mistake, but I couldn't kick her out when I needed a masseuse.

I regret the hateful words that spilled from my lips in front of everyone to the one woman who didn't deserve an inch of my abhorrent attitude. My goals and pride got in the way, and then it was too late. She left. Everything I gave her was there in the apartment. She only took the things she came with when she moved here from South Dakota. Which was nothing but the clothes on her back.

"I told you I don't want to talk about Briana. I know I fucked up, and I'll own it."

"Have you? Because Giselle doesn't want to be around you unless she has to since it happened, and it's been three years, Jaden. For three years, she hasn't physically seen Brie. They only talk by phone, which lasts ten minutes if she is lucky."

My brows rise, surprise etched on my face. "I didn't know, Nate. I'm sorry. Is she okay?"

He follows me to the locker room as the lights turn on, sensing us walking through. "That's the thing. We really don't know. She tells Giselle she has been fine. Working and keeping to herself. When Giselle invites her over, she quickly declines. Blames it on work."

"Where is she working?" I ask, entering the closed shower.

He lets out a breath that I hear through the door before turning on the shower until the water is scalding.

"Don't have a fucking clue, brother. She won't say. She doesn't talk about herself. Giselle thinks she is avoiding her but doesn't want me to interfere. Giselle also told me to tell you she wants you to leave her alone."

"No offense to Giselle." Grabbing the towel to dry myself off before opening the door. "I have left her alone. I hate to admit it, but I'm no good for her. I never was. And I don't deserve her."

"Then I guess you don't have to worry about her. Keep your attention on your next fight card and keep fucking your ring bunnies. That's all you need, which makes you happy." He moves to walk out while I'm getting dressed.

Following him to the gym entrance, I ask, "What is that supposed to mean?"

He walks outside after setting the alarm and locking up. "It means you are happy with things the way they are and shouldn't worry about it. I promise not to bring her up anymore."

Is he shutting me out from talking about Brie? Does he think I'm happy getting my dick sucked or fucking some random ring bunny? That I don't miss her. I won't admit it to anyone, but I miss her. She was perfect. She never asked questions and never judged me. She respected my boundaries of not bringing her to my house. When she questioned me that day, I wasn't used to it. Everything I did was on my rules, time, and how I wanted them. She had every right, though. If I saw some guy, she'd had a fling with from the past rubbing on her, he wouldn't be breathing.

She was never wrong. I was wrong, and it kills me. I hurt her. I failed us. The only thing I could do was make sure she was safe.

Guilt claws my insides. I don't know if she is safe because I don't know where she is.

Opening the door to my Zenvo, I call out, "Hey, Nate?" He stops in front of his car and turns around. "Is she safe?"

He scratches his brow. "I guess so. She must be." I nod and slide into the car, and head home.

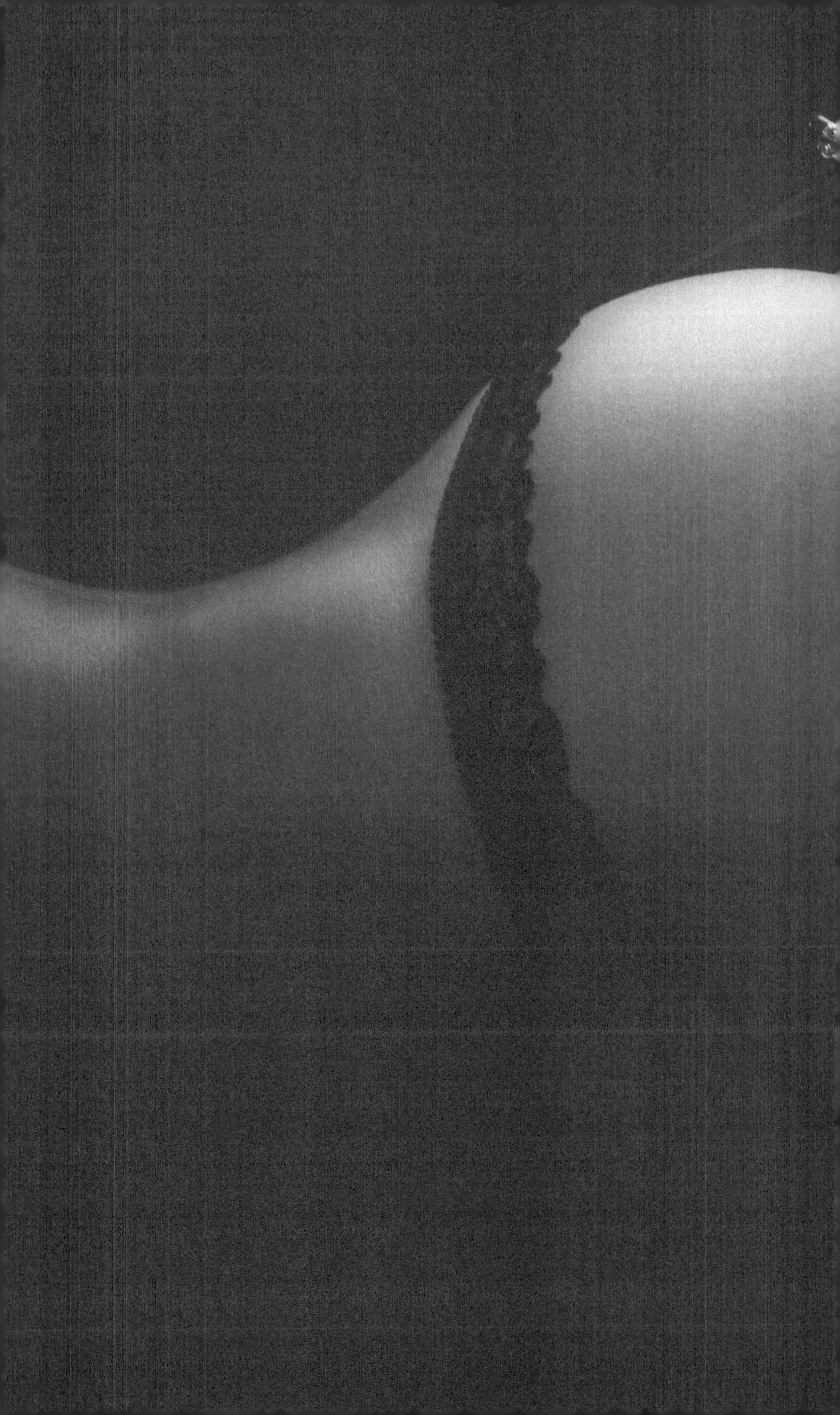

CHAPTER THREE

Briana

I wake up, bolting up from the corner of the floor in my blacked-out bedroom, taking deep breaths in sweat from another nightmare.

It was the first time they came inside my room to brutally rape me. It was after I fell for Jace, and he spread rumors about me that I was a whore like my mother.

News like that in a small-town travels fast.

My mother's drug dealers and drug-addicted friends got wind of it. Guess they figured it was true, and they should try their luck when my mother passed out from her last hit. No matter how hard I pleaded. No matter how hard I fought them, pushing the small dresser to block the door. It was no use.

When an addict is on his high, it's like they have super-human strength.

When it was over, the next morning, I went to a discreet clinic that addicts frequent and told them I was hooked on drugs and don't remember what happened. The nurse didn't believe me, but I insisted it was true, denying the help for drug withdrawal and instead got treated for other stuff like my swollen eyes, busted lip, and vaginal tearing.

They made sure I didn't fall pregnant and treated me as a rape victim. I lied about my age since I was seventeen and changed my birth year to reflect that I was an adult. The people going in and out of the clinic were so strung out, and being from a small town, no one questioned much since it was a free clinic for addicts.

No one back home knew I was being raped except the ones who did it and my mother, and that fateful night when I mistakenly brought Giselle with me to help my mother.

Giselle and the guys only thought it was Jack, but there were two more.

It happened more than once, but those memories are inside my head, and no one needs to know. The guilt doesn't help. Giselle is the only one who would care, and she can do nothing about it.

Everything in my apartment is black. My bed with black sheets, black painted walls and furniture. Everything is dark, like my life.

Making my way to my black-decorated bathroom to shower and clean the drenching sweat from my body, I let the tears from what I had to endure last night fall.

When I blink under the spray of the shower, my eyes sting from crying last night, shame and regret filter inside me.

It was my first time in the VIP room, and what did I do? I dry-humped the guy.

I'm officially a whore.

That is exactly what they said when I was in high school. It wasn't a lap dance; I basically got the guy off, rubbing my lace-clad pussy over his cock encased in his pants. He wasn't bad looking by any means, and every VIP is screened medically, so I have nothing to worry about.

He paid me double, which made it worse, never having done that before. It was humiliating and something I hated doing with every fiber of my being. Maybe he paid me double because I embarrassed him by not even getting aroused, or maybe for getting him off.

I'm so numb. Men only see me as a piece of ass. It's why I

have sworn off dating. What is the point? When a decent guy finds out how I pay for school and pay for my apartment, they will treat me like a stripper or, worse, a whore.

Who would want a damaged woman like me anyway? I'm fucked up, and there is no hope for me. No therapy can fix what was done.

I have no one except my best friend, Giselle, and I don't want her to see me like this.

It's like my body goes with the motion with no feeling, empty, and all I want to be is alone.

When I dance, it is the only moment I can breathe.

It was never supposed to be like this; I was in love with a man I thought cared deeply for me. He threw me out of his life and back into the life I had before I met him, except this time, I only hope to make it out. Meanwhile, the darkness is where I sleep, reminding me that I'm not worth anything.

The only thing I look forward to is accomplishing school. I have one thing going for me, and I'm doing it on my terms. I want to be a physical therapist for combat fighters. I almost gave up after Jaden ended it. I had no money or place to stay and had to start over.

He never called me.

He never reached out. Not even to see if I was okay. That is when I knew I meant nothing to him.

Jaden "The Destroyer" Cyprus is living his dream undefeated. It's hard not to see his fights promoted and discussed on the news and social media. This is Las Vegas;, fights are the main events.

Equinox has a few fighters that walk through its doors, but I try to avoid their advances and offers for private dances. I'm not interested in anyone because none see me. They only see a good time. Guys look at my body like they are shopping in a meat market. They don't care about my feelings, who I am, or if I find them attractive. Their language is sex and money.

Dancing is one thing, but what occurred last night is something I've never done and never thought I had to do. The ultimate sacrifice for a better life on my terms. Even if it left me empty and alone. It triggered the memories.

The only difference was that I agreed and knew the risk and what it would entail.

He got what he wanted. Next time, he would pick another girl that wasn't a bitch right after.

CHAPTER FOUR
Briana

It's Friday night, and Equinox is at capacity, with most of its members and special guests in attendance. The mystery client from the VIP room last Saturday night has not returned, and I'm relieved. Marcus saw my worried expression when he asked me how it went. He assured me I didn't have to take another client and I could just dance my set on the floor, and all was good.

Marcus is also in charge of the safety and VIP rooms. He makes sure the members keep themselves in line following agreements and negotiations with the girls.

It's my turn on the floor, and the club has a runway-styled floor with the end having a single pole close to the audience for their enjoyment. There are also three poles on the main stage in the back, and the best part of Equinox is that when you dance, you do not have to go nude.

Looking down at my outfit behind the curtain, the bright neon lights reflect the club's darkness, casting a glow on the runway floor, making my outfit sparkle. I adjust my pasties on my braless breasts and tweak the shortest boy shorts I think exist. They are so short that they're almost a thong over my fishnet tights.

"You're up, Coco. Not an empty seat in the house. If anything happens or someone gets out of line, just remember I'll be standing on the side, and security will rush in ASAP." I adjust my six-inch satin glittered heels.

Looking up at Marcus's monstrous frame, I smile. "Thanks, Marcus."

Thank God he's married and loves his wife way too much. He reminds me of an older brother I wish I had. One that would watch your back no matter what. A big brother that wouldn't let drug dealers rape their sister or put up with a drug-addicted mother.

Walking out to the floor, I grab the pole in the middle for my set. The lights shift, dimming low, and my heart sinks when I turn my head to look at the crowd.

The man from the VIP room is watching me at the end of the runway in front of the last pole. His eyes are black as night, and there is a man in a bulletproof vest standing behind him. It must be his bodyguard. This means my assumption of him was right, and he is dangerous if people want him dead.

"Fallout" by Unsecret & Neoni begins to play through the club's speakers, and I start my set as I climb the pole, beginning with a split and turn upside down, letting my hands hold me steady.

The crowd shifts in their seats as I climb up to the tallest point of the pole near the ceiling, waiting for the hook to drop. I place my body upside down with only my thighs holding me.

When the song's hook drops, I drop with the sound of the beat. The pole slides between my thighs, and I skid to a halt before my head can hit the floor. My hands are spread wide like I'm floating suspended in the air right above the shiny black polished surface of the stage.

"Shit, did you see that?" a man from the crowd says.

The beat changes, my legs let go of the pole, I crawl on my hands and knees down the runway floor in a rhythm to the song, moving toward the pole on the end near the man I'm trying to avoid with my gaze.

He makes me feel on edge. He watches me like a predator hunting his prey. "Hurricane" by Fleurie plays, and I dance to the song and breathe through the darkness to the slow cinematic silence.

He stands when I make my way down, and my stomach clenches in fear. The nearer I get, the more I can see his expression. It is blank and unreadable, reflecting the way I feel. I twirl on the pole, ending the set in a split.

When I stand, he is gone. Like he was a ghost, and I imagined him sitting there. One minute there and the next gone.

Walking to the back to throw on a robe and cover my exposed body, Marcus walks over to me with a worried expression, stopping me from heading to the changing area.

"Coco. Your VIP has arrived and booked the rest of your shift." I nod reluctantly and walk toward the VIP room with Marcus trailing behind.

If a VIP requests you again, you can't refuse.

Opening the door to the same room as last week, he is waiting for me with a folder, making me frown. "Hello, Coco. Your performance was… impressive. I enjoyed it very much," he says.

Ignoring his compliment, I ask, "What can I do for you this evening?" He knows I am being sarcastic and playing on his ego from last time and how he made a mess of himself.

He gives me a grin. "Come and sit across from me in the chair. I have a proposition for you. You don't have to agree. You can walk out of here, and I will still pay you for your time, requiring nothing further. I just want you to hear what I have to offer."

Sitting down, I face him while adjusting the robe to cover

my exposed thighs. His eyes follow my movements, and my skin crawls with annoyance.

"Okay. Let's hear it."

He chuckles at my flat tone. Holding the folder in his lap, he removes his gold cuff links from his pristine white dress shirt, rolling them over his strong tattooed forearms like he's getting ready to wash dishes and doesn't want to get his sleeves wet.

Once done, he relaxes his posture by widening his legs on the chaise facing me. "Open your robe. I want to see your breasts." My nostrils flare, but I try to mask my annoyance. I swallow thickly because I'm not sure if he is trying to fluster me or wants to remind me that I'm here to pleasure him.

"Okay," I say flatly, giving him a cold, empty stare, opening the sash on my robe and letting it fall open. My head tilts to the side, challenging him.

"Much better. I find you stunning, and I might as well have a great view while we discuss the proposition I have for you. I'll have you know that I am a very generous man. I will not bore you further. So, I'll begin. My name is Ethan Carter, and when you search for my name, you will find that I'm a billionaire who owns several conglomerates. I have fathered no children, though the media has tried to look for cracks in my reputation, and so have all the women trying to worm their way into my good graces. Your name is Briana Jameson. Born in South Dakota to a drug-addicted mother currently incarcerated."

Bastard.

I squirm in my seat, giving him a cold, hard stare of pure loathing. Rich prick has no right to investigate my personal life or my past. He gives me a triumphant smirk.

"Fuck you," I say, seething, my breaths coming in and out faster than before.

"I would, but you see, I am still in love with my dead wife, and I think I always will be. She died seven years ago, and I can't move on. The pussy my cock wants to devour is inside a coffin six feet under. I know these things about you because I'm in business with the same organization your ex-boyfriend does."

"What does any of that do with you and what you want?" I know he is referring to Jaden and his dealings with the Mafia. I don't remember specifics, but I'm not stupid. It was how effortlessly they handled the Jack situation.

His eyes turn black as night, and I swear they are soulless. Dark like my own. He licks his lips, and his gaze travels slowly over my exposed breasts until it reaches my eyes.

"You're the first woman that has been able to give me pleasure. I'm not interested in vaginal penetration except with my tongue. I'm interested in other ways you could appease my manly needs. It would only be for a month. I know you are completing a program as a physical therapist, and I will pay the entire cost of your education. I also will purchase a generous mode of transportation. I know you love your motorcycle but the fact that it is a death trap, you are no use for me if you are lying dead on the pavement."

My eyes narrow because he knows a lot about me. It's too much for comfort, but I remember that Equinox is full of members with money, and some men are with the Mafia. My hands shake, he sees my nervousness, and his face hardens in anger. He shifts in his seat.

I flinch instinctively. "I'm not going to hurt you, Briana. I researched everything there is to know about you because I would like you to agree. I will still pay for your time if you are uncomfortable with the arrangement. If you are interested in my offer, clothes will be delivered before your session here, and it's for my enjoyment."

Averting my gaze, I stare at the wall, realizing what he is asking. He wants me to be his toy.

"You want me to be your toy."

He grins. "Something like that." He sits up and leans his

forearms on his knees, and I glance at his face, noticing the smoothness of his skin for the first time. His straight nose and dark lashes frame his dark eyes the color of midnight.

"My guess is that is how you feel these days. Dark, broken, and with no room for emotion. See, we share something in common. It's there because I saw it today and the last time you were in my lap. You also weren't aroused while you rubbed your pussy over my cock. Not a flicker of emotion. It feeds me, and I want to feast on it. It's like playing in the dark without seeing who is really there."

"You are sick," I snap.

"So are you."

"I'm not sick because I don't use people, nor do I dig up dirt from their past and use it as a way to break them down. To get them to agree to a sick fantasy."

"Maybe. But here is the thing. I will get you for a month, and you will get something you don't have."

"Yeah, what is that?"

His eyes glitter, black and sinister in the dim light as he leans back in the chaise again.

"Power. You will be known everywhere you go as the woman who did the unthinkable. You have gotten the attention of the infamous Ethan Carter. The billionaire has not been seen with a woman since his wife's untimely death. You will also understand what it is to have a man treat you like a beautiful woman should be treated. Not just sexually but in the real sense. Not like Jaden Cyprus. I'm sure he didn't treat you all that well. Maybe sexually, but we both know he does that with all his ring bunnies. Especially since you ended up here. Back to where you started after high school before you two met."

The knife he is twisting inside my chest at the mention of Jaden and how things ended gives me the determination to accept this man's proposal.

He pointed out how Jaden quickly got rid of and replaced

me. He didn't stop me that day; he let me go, making me realize my love for him was unrequited, but that was then, and love is not a factor in my life. Not anymore. All that is left is a dark abyss.

My goal is within reach. There are certain things I will not do, and I will make sure these things are clear to Ethan Carter.

I cross my legs, exposing my fishnet-clad thigh.

He watches my movements intently while adjusting his cock through his pants.

Rolling my eyes, letting him finish adjusting himself, I tell him, "There will be certain things I will not do or allow you to do."

"Fair enough. Name them."

"No hitting, slapping, or third parties. Your dick will not go inside me, no blindfolds, bondage, anal, or gags."

"I wasn't planning on doing any of those things, so we are good—"

"One more thing."

"I'm listening."

"No kissing on the mouth."

"Why?" he asks.

"It's too personal." He nods and hands me the folder with an NDA to sign.

"One month is all I ask, and if you feel uncomfortable, all you have to do is tell me to stop, and I will stop. I will draw up everything we discussed in writing for you to sign. I will request one appearance outside of this club."

"Okay. Anything else?"

"Yes, there is one more thing I want clarified."

"Okay."

His voice is rough as he says, "I will not fuck your cunt with my cock, but I will stick my cock in your mouth, and I will return the favor by fucking your cunt with my tongue. No fake orgasms. I want you to physically come, preferably in my mouth. I want to know how you taste and see your beautiful face come undone because of me."

Glancing at his unreadable expression, he says the words I never expected to hear. What I expected was more like how I was going to pleasure him and what he wanted me to do.

My heart is racing at how forward he is describing what he wants to do to me and how he expects me to act. At least he won't fuck me in the true sense, and I don't have to take any more VIP guests in a back room. He is the only one, and it's only for a month, I tell myself silently. He wants nothing else but what is agreed upon.

"Okay."

He smiles, motioning me over with his finger. I rise up from the chair and walk over to stand between his legs. When I glance down at him, my face is devoid of emotion. The numbness begins to claim me. His fingers slide the robe off my shoulders, letting it pool at my feet.

"Kneel," he demands.

Carefully kneeling between his legs, I steady myself by placing my hands on his hard thighs over his trousers, careful not to bend my ankle, sliding each heel under me. His eyes travel to where I'm touching him, and his eyes darken with desire. This man is in love with his dead wife, so he says, but his expression right now is filled with so much lust.

He palms my breasts, removing the pasties carefully. And I let him.

This man screams control as much as I silently scream for him not to touch me.

Once he gently removes the sticky pasties, my nipples are hard. Not because I'm aroused but because of the temperature of the room. My body involuntarily shivers, and he notices. A normal man would offer his coat or make sure a woman finds warmth. Not this man. I'm not his girlfriend or a fling. I'm his toy. Bought and paid for in a transaction for one month.

His response is to dip his head and take my nipple inside his mouth and suck. My body jolts at the suddenness of his action. My fingers instinctively find his hair, running through his silky black strands. Not in pleasure but to control his assault on my breasts. His tongue swirls and sucks on one, and then the other is met with a deep groan coming from his throat.

When he has his fill, he moves to stand, causing me to fall back on my heels. I tilt my head up, watching his hard erection, tenting his pants. He removes the buttons of his crisp white dress shirt, and my eyes admire the smooth expanse of chiseled muscle when he removes his shirt, placing it on the chaise. His body is covered in tattoos like he belongs in a gang, but I know he belongs in the Mafia. He has a particular mark on his inner wrist, I recognize. Jaden has the same tattoo, but Jaden has more lines than the one on Ethan's inner wrist. I don't know what it means, but they must know each other. This man knows Jaden, and he must know Nate. He walks over, undoing his belt, and my expression must have sheer panic written all over it.

"Relax, I just want to feel you close to my skin when you straddle my lap."

He occupies the chair I vacated, and I'm nervous. I haven't touched a man since the one I gave my heart to, the one that shattered me three years ago.

I close my eyes and listen to his instruction, and it is at this very moment I know I am truly lost. I don't mean to do it, but I have to. The act of self-sacrifice. A haunting echo goes off inside my head. A war cry in silence.

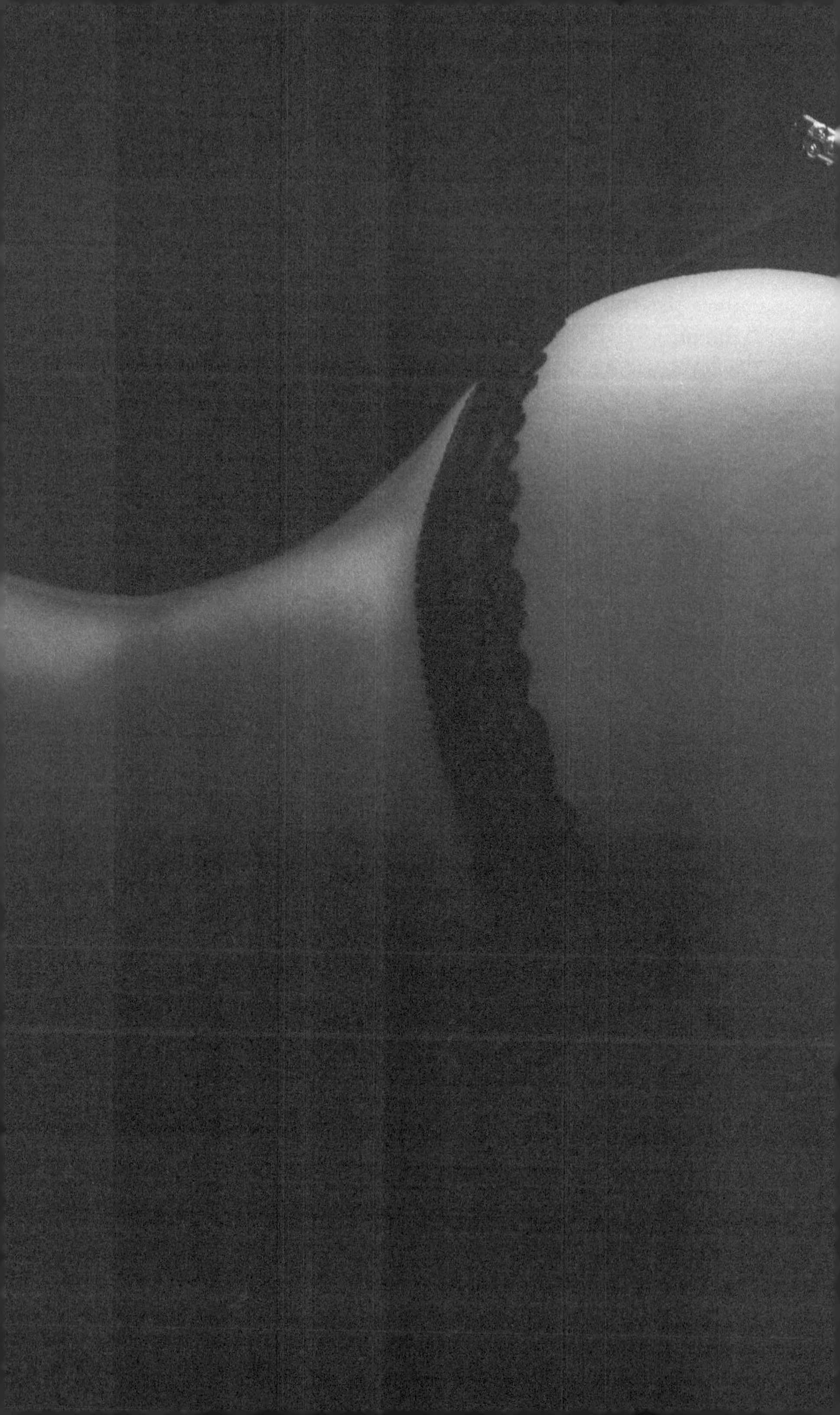

CHAPTER FIVE

Briana

"Take off your panties, everything except your heels and tights," he demands.

I do as he asks and slide them off my thighs slowly as his gaze follows the movement of my fingers.

Standing naked except for the black fishnet tights and platform heels, his eyes are fixated on my hairless pussy. His hand fists his cock from tip to shaft, with pre-cum glistening from the tip.

"Sit on my thighs."

I release a breath I did not realize I was holding and brace my hands on his shoulders. I carefully sit on his lap with his hard erection, standing erect like a steel rod between us. His hands grip my thighs, sliding slowly to my ass. His mouth tenderly places kisses on my chest.

"See how hard I am for you, beautiful? I want you to slide as close as you can so your pretty pink cunt can rub on the shaft of my dick."

Staying silent, I comply, opening my legs wide enough so that my clit rubs on his length.

When I get close, the movement allows the glow of the lights in the room to shine on his impressive length. Ethan Carter has an impressive cock and is a handsome man, but I'm a human toy to meet his needs.

When I move my hips in a circular motion with my hands on his bare muscled chest, he lets out a hiss when the slit of my pussy opens slightly. His pulsating cock feels my sensitive nub as I continue to stroke his shaft. His hand slides into the blonde strands of my hair near my scalp, pulling me closer to his lips so he can whisper in my ear. "You are a very sexy woman. Do you know what I love the most about you?"

"What?" I whisper.

"Your darkness. It feeds mine, and I see it in your eyes. It wreaks havoc with my own."

"What he is saying is crazy, but I understand him. This is not about love or meeting someone new or about the past. It's about the present and how you can feed your demons so that they can spare you from taking you down under.

This man scares me because where I want to be free of it, he wants to stay in it. He wants to play while his soul is broken into a million pieces, lost in his bleakness. He wants me to respond to him while giving him his carnal release. This is a preview of what I'm signing up for. A glimpse of how far this will go, and he is giving me the option to walk out of it tonight. The only problem with getting up and walking out and telling this man to go fuck himself is what the hell am I going to do to pay for the remaining balance of my degree and clinical hours at the center. Take another VIP in another room? What if he is nasty and worse than Ethan? Then, I would have to take another until I could support myself dancing on the main floor, taking different men in the back. I involuntarily shudder at the thought.

"Are you okay? Are you cold, beautiful?"

My mind wanders back, and I realize I have stopped moving, but when I look down, his cock is painfully hard, and then my eyes meet his dark orbs.

"No," I say breathlessly, and I continue to move again. His fingers snake up my back in a tender caress.

Biologically, my body responds to the nerve endings under

my skin with my nipples hard as twin peaks. He notices my body's reaction, and he grins, moving his left hand between my thighs; he touches the most intimate part of me with his thumb rubbing his precum over my clit. Arching my back, my hands find the side of his face, and he nuzzles his face on my breasts as I ride the outside of his shaft.

"That's right, beautiful. I want you to milk my cock and let my cum drip over that sweet pink pussy."

God help me, I mewl at his words. Moving at a faster pace, I find a rhythm that causes him to groan and me to moan.

He takes my nipple in his mouth, and he softly bites and nibbles my velvet skin, causing my pussy to drip, coating his shaft, and the noise of my rubbing echoes in the room. It's different from anything I have experienced. It's a need and no emotion. No regrets. A simple transaction between two adults with a dark past. I moan, and he holds me so the contact between his cock and my pussy is tight and wet, even if he is not inside me.

"I'm going to come, my dark angel. If you don't come, I will make sure you do."

His brow furrows, and a hiss escapes his lips as he comes hard. Hot cum spurts all over my stomach, pussy, and his pants. A deep groan comes from his throat when he looks down at the mess he made. He pushes me back slightly and runs the head of his cock up and down my clit, smearing his hot cum all over the outside of the fishnets covering my pussy. "I've made a mess, princess," he says, lifting me so he can stand.

My legs wrap around his waist as he lays me down on the chaise. He is between my legs, hovering over me with his semi-hard cock near my slit. He rips the hole at the crotch of my fishnet tights wider so he can brush the head of his cock full of cum all over my pussy, mixing my arousal with his cum.

Raising myself, resting on my elbows, I watch until he looks up and smirks, dropping to his knees and ripping my tights so he can lick my pussy. He places my legs over his shoulders, and I try to not hurt his back with my platform heels while he laps my pussy.

"You taste so good, beautiful," he says against my lower lips. "If you tell me to stop. I will. Okay?"

"Okay," I say, a moan escaping my lips.

"Do you want me to stop?"

"No."

He smiles and slides his tongue inside my pussy and fucks me with his tongue relentlessly. He sucks and swirls his tongue, and my body responds by flooding his mouth. Three years of not having a man pleasure me build inside of me like a quaking inferno. I'm panting and moaning, lying on my back as Ethan satisfies me, making me come so hard.

I moan, and when he senses I'm coming in his mouth, my pussy walls clench around his tongue; he swallows every drop like an animal that has been kept from drinking water.

His head rises from between my legs, and he glances at me with triumph, licking his lips. My legs carefully slide off his shoulders, shaking. He bends and finds my panties, cleaning both of us the best he can. He hands me my robe to cover myself. When he makes himself presentable, he slides two fingers over my cheeks.

"I will be in touch," he says, leaving the room.

The next day, as promised, a courier drops off a package that has an emerald-green crepe Valentino minidress with a dangerous v cupping my bare breasts with gold matching Valentino pumps. It is summer, and the warm Las Vegas heat still lingers in the air caused by squelching hot summer days. The dress leaves little to the imagination.

Ethan loves to dress me in daring outfits that accentuate

my figure to the maximum ability without leaving me naked when he meets with me at the club.

This is the first and only public outing he has required me to attend. I agreed to accompany him when he outlined it in the terms of the contract.

I couldn't turn Ethan down because I signed an agreement with him, but after tonight, whatever happens, it is the last time I will see Ethan outside the club under these circumstances. He has paid everything up to this point, from my past loans to my current semester. I have to figure out the last part. Being Ethan's toy is not something I am proud of; I am tired of doing something I don't feel comfortable doing. This is one of them. I will treat this last night with Ethan like a one-time thing. A date with no strings attached.

Glancing at myself in the mirror, the dress is gorgeous and hugs my curves flawlessly. To finish the look, I applied makeup with a smoky eye and a shiny nude lip. He didn't say where he was taking me, but I can imagine it is somewhere where there will be pictures and paparazzi. I imagine Ethan has a purpose, and I intend to look pretty on his arm. My guess is to calm the rumor mill stating he has been depressed and unstable since his wife's passing because he doesn't socialize or interact publicly. When I looked him up before I signed the contract agreeing to his terms, women claimed he had fathered their children and slept with them multiple times. One claim was that he was a drug addict or mentally unstable in his depression.

In his line of work, investors prefer to avoid investing or conducting business with an unstable individual.

A knock sounds through my front door; my instinct is to grab the bat, but my phone pings with a message from Ethan.

Ethan: My driver is at the door to pick you up.

Briana: Okay.

Well, at least I know who is at the door. I place my bat on the bed, but I am surprised Ethan didn't come and knock on the door himself. Ethan is a control freak, and he craves control in all situations.

Thomas, his personal bodyguard, greets me when I open the door. "Hello, Dr. Jameson. Mr. Carter is waiting in the car."

"Hello, Thomas."

When I reach the black Rolls, Royce parked out front, Thomas opens the door, and I slide into the luxury cabin of the car. The rich leather touches my exposed skin. The dress I'm wearing means a lot of skin.

Ethan is sitting to my right in a crisp white dress shirt open at the throat, exposing his colorful tattoos from his chest and snaking up his neck. The sleeves of his dress shirt are also rolled up, and more ink is exposed over his strong forearms, hinting that Ethan Carter is not your typical businessman. He is ruthless and works directly with the Mafia or was born in it.

"You look stunning," he says, surprising me with his compliment.

"Thank you. You look… nice," I say awkwardly.

He turns his body slightly in my direction, and I let out a nervous breath, aware of the sound of Thomas entering the driver's side and the car's light turning off, basking us in darkness except for the little lights on the car's doors.

Ethan turns on the cabin's light, and the glow illuminates his dark eyes and black hair. His jaw is sharp and clean-shaven, and he looks very handsome. The scent of his crisp and exotic cologne hits my senses from his movement.

"We are going to a fundraiser hosted by one of my companies. There will be paparazzi and reporters, and they will ask you questions about us. You say nothing and let them make their own assumptions. The mystery of our relationship will give you a glimpse at what I promised you."

He means power.

My association with him and the woman that has caught his attention after his wife's death will give me what many women secretly crave. A chance to be on the arm of the handsome billionaire, Ethan Carter. If people only knew he was a control freak and, if my assumptions are correct, a Mafia king.

Ethan shifts uncomfortably in the seat next to me as my thoughts ramble, and I'm silent. I tilt my head to gauge his reaction and see what he expects of me.

"Is everything okay?" I ask.

"No. I need to ask you to do something for me before I embarrass myself at the fundraiser," he growls.

I raise a brow, wondering what on earth could embarrass this man. He radiates wealth and power. When he palms his hard cock over his tailored dress pants, my eyes widen. His dick is painfully hard, straining against his dress pants, and he seems unable to calm himself.

"I'm sorry but seeing you in that dress and the scent of your skin next to me is driving me insane."

He sends a text message on his phone, and suddenly, the car pulls over discreetly.

My breathing picks up in anticipation, wondering what type of pleasure he wants me to give him without ruining my dress and arriving like I was just fucked in the back seat of his Rolls. I'm sure no words would make a difference anyway. I agreed to his terms and will fulfill my part of the agreement.

Besides, Ethan is not bad to look at, and he has an impressive cock. He is hard and cold but gentle.

My hands grab my waist-length hair, moving all the strands to one side so I can slide my body as close to him as I can in the back seat of the car. My fingers undo the buckle of his belt and unbutton his slacks. He reaches inside his boxers, and the exotic scent of his cologne causes my heart to pound. I'm so nervous. He always takes what he wants from me at the club, but always within our terms. His hard cock springs free when he releases it from his boxers. The head of his cock is angry and glistening with precum.

He gives his cock a hard stroke. I watch as a beading drop of precum pools at the head, about to spill. My eyes meet his, and they are full of lust. His eyes travel to the deep cut on the front of my dress, and his hand slides inside to cup one of my breasts. His eyes briefly close when his fingers play with my nipple.

"I need your mouth on me, beautiful," he rasps.

His eyes snap open when he feels my nervous fingers undoing the buttons of his dress shirt to not ruin it with makeup or his cum. He lets out a hiss when my fingers brush his erection and the taught skin of his stomach. The man is inked everywhere and is such a contrast against the crisp white dress shirt.

The man honestly just needs to get laid already. I'm not talking about blow jobs and rubs of my pussy against his shaft. I mean, a good hard fuck. What kind of man makes a sexual agreement that involves money, the cost of her tuition, and a quarter-million-dollar car and doesn't fuck her? It is like he wants to torture himself over losing his wife. I get he loves her even after her death, but this is just insane.

My thoughts travel to Jaden, and my pussy gets wet, but then another thought takes me by surprise. The mention of the ring bunnies he fucks after his fight when the media show-cases his wins. How he has different women on his arm when he takes a picture.

My hand finds Ethan's hard cock, and his breathing picks up.

"Briana. Fuck."

"Do you have a condom?" I whisper.

I want to break the rules. I want to fuck Ethan. No emotion. No strings. A hard, casual fuck. He needs it, and frankly, so do I. I'm tired of being in love with someone who doesn't love me. I want control over my life and over my body.

Men always take from me, cast me aside, and move on. Not anymore.

Ethan digs into his pants, opens a sleek black calfskin leather wallet, and produces a condom. I tear the wrapper with my teeth, and he frowns.

"Why do you need a condom?" he asks gruffly.

"Why do you need one? When was the last time you stuck your cock inside a pussy?"

I'm shocked at my filthy mouth, but my thoughts are in the current moment with Ethan. Him asking me to suck his cock because he is too aroused to go into the fundraiser. Then Jaden showed up in my mind, and the fine line between love and hate for the man that I love blurred the lines in my moral compass. I'm not in love with Ethan, but a quick fuck does sound good right now. The hurt from my past, mixed with Jaden's betrayal, has me feeling some way.

"Since my wife," he says softly.

The hurt can be felt when he mentions her, and I'm almost hesitant, but then darkness consumes me and replaces the feeling with vengeance. For once, I make a decision I thought I would never make. My hand slides the condom over Ethan's cock, and his eyes dip to my fingers, watching my movements as I slide the thin scrap of my panties off my legs.

"I haven't fucked a man since Jaden tossed me on my ass from his gym three years ago."

My legs straddle Ethan, and his condom-clad cock is resting against my bare pussy. My dress is bunched at the waist, and my thoughts are in overdrive. I rise on my knees to take him inside me slowly, inch by inch, and I'm glad the Phantom has a privacy window, and Thomas cannot see what is going on in the back seat of the car.

My eyes close, trying to relax so my walls adjust to Ethan's size. He groans, and his neck muscles strain. I know Ethan is holding himself back, so I whisper in his ear, "Fuck me,

Ethan. I'm letting go this once, and you should too. I know you wouldn't hurt me. Give me what I want."

A growl escapes his throat, and he lifts me like a doll. He lays me gently on the back seat of the car. He fists his cock, wet with my arousal. He brings his hand to his mouth and licks his hand, swiping his tongue, tasting my arousal, and begins to stroke his shaft.

"You taste so good, gorgeous. I'm going to fuck that sweet cunt until your eyes roll back in that pretty blonde head of yours. You are giving me a gift I have no right to take."

"You have spared me the need of having random men touch me because the one I loved didn't want me."

His eyes travel downward toward my legs, spread open, and then back up. The next words out of his mouth are controlled and deeply measured.

"Jaden Cyprus is a fool to have let something so beautiful slip between his fingers. When he finds out that I was balls deep inside of you, he will realize the depth of his mistake."

He slides inside of me, deep, and my eyes roll back at how big his cock feels. He pounds into my pussy like a man on a mission. The sounds of our skin meeting together in frantic succession, bounce against the interior of the luxury cabin along with his grunts.

My hands slide up his muscular chest, and even though he is not Jaden by any means, a woman can appreciate how gorgeous Ethan Carter is. The man is sinfully hot but emotionally unavailable. His wife was a lucky woman to have him between her legs every night.

He tilts my chin with one finger. His dark black eyes meet mine, full of lust and pleasure. "Come for me," he demands, "I want you to come all over my cock."

He slides his hands under my ass and pushes deeper.

"My god. You feel so fucking good. Fuck me, Ethan," I cry out between breaths.

His dick swells inside me when my words reach his ears.

My hands caress his muscles underneath his shirt. My mouth licks the skin from his neck.

"You are so fucking sexy. Your pussy is heaven," he says, pulling out and sliding back in until he is deeply seated as far as he can go. He repeats the movement, and my orgasm builds.

"Do you like my cock inside that tight pussy?"

"Yes," I moan. "Ethan… I'm…close."

"Fuck," he says, thrusting into me savagely.

He fucks me hard and fast. I couldn't even cry out until after the wave of my orgasm slammed into me.

His jaw is clenched while he pounds me, thrusting his hips as my pussy clenches his cock. When he's about to come, my eyes widen as another wave of an orgasm roars to life. Ethan's stare is savage. He looks like a wild animal finally released from his cage.

"Harder!" I cry out against his neck, sinking my teeth into the skin by his throat. He fucks me harder and faster. I moan, "Fuck, yes." My muscles are strained to the limit, my nipples bounce with each thrust. Skin slapping. Goose bumps rise on my skin like fire and we both come with a groan.

After a minute, he doesn't get up, his cock still inside me. His breath heating the skin on my neck.

"Did I hurt you?" he rasps.

"No. I liked it."

"Good."

His skin is slick with sweat. I clothes are wrinkled, but we couldn't care less or have fucks to give.

"Are you relaxed now?" I ask adjusting the top of my dress.

He chuckles, taking care of the condom and fixing his clothes the best he can.

"Yes."

"Good."

If he can be calm and collected like we are going over the weather, then so can I.

"You realize we are going to look like we just fucked."

"We did," I point out.

"Yeah, but everyone will know."

"If you want to drop me off. I'm okay with that."

"No. I want you by my side tonight. No exceptions."

"Okay," I say, smoothing my hair and reapplying lipstick without a mirror.

CHAPTER SIX

Jaden

"Hold the bench and don't move."

"Okay, like this? Do you like it like this, Champ?" she asks.

I'm fucking a ring bunny, trying to get my adrenaline to calm down after a fight. I just won against a fighter named Barrera by TKO, and I'm still undefeated.

"Yeah, just like that," I tell her, making sure I have two condoms on in case the first one breaks. I don't trust these girls and have no interest in drama much less getting one pregnant.

It's a quick fuck.

I slam into her, holding her hips, and she yelps when I take her rough.

I pump into her as sweat drips down my back. She is not as tight as I would like.

"Yes, you're so big," she says after a moan.

I roll my eyes, pumping into her, wishing she would shut up. My thoughts focus on one woman. The one who could make me come with just her beautiful smile and perfect body, and empty into the condom. My blonde goddess. The one girl who reminds me of a Barbie doll. Brie.

Pulling out of her, I'm not even sure if she came or not. Call me an asshole but I don't care. She straightens and pulls her short skirt down.

When she turns around, I already have the condom taken care of, my shorts pulled up, and bag on my shoulder, ready to head out the door.

The guys are outside, waiting for me by the exit.

"You want to do this again?" she asks hopefully.

"No," I say in a flat tone.

She lowers her eyes, wringing her hands.

I sigh, knowing I'm being a dick, but if I wasn't a fighter or undefeated, she would even look at me. She is what my boys call a sack chaser. Another term for gold digger.

This woman doesn't know me, and she bent over in a musty locker room in an arena to get fucked by a guy she saw on TV.

"This is a one-time thing, and it will never happen again. I don't even know your name," I say, walking out.

"Tiffany. It's Tiffany," she calls out again as I'm striding down the hallway toward Nick, Nate, Jake, and Kyle.

Nate quirks a brow. "She got attached after twenty minutes?"

"Yeah, let's get the fuck out of here before she thinks I'm waiting for her to come over."

They all chuckle as we walk out to the blacked-out Escalade.

"Hey, there's this club we should head out to tonight. To celebrate the win. VIP members only. I got an in from a guy I know who is a member. He pays half a million a year just to be a VIP, but the dancers are gorgeous. He can get us guest passes for tonight," Jake says, looking at me.

My curiosity is piqued because of the high price tag. "What kind of club is this that you have to fork over half a million a year to get into VIP?"

"It's called Equinox, and it's for the super-rich. The ones

that don't want anything to leak out. The type of place you need to know someone with deep pockets, or have deep pockets."

"You still haven't answered my question, Jake."

"It's a dance club with the most beautiful women, like a strip club. Handpicked for their dance skills as well as looks. Every girl is clean and must sign an NDA. Whatever happens there stays there. The girls even have a choice not to accept the VIP clients' requests. It's consensual, and everything is negotiable, if you know what I mean."

Nate glances at me and then back at Jake. He knows what club this is, and so do I. We run with the Mafia. Not as much as before but we've heard about Equinox from Mafia leaders, but we haven't frequented strip clubs since the Porcelain Dollhouse.

I haven't been to a strip club since I met Briana. The Mafia is how we started the gym and got the funding to go pro. Social media is the hype, but everyone knows it costs money to make money.

Nate speaks up first, "Count me out, brother. My girl would kick my ass."

I nod, expecting as much. My best friend and brother from another mother is crazy in love with Giselle. I was like him once. I could've had that.

Well, I had it, and I threw it away. Kicked her out of my life. Then I remind myself it was for the best. If you care for someone, you want the best for them, and I knew I wasn't the best for her. She is better off without me. Even if I still think about her when I'm fuckin' random girls I don't give a shit about.

My phone vibrates with an incoming text.

> Janine: Congrats on the win. Do you want to come over so I can work out your muscles?

That is the last thing I want to do. Especially at the apartment she moved into, which I regrettably told her she could rent from me after I broke it off with Brie and she left. I wanted to erase the memories I had with her there. It reminded me of her beautiful moans when I took her on the counter, against the wall, and on the bed.

> Jaden: No. Good night, Janine.

I don't thank her for congratulating me because it will give her the courage to continue to try to get me alone with her. *Not happening.* Janine is becoming an annoyance. The only thing I need from her is in a professional capacity. The massages on my shoulder relax my muscles, but the pain comes back.

> Janine: Okay. I'm at the apartment if you change your mind.

Fat chance.I had to stop her a month after Brie left when she wanted to kiss me and grab my cock through my shorts in the back room of the gym.

I don't respond and slide my phone into my pocket.

"Jake."

"What up?"

"I'll go," I tell him.

"My man. I'll text you the address," Jake says with excitement.

Twenty minutes later, I'm walking through the front door of my clean, minimalistic, empty home. My phone vibrates in my pocket, and I look at the notification with the address to Equinox.

I park in a discreet parking garage next to rows of ultra-luxury vehicles; Jake, Nick, and Kyle park their sports cars next to mine.

"Ready, Champ?" Jake asks locking his car with a knowing smile.

"Yeah, let's go," I say, following him toward a single black door with a bouncer wearing a tailored suit built like a house.

He nods to Jake and says something in the mic in his hand.

After three minutes, we have special bands that read all-inclusive for one night only. I turn my wrist to look at the bold letters written across. NO VIP. I could change that tiny detail, but I'm here to blow off steam and celebrate with the guys. I know they are excited about me winning and just want to have a good time.

We follow a hostess in a short skirt that Nick is blatantly checking out. She leads us to a table to the left of the stage. To our right is a tall man with dark hair who screams wealth, with a bodyguard standing behind his chair. His table sits right in front of the last pole, at the end of the stage set up like a runway in Paris on fashion week.

This place screams wealth with the most expensive, alcohol, cigars, and Food. A place for millionares. Some are even billionaires.

I recognize the man on our right, Ethan Carter. We move in the same circles and even have ownership investment in several companies. He comes from wealth and privilege because his father is a Mafia king. We only respect each other because of our business with important leaders.

Men like Ethan Carter scream power and danger with a huge mix of wealth. He is not old. If I'm not mistaken, he is around my age at thirty-two, with a strong build. He is always into some dangerous shit that cause people to try and end his life. His head turns in our direction, his dark eyes land on me, and he smirks.

"Who the fuck is that asshole?" Jake asks, lifting his chin in the man's direction.

Cracking my neck, I stare the asshole down. When Jake looks over, the bodyguard notices the tension and crosses his arms over his chest in a defensive pose.

"His name is Ethan Carter," I say low enough so no one near our table can overhear. He is a billionaire and probably the richest man in the room besides me. He owns numerous conglomerates all over the world. He lost his wife seven years ago in a car accident and has never been serious with another woman. They say she was the love of his life."

"Well, if they could see him now. I don't think his dead wife would approve of where he is spending his nights," Kyle chimes in.

Nick chuckles. "Someone or something must have his attention for him to be here. I guess we will find out."

"It's like getting information before TMZ," Kyle adds.

The lights change. A big motorized screen behind the three main poles lowers slowly. The shiny black floor is like in a runway but the stage is set up like concert or music video.

The hostess who sat us at the table brunette with small breasts pushed up by the lace corset walks over with a tray with a bottle of Macallan 18 and four glasses.

Smiles demurely placing them in the table. "Compliments of Mr. Carter. Congratulations on your win, Mr. Cyprus," she says and leaves.

The four of us turn our heads like robots and watch the asshole raise his glass in a mock toast.

Sitting upright in my seat, I give him a hard stare. My stomach clenches with annoyance because something isn't right.

I came here to relax, ease my mind, and not get irked.

Jake pours me a glass and I take it in one go, the infamous burn as it goes down, coating the lining of my stomach. Jake pours me another. I need to slow down. I have been training, and my body hasn't had alcohol in a while.

The seats begin to fill inside the club, and the men focus on the stage like waiting to see a famous artist in concert for the first time. Fascination and excitement can be seen marred on their faces. Ethan loosens his tie and removes his jacket, rolling his sleeves on his tattooed forearms. My eyes are trained on the stage because whoever they are all waiting for must be something to get all the attention in the room.

The sound of a piano sounds through the speakers as "Breathe" by Fleurie begins to play. The lights shine, revealing a woman with angel wings twirling in a vaguely familiar silhouette. She twists on the pole, her leg in a split as the song picks up in tempo. My head tilts to the side because I can't see her face. Her split is flawless, and when her wings spread out, it's the most beautiful thing I have ever seen.

"Wow," Kyle mouths.

She walks like an angel with wings when the hook drops down the runway with over-the-knee black velvet boots and a bodysuit with a dangerous slit down the middle. The lights turn on, and a glow is cast on her body as she struts down the runway. A fan turns on, blowing her platinum-straight hair like a gust of wind.

My stomach clenches in a vise. The girl I let go, the one above all others, is dancing with her beautiful body in front of all the men in the room. I wish I could claw their eyes out.

"Is that? Holy shit," Nick says.

Nick glances at me, and Jake lowers his gaze. My expression must reveal everything that I'm feeling. Anger, regret, sadness, and self-loathing. My eyes water, my nostrils flare, my chest rising and falling. Fuck. I swipe my hand over my face, not believing my eyes. Hoping this is a dream.

She stops when the music's over. She notices me at our table, but then her head snaps toward the man I now despise with every fiber of my being. She slides the straps holding the wings, and the motherfucker stands to help her. His fingers slide down her delicate arms, removing the elastic with familiarity. Intimacy. Rage boils inside my veins.

"Chill, Jaden," Nick says.

She straightens, but her expression is not adoration or love. It's cold, dark, and empty. Her eyes find mine, and it guts me, tearing my insides to shreds like a meat grinder. She averts her gaze. What I see terrifies me. That is not my Brie. My Brie smiles and looks human. The Brie in front of me is a shell.

When you look into her beautiful eyes, there's nothing inside. My hands grip the glass, and it feels like I'm about to break it into tiny shards.

"Still Your Girl," by Fleurie plays, and she grips the pole with the soft voice echoing through the room.

She climbs the pole to a dangerous height; every eye in the room is aimed at her perfection. When the song drops the hook, she slides down at an unsafe speed, stopping right before she can touch the floor. The song ends, and she lies on the floor with her back arched and arms spread wide like a flying angel.

"I have never seen shit like that," Jake says with his mouth agape.

"You are not helping, Jake," Kyle whisper-yells.

I'm silent, watching intently. She must have one more song because she is waiting. You can feel the anticipation in the room. You can feel it.

A familiar artist plays, one I've heard before when she danced with Giselle.

"Ultraviolence" by Lana del Ray. It's haunting.

I realize I didn't just hurt her. I obliterated what was left of her. She's back dancing in a roomful of potential predators that will use her.

This is how she is surviving. I fed her to the wolves. The small light she had is gone.

In my selfishness, I failed her. She was never supposed to

come back to this life. She is too smart and beautiful to be here. A woman with her past shouldn't be in a place like this.

That asshole next to me knows who I am for obvious reasons, but his smirk tells me one thing. He knows. His smirk is one of triumph, and I played right into it. My eyes are trained on her fluid body movements as she removes the body suit, and I frown.

"Is she taking that off?" Nick asks.

She slides the body suit off and is left in tights, a bikini, pasties over her nipples and her gorgeous breasts on display. My dick is suddenly rock hard in my designer jeans, straining against the zipper.

"Fuck," Jake says, and out of respect, the guys try to look away. My fists clench in my lap, and I'm a mess. My emotions are all over the place, mixed with arousal and anger. The anger aimed mostly at myself and the dipshit one table over claiming her. Like she is his property.

The asshole looks my way when her set is over, and she walks from the stage.

"Our queen of darkness, Coco." Is announced through the overhead speaker, and every asshole in the room gives her a standing ovation.

After fifteen minutes, she walks out by the tables in a silk robe with sexy mink heels. Her blonde hair is longer in platinum waves contrasted against her gold sun-kissed skin. My cock thickens painfully as my eyes outline the firmness of her breasts under her robe. My gaze travels down her thighs, noticing the robe is short. With each step, I catch a glimpse of her lace panties concealing her pussy.

Jake glances at me nervously because he knows I'm livid.

"Get me a room with her. I don't care what they charge. Now," I growl.

"I'll be right back. Let me see what I can do," Jake says, getting up and walking toward a tall, built man in a suit that must be the manager.

She passes by our table, and when I glance at her, my heart breaks into a million pieces. She looks at me with emptiness and hate. Kyle and Nick try to smile at her to ease the tension, but she doesn't smile back.

She says, "I heard about your fight. Congratulations on your win." Her head tilts in the asshole's direction. After tense seconds, she says, "If you will excuse me, someone's waiting for me."

Before she leaves, I circle my hand around her wrist, halting her. She pulls it from my grasp like she was burned. "Don't touch me," she seethes.

"I'm sorry. I didn't mean to make you feel uncomfortable. I need to talk to you."

Her eyes narrow to slits. "I have nothing to say to you. I have no interest in hearing anything you have to say. If you want, I can have the manager of the club find someone to entertain you tonight so you can celebrate your win. He can also include your friends. Would you like one, two, or three girls in the room?"

My jaw clenches in annoyance. "Whatever I can have with you is what I want."

She quirks a brow. "Only one person is on my list, and he doesn't share."

The mention of a man in her VIP list she must be fucking has me seeing red. Jealousy rearing its ugly head because I know it's that asshole, Ethan Carter.

Giving her a challenging smirk, I say, "Then I guess he will have to make an exception."

Her eyes flash in a dark challenge.

Jake returns, and his eyes widen when he spots Brie. "Hi," he says to her nervously.

"Hello, Jake," she says as the man who must be the manager walks up to her.

She looks at him and then at me, knowing I was already ahead of myself. I'm wearing a black hoodie, and I pull my sleeve up and show him a glimpse of my tattoo, and his eyes widen. He recognizes it like I knew he would because, like I said, we know who runs this club.

"Coco, Jaden, 'The Destroyer' Cyprus, has respectfully requested a room for a private dance."

"No problem, Marcus. Please let Ethan know I will see him tomorrow." My face contorts in rage at her mentioning the man by his first name.

"Let's go, Champ," she says.

She doesn't address me by first name, and my stomach sinks. Fuck. Rising from my seat, I follow her as she sashays toward a long, dark hallway with blood-red carpet and dark-brown wood molding. This area doesn't smell of stale cigars but like a designer boutique with expensive perfume and champagne.

She opens a discreet room that leads into a comfortable area with a velvet sofa and a minimalistic table. To the left, there is a private dance pole. There is also a chaise big enough to lie down on, and my eyes are taking in the room equipped with a panic button.

I inwardly sigh with relief she could at least call for help if she was ever back here and someone was trying to hurt her. She motions for me to sit on the couch, and a knock is heard from the door. She walks over to open it, and a woman walks in with a tray, places it on the small table to the side of the couch, and quickly leaves.

"Would you care for a drink before we start?"

"No. I want to talk."

"I'm not interested in anything you have to say unless it's regarding the rules. If you are not interested in the lap dance. I can fetch someone else, or I can quietly leave."

The muscle in my jaw ticks faster. The blood in my veins boiling, but if I kept her here, she would not go back out there. I'll take in the pleasure of having her on top of me.

"What are the rules?" I ask.

"Your pants have to be left on, but you can take off your shirt. You can touch me if I allow it."

"Do you?"

"Do I what?"

I smirk. "Allow me to touch you. You were jumpy when I grabbed your wrist earlier, and I don't want to break the rules. Since this is a different setting. I want to make sure you are comfortable with me touching you," I say, looking around the room at what it offers.

Her breathing increases as she contemplates her next answer. Her expression is blank as she stands before me, looking down while I sit looking up at her.

Her light eyes turn dark, and it's not with lust or desire. It's with the same coldness I saw earlier when she was on stage.

"I would prefer you not to touch me."

Ignoring her indifference, my fingers grab hold of the hem of my shirt, and I pull it off over my head. Her eyes immediately caress my thick, muscled chest down to my abs. My head tilts when she silently removes the robe, and I almost hiss audibly because her body is flawless. Her ample breasts, a small waist I can wrap my hands around with flared hips, the dangerous curve of her ass, and the most beautiful face I've ever laid my eyes on. She is even more beautiful than I remember.

My cock hardens to attention at the woman it has craved for the last three years.

"Everywhere. I want to touch you everywhere."

"That's what they all want."

That was not the answer I expected. Makes me wonder how many have tried. How many have tried to force her, and the rage I've been keeping in chains is close to breaking free. Tempting me to throw her over my shoulder and take her out of here.

Music begins to play, and she walks over and straddles my lap. Her scent of vanilla permeates the air around me. My hands touch her waist, and I position her over my hard dick so she can feel how hard she makes me. My lips find the place between her breasts, and she arches her back, holding onto my shoulders.

I take my fill of the scent of her skin, kissing her. She gasps when I lift her in the air, not giving a fuck about the rules.

"There's one thing you forgot, baby. I don't follow the rules when it comes to you. I break them."

Placing her on the comfortable chaise before she can protest, I'm between her legs, rubbing my hard erection over her covered pussy.

My head lowers to nibble her ear while I grind into her pussy, rubbing her clit. She watches me with no emotion. Her response was confusing; she didn't moan or smile like I remembered. Her pussy is not drenched like it used to be. This feels off and wrong. I stop. Her eyes look bleak and nonexistent when my gaze finds hers. This is not her. This is not my girl. This girl is empty. Her legs relax and she turns her head away from me.

"Are you done?" she croaks.

My heart sinks. I swallow hard because, for the first time, I feel like I'm forcing her. She doesn't want me.

She stiffens when I get up off of her, and she tries to cover herself with her hands while quickly looking for the robe.

"I'm sorry," is all I say.

What could I say? I fucked up, and I'm no different than any man in this place. Taking advantage of her and her position. I've never felt more disgusted with myself.

"Please don't ask for me again. You've done a great job staying away and forgetting about me. I want nothing more than for that to continue," she says.

"Brie. I-I can't. I'm not going to stay away," I tell her, backing her against the wall. My finger tilts her chin up so she can look at me. "I'm so sorry, baby." Her hands drop to her sides, and her robe opens, revealing her delicate skin.

My fingers quickly find the sides of the silk material, and I close it, wrapping and tying it together, covering her. Her gaze is still trained on mine, standing motionless with her plump pink lips slightly parted.

The backs of my fingers gently trace her soft cheek tenderly. Lowering my head toward her lips, my lips brush hers softly.

"I miss you," I say, whispering before my tongue finds hers in a kiss. Our kiss. A kiss that is so soft and tender. She places her hands on my chest, and when I think she will push me away from her, she rests her palms flat on my heated skin. My heart speeds up as she meets my kiss. A kiss I've missed because I may have fucked ring bunnies and random chicks, but I've never kissed them on the mouth. She is the only woman I have ever loved kissing.

"You are so beautiful," I say, breaking the kiss. "I apologize for treating you like that on the chaise. I'm truly sorry." She averts her gaze. "Brie, please look at me."

"Times up. I need to go." She moves away, and I back up, giving her back her personal space. Her response is like an ice bucket of cold water in a hot jacuzzi, but I let her go. She leaves the room, and I stand there contemplating my next move.

CHAPTER SEVEN

Briana

I never thought I would see him here in this club, of all places. He saw me, and he saw Ethan.

He saw how Ethan touched me, and his expression was murderous. I'm not sure why he even cares. What did he expect? That I would run into his arms, and he would whisk me away?

After the way, he treated me and kicked me out of his life after I fell in love with him? I gave him a part of me. The only part I had left, and he shattered it. My love meant nothing to him.

He showed me what I meant to him. A pretty face and body. No different than any other man who has laid eyes on me and shown interest.

He reminded me tonight when he rubbed himself on me. Before, I craved his touch. I would die for it.

Until he showed me how he felt about me. Pretty to look at with a dose of pity. No, thank you. I'll take my chances with Ethan and our agreement. I let him kiss me so I could leave, and he wouldn't push. I was so close to pushing him off me, but I let him. I shouldn't have, but I did, and I hate myself for it.

I walk out to my motorcycle with my helmet in hand. I bought the bike when I made money the first month I danced at Equinox. I bought it used, but it was modified and in good condition. I took professional lessons at a speed track by a company that teaches amateur riders. I thought it would be a therapeutic way to release the heartache caused by the man standing in the garage with his boys, trying to figure out my mode of transportation.

He spots me toward my Yamaha R1 with my shiny black tights and motorcycle jacket. My blonde hair was braided to the side with my motorcycle boots thudding on the concrete, causing his boys to take notice. His brows rise when he sees the helmet in my hand and finds the bike parked.

"No fucking way. She rides that thing?" Jake says.

"Is there a problem?" I ask, glaring at Jake.

He slides his hands into his pockets. Shaking his head. "No. Just surprised. My bad."

Giving them a smirk, I place my helmet on the side mirror of my bike to pair my phone to the helmet speakers and set my playlist to play. I power on the bike.

"I'm following you," Jaden says. My head turns to look at the Zenvo, idling.

Giving him a smirk, I say, "You were always a flashy guy. I guess some things never change. Are you sure you can keep up with that overpriced waste of money?" The guys chuckle.

"Are you sure you can handle that big bike?" he quips.

Licking my lips slowly, his eyes follow the movement. Admiring him in the well-lit garage compared to the darkness of the club, his black hoodie does little to hide his appeal. In the back room of the club, I noticed his body, chiseled to perfection. It reminded me of our kiss; his expensive cologne was still on my skin. If he was good-looking before, now the man is pure perfection. Everywhere.

"I guess you will just have to find out for yourself." I pause for effect. "If you can keep up." I place my helmet on to play Revolution by UNSECRET, and he briskly walks to his super-car, sliding inside and revving the million-dollar sports car while Nick slides in the passenger seat. Jake and his other friends follow in their respective sports cars.

Revving my bike's engine with the modified exhaust and power commander, he watches me as I expertly slide my gloves on before I mount the bike and roll it backward from the parking spot. Revving the bike hard, the sound echoes in the garage, giving the guard at the club's door the cue that I'm leaving.

Marcus walks out and fist-bumps me, a silent signal to ask if I'm okay. I nod because he knows I can't hear him well with the engine and music. He gives the guard at the door the signal that I'm good. Marcus takes care of all the employees, especially the dancers. Some guys can get out of line.

When I hit the main road, I am revving the bike as I take the highway and fly through the lane to the rhythm of the music. Jaden and Jake try to keep up, but I'm lighter and faster.

I take the curves, leaning so close that my knee almost touches the road's pavement. The exhilarating feeling, the adrenaline coursing through my veins as the freedom from the wind runs through me. This is my therapy. The speed is my drug to withstand the upcoming darkness that waits for me in my dark bedroom.

Getting off at my exit, his car moves up next to me. "Are you fucking crazy?" he roars.

I give him the middle finger and leave him far behind, losing him in my side-view mirror. My intention in speeding off was for him to need to find out where I live. He must think I'm unhinged by how I was riding my bike, but I don't care. Jaden is my past, and he ensured I wasn't in his future.

The kiss we shared in the room brought back memories of my love for him, and that scared me because loving him again was not an option for me. The way he treated me and left me alone all this time showed me I wasn't an important part of his life like he was for me. He has been fine without me, unde-feated as a pro-MMA fighter.

He doesn't need me like I needed him. It's too late. I have a man who wants no love or emotion and is safe. No pity, no feelings. Just feeding a need without giving myself to that man entirely. Even if it's only temporary.

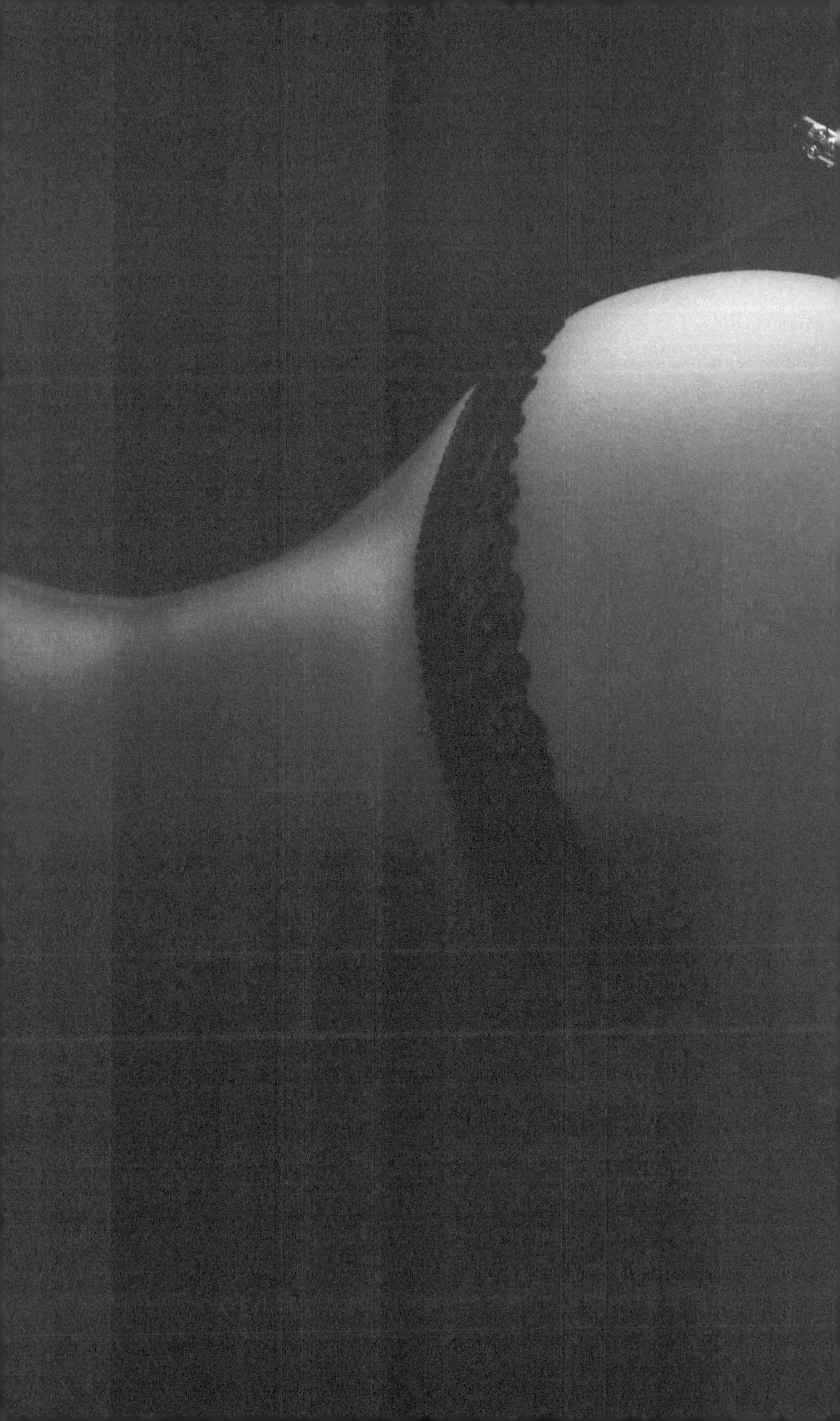

CHAPTER EIGHT

Jaden

"Come on, pick up, Nate." The phone rings as I dial Nate's number after Brie took off and I lost her.

"This better be good because it's three in the fucking morning, Jaden. Someone better be in trouble or something."

"Nate, wake up, Giselle. I need Brie's number," I tell him breathlessly. I've been driving everywhere down every street, looking out for a motorcycle with a sexy female dressed in skintight black riding gear.

"Are you out of your mind? Fuck no. I'm not waking up, Giselle."

"Please, Nate. I found Brie, and I lost her. She's dancing at the Equinox."

I hear cursing in the background. "Nate, are you there?"

"I have you on speaker, and Giselle is listening," Nate says.

"What do you mean she is dancing, Jaden?"

"Jake took us to this club called Equinox. It's a private club for the super-rich. Let's just say she is the star of the show. Her one and only VIP client is Ethan Carter."

"Ethan Carter, the billionaire? The same…"

I interrupt him. "The one and fucking only. I requested a

lap dance from her in the room through the manager, and let's just say, she is not the same Brie." After a few seconds of silence, I hear Giselle's muffled crying.

"I hate you, Jaden," she says, sniffing through her tears. "That is why she avoids my calls and doesn't come around anymore, and it's because of you. It's been three years. You should have never treated her like that. She loved you. She loved you so much. She's hurting, and I'm not there for her. You don't understand."

She was in love with me. I treated her like a piece-of-shit hookup and let her go, all the while she was in love with me? Not anymore, asshole. She can't stand you touching her. She won't even look at you.

"What don't I understand?"

She takes a lungful of breath. "There is more to Brie that she doesn't let on. She hides it very well. Let's just say she liked that you never took her to your house because it was convenient. Something she didn't want you to see. Except…"

"Except what, Giselle? Tell me. I'm not going to let anything happen to her. I regret what I did. From what I saw today, I know she is not okay, and I need to help her. I want to be the one to do it."

"Something more happened when she lived with her mom. She never told me, but I can imagine it wasn't good. She was handling everything well until that night when…"

"You don't have to say it. I know. Keep going." It pains me when she mentions that night and what those animals did to them.

"She feels bad about it and blames herself, but you took care of it, and she felt safe. I feel safe."

"And then I'm the asshole that fucked it all up by treating her like shit and kicking her out of my life like she meant nothing to me."

"Yeah, that," Nate chimes in.

"Fuck. I promise to make it right and help her. You have my word."

"Alright, brother. Giselle will try to call her, and I'll text you her number. Another thing: while I have you on the phone. This fight is being set up by Fighter Promotions, a guy named Zavier' The Sergeant' Morales coming off an injury. Count this night as a freebie, and no more drinking. Got it?"

"Yeah. Got it. See you guys later."

Lying in my bed after dropping off Nick, I dial Brie's number Nate sent me via text, which goes straight to voice-mail. So, I sent her a text.

Jaden: Nice try, sweetheart. Get ready, because I'm coming for you.

Picking up the picture on my nightstand, I glance at it. It is a picture of Brie.

I speak to it like she can hear me. "We all have demons, baby. I will find which ones are yours and fight for you."

Kissing the picture and setting it on the nightstand next to my phone on the wireless charge mat on my nightstand, I let sleep take me to the nightmares that plague me.

The feeling of many hands touching me has me springing up from the bed drenched in sweat. I'm panting from another nightmare. It must have been going on for a while because the sheets are off the bed and my phone is on the floor near the carpet.

The picture frame is clutched in my hand in a tight grip. Looking at it, the feeling of longing rises within me, making me forget my pain. The inner turmoil haunts me because there is this feeling there is one person probably going through worse, and my selfish ass was too stupid to notice.

Pulling up to the gym, I've been checking my phone all morning like a lovesick fool, hoping Brie would text me back.

Checking it one more time before getting out of the car, Nada. No text or return call. This will be more difficult than I thought. I've never been ghosted or ignored by a girl.

Opening the door of my car, I notice a black Bentley GT convertible. When I enter the gym, the guys notice me as I walk over.

"Yo, Jaden." I give Nick a chin nod heading to my office.

"Who's Bentley?" Nick asks.

I shrug my shoulders. "Fuck if I know. Did Nate buy Giselle a new car?"

"Nope, her SUV is parked in the corner," Jake says.

"Those are some pretty sweet wheels," Charles says, sitting behind the reception desk. "Bentley Continental GT convertible." He whistles. "Very expensive and very classy."

"That's brand new," Kyle says, walking in and pointing at the topic this morning. He gives me a questioning look.

"Don't look at me, it's not mine," I say, shaking my head with my hands up.

Nate walks in the front door of the gym, probably from seeing Giselle at the studio.

"Yo, Nate. Is that sweet ride yours?" Nick asks.

Nate glances at me with an expression with me pinching my brows. "No, it's someone that came to see Giselle," is all he says. His eyes never leave mine. He places his hand behind the back of his head.

"Whoever it is, tell me."

"Briana came to see Giselle. She's in the studio." My stomach clenches like a young schoolboy anxiously waiting to see his crush. An idea forms in my head.

"Bring her here. If I go over there, she will probably leave."

"I don't know, Jaden," he says, shaking his head in denial.

"Tell her Charles wants to see her. That he wants to say hi."

"That is childish and a setup," he quips.

"Come on, Nate. She won't take my calls or answer my texts. I need to see her. I want her to know she is welcome here whenever she wants. I'm trying, but I don't want to piss her off any more than she already is with me," I plead.

He scoffs. "I should record this, Jayden 'The Destroyer' Cyprus after a girl." He takes a deep breath and rolls his eyes upward. "Fine, but you owe me. Charles, I'm going to try to get Brie to come over, I'm telling her you are asking to see her," Nate tells him.

"That is Brie's Bentley? Did she graduate already?" Charlie asks.

Jake snorts and I give him the death glare. "My bad, Jaden," he quickly apologizes.

When Nate leaves for Giselle's studio, everyone's eyes are trained at the entrance of the gym, waiting for Brie to make her appearance. *Come on, baby.*

Fuck, this is nerve racking. Is this how women feel when they are waiting to see the guy they are crazy for?

Not wanting to look like a desperate teenager, I walk over to the cage and watch Kyle and another kid named Brian train as sparring partners. Brian is my newest fighter and a hothead that thinks every girl wants to nail him. He is a good-looking kid but a little too cocky. Reminds me of when I was in my mid-twenties.

"That's it, Brian. Go for the takedown."

The kid listens. *Boom!* The kid takes Kyle down, the sound echoing when Kyle's body hits the mat. My fingers are hooked through the holes of the black fence around the cage holding the weight of my arms and anticipation swarms inside my gut. Once Kyle taps out, Jake rings the bell so Brian can release him.

A rich female laugh assaults my ears and my heart clenches in my chest. Her laugh is like music to my dark soul, bringing it to life. All the fighters look over to where Briana is laughing and talking animatedly to Charles. Briana and

Giselle call him Charlie and the old man gets red in the face when they converse with him.

My gaze travels over her body in her tight black leggings and matching crop top sweater, showcasing her smooth, toned stomach. Her platinum hair is straight, with a slight wave at the ends just above her ass.

"You got the bug, Champ?" Nick says, pointing out that I'm ogling Briana from the back side of the cage, hanging on it with my bulky arms to hide my face between my arms, trying to look inconspicuous.

"Yeah, I got it bad," I tell him.

"Who is that?" Brian asks, wiping sweat off his forehead. "She is so fine. I have never seen a blonde girl look that fine."

"Keep your eyes to yourself and dick in your pants. She is off-limits," Jake says.

"Why?" Brian asks, placing his gloved hands on his hips. "She your girl?"

"That is Giselle's best friend, they are like sisters. She also used to be Jaden's girl," Nick explains. Silently thanking him for leaving out the part about how we broke up, and I was to blame for treating her in the worst way possible.

Brian glances at me and then at her. "You still want her, don't you?" he asks me.

"Is it that obvious?" I ask him.

"Hell yeah. You can't stop staring at her. With all due respect, I wouldn't blame you. She must be amazing to have your attention like that. I have never seen a girl have your attention for more than a quick lay."

She walks over and for the first time, I'm nervous around a woman. I thought of asking why she didn't answer my calls or texts like a jilted lover but realized that if I want to even have a simple conversation with her, that is not the way to go about it.

I'm curious as to how she has that car but a sinking feeling in my stomach tells me I will not like the answer. That car is definitely not her style. I'm the flashy one and she would always complain about how much money I would spend on her. One thing I loved about Briana is that she is not shallow or interested in my money.

She isn't interested in fame either. She is the type to avoid the paparazzi, and I'm thinking it's because she doesn't want people to find out things that she'd prefer to be hidden. Whatever she is trying to hide, I will find out.

Charles follows behind her over to the cage. "Hey, Jaden. Look who dropped by to say hello." He beams.

"Don't get too excited, old man," I say playfully.

"I actually came by to say hello to Charlie but didn't want to be rude and not say hello to everyone else. I apologize if I interrupted anything. I know you told me you never wanted me back here, but Nate told me that Charlie wanted me to come in and say hi. I'll be out of your hair in a minute."

I grimace at her mentioning my having told her to leave and never set foot in the gym. That she has to explain herself as to why she set foot inside it makes me ashamed of myself. My gaze finds hers and my hands are still on the fence as I turn and face her. "You can come in here whenever you want."

I want her to come here. I have missed her presence everywhere. The sound of her laughing when I would make a joke, the softness of her skin, the smell of her hair, and the sounds she makes when I'm inside her.

In my selfishness, I let her go and I'm terrified she will never want me back in her life. She doesn't look at me the same. She glances at me but that spark inside her when she would check me out, stroking my ego, is gone. She's trapped inside herself like a web of dark thoughts and awful memories. Memories I'm part of and not the good kind.

"I'm sorry about last night, I overreacted," I tell her. She crosses her arms over her chest defensively but her cropped sweater rises, and my cock begins to get hard. Thank God for groin protectors. Her small waist is exposed and when she places her weight on one leg over the other, causing her hip to jut out, the dangerous curve of her ass is visible from where I'm standing on the perimeter of the cage. My eyes travel over her, and she raises an elegant brow.

"Which part? When I spanked you in your overpriced waste of money or before?"

"Both," I quip.

"No way. She beat you in your Zenvo? With what?" Brian asks, pointing to the Bentley. "That?"

"No, brother. She beat him with a modified R1 motorcycle. I was there. She can definitely ride," Nick says.

"Is that your car?" I ask, knowing in the pit of my stomach that I will not like how she got it.

"Yep. Unfortunately, it is."

"I'm surprised."

"Why?" she asks.

"Because that isn't your style. It's flashy and overpriced," I say with a smirk.

"So was the Porsche, you bought me," she counters.

"Is that why you left the Porsche and everything else I bought you?" Her foot taps in annoyance and I know I'm pushing my luck right now, but I want to know who gave her the fucking Bentley.

"I never asked you to buy me those things."

Not letting her redirect the question, I ask her again, "So, who gave you the Bentley?" Her eyes flash and her tongue slides across her lips, the tension in the air rising. All the guys are paying attention and listening intently to our exchange.

"It was a gift."

"Who gifts a Bentley?" Charles chimes in.

She turns around and says to Charles, "Someone with a lot of money that doesn't see it as a huge expense."

Charlie whistles in amazement as he moves toward the

cage. She turns her body back around, tilting her head to the side and I can see the profile of her perfect face.

"Sweetheart, whoever gave you that beautiful car as a gift is definitely a man and is crazy about you. Are you holding out on this old man and not telling me you have a rich boyfriend somewhere?"

My head snaps up and I rise to attention at the mention of her having a boyfriend. My hands drop from the cage, and I clench them into fists.

She giggles and she looks down at her feet, her platinum hair sliding forward. "No, Charlie. I don't have a boyfriend. It was a gift. I'm single and unavailable, old man." She looks up and gives him a wink.

Charles blushes when she gives him attention. "So, who's the lucky guy?"

"You're not going to let it go, are you, old man?"

"Nope. I need to make sure you are safe and not being taken advantage of."

She blows out a breath. "Fine, Ethan Carter bought me the Bentley."

"The billionaire with all the bodyguards? The one that made the cover of Forbes?" Charlie asks, surprised.

"That would be him," she says, glancing around nervously.

My nostrils flare in anger. That motherfucker.

Jake, Kyle, and Nick exchange knowing glances. I'm guessing I will pay a visit to Mr. Carter to see what arrangement he has with Briana because she is definitely not going to tell me.

"You didn't return it? You didn't tell him it was too expensive or that you didn't like it?" I question her. I'm jealous as fuck. I know I have no right to be, but she is driving around in an almost half-million-dollar car gifted by another man. I'm fucking livid.

"I actually like the car. He knew I would like it is what he said, and I guess he was right."

I flinch like she took a swing at me. Her implying I don't know what she likes or would have liked, and it makes me feel like I never took the time to get to know her— to pay attention to the things she found beautiful or what was special to her.

"I'm sorry I left all the stuff you gave me behind. Under the circumstances, you can understand why it was best that I left quietly. It was what you wanted. I'm sure… what was her name?" She puts her index finger over her mouth, trying to remember my massage therapist's name. "Janine. I'm sure Janine was thrilled when you let her move into the apartment. She got all this cool free stuff." She shrugs her shoulders.

It's like she is twisting a knife in an old wound of my own making. I'm such a coldhearted dick. She was in love with me, and I tossed her out because she saw what I didn't see. A woman trying to seduce her man and coming between us. In reality, I'm to blame for the failure of our relationship. I put our relationship on the line by hiring Janine in the first place, never once thinking how it would make her feel.

I know I'm an asshole regarding women but with Briana, it was different. It has always been different. Her living in the apartment I provided her and driving the car I bought her. She is the first woman I have ever taken care of like that. Then I pulled the rug from under her and treated her like shit. She has every right to want to spit in my face.

A cough is heard from my right as Brian shakes his head, listening and piecing together how everything went down.

"I'm sorry," is all I say to her, swallowing my pride.

"Me, too. Looks like it worked out for you. You're undefeated and you've got everything you ever wanted. I truly wish you the best. I wish you… all the best." She looks at her phone. She is trying to compose herself and look busy. "I've gotta go. Good luck, guys, and stay safe."

She leaves, and I follow her outside to her car, chasing after her.

"Brie, wait," I plead, stopping behind her. At the sound of my voice, she stiffens.

"What, Jaden," she snaps.

"Turn around and look at me," I demand.

She slowly turns around and my head lowers and I catch her lips with mine and she melts into my arms. I hold her against my chest while my tongue traces the inside of her mouth and twirls with her tongue. The kiss is frantic and needy, like we are starving and haven't eaten in days. My hands slide under her cropped sweater to the skin between her breasts that is exposed. She moans and I break the kiss to give her some air.

We are both panting. I want to carry her to the office and show her how much I've missed her, but I can't. I want her to know that she means more than just sex, she deserves to be treated like a queen and I want to be the one to treat her like one.

We don't kiss other people on the mouth. It is a promise we made. Like a pact. When we were together, I never promised a forever or marriage to her.

One thing I promised was that I would protect her, and I failed. In my selfishness, I didn't keep my promise and broke my word. Pride wouldn't let me go after her and I lost her.

My hands slide down to her plump ass and I look down at her.

"Come to dinner with me?" I ask.

"I don't think that's a good idea."

"Why?"

She looks away. "I can't, Jaden. We're over. We've been over."

"Nothing good happens when it's easy. I know I treated you badly and I am so sorry, Brie. I really am."

"It's too late, Jaden. I can't."

"Is it because of him?"

She pulls away and unlocks the door of the car and I stand back, giving her space. "I gotta go," she says, ignoring the question.

Fuck. I rub my hand behind my neck, not caring if I look desperate. "If I call or text, will you answer me, please? I want to make sure you are okay. Will you give me that?"

"I'm not your concern anymore. I haven't been for the last three years."

I let her go reluctantly and watch her as she drives off.

"It is not what you think," Giselle says as I whirl around to see her standing there by the entrance of the gym with Nate.

"Whatever it is, I'm going to find out," I tell her.

"She is on her way to the center to give physical therapy to combat athletes. I'm so proud of her."

"What is she doing with Ethan Carter?"

Giselle sighs. "I don't know. That part she left out, no offense to you both, but guys with money and power usually have women sign NDAs. She can't discuss anything even if she wants to, but whatever it is, it is temporary, and I know my best friend. It is just… convenient."

My fists clench. "What do you mean convenient?"

"A transaction, brother, an agreement," Nate chimes in.

"Then I guess I need to pay Mr. Carter a visit."

"Are you crazy?" Giselle says with wide eyes.

"Babe, you know there is no stopping Jaden," Nate tells her.

"Do you need me to go with you, brother?"

"Nope, I got this."

"Well, don't do anything stupid. Even if we are higher in rank, he still moves in our circle." Nates says.

We both ran an updated search already on Ethan Carter. He runs a dirty shit show behind the scenes. He runs in the same circles we do. He knows who we know, and vice versa, we are involved in different areas. But he doesn't know the lengths I will go for her.

CHAPTER NINE

Jaden

Walking into the building of Carter Enterprises, I am met with a young receptionist in the lobby. Giving her a smile, I tell her I'm here to see Ethan Carter and give her my name. She walks around her desk to try smoothing her tight pencil skirt. Looking at her face, she smiles coyly at me. I avert my gaze with an eye roll, letting her know I'm not interested.

A phone rings, and she walks slowly, sashaying to answer the phone.

"Yes, Mr. Carter. I will send him in," she says through the phone.

She gives me a smile. "You may see him now. Right this way." She leads me toward the double doors that open to an elevator. She swipes her card to the thirty-fifth floor.

The elevator stops, and the doors open to a modern office with a large wood desk and two chairs. Ethan Carter is standing, giving me his back, looking out the floor-to-ceiling window.

"I know why you came here. It's because of her."

Her meaning Brie. I walk closer and stand between the two

chairs, looking at my surroundings. We are alone in the office. There is a black leather sofa to the left with a bar on the right, but no one else. No security. No bodyguards. Interesting.

Glancing at the man in the four-thousand-dollar suit, I notice he isn't thrilled to see me when he turns around, but I expected it. He knew I would pay him a visit sooner or later once he saw me at the club.

"I questioned her, but she wouldn't say. She kept true to the NDA you made her sign."

He chuckles. "Please have a seat."

"I didn't come here for a chat. I'm not one of your business associates."

"Indeed, you aren't, Mr. Cypress. I know you have done your homework about me to make sure she is safe. I don't blame you. I would have done the same and done my homework regarding you and Briana."

Taking a seat, I clench my fist to keep from reaching over and laying his ass out. His dark hair and eyes tell me he has a hidden temper, but he doesn't understand I'm strategic and tech-savvy, not just skilled in martial arts. I'm also a billionaire, like him. I'm more private about my business dealings and open about my fighting career.

He takes his seat behind his desk, and after removing his suit jacket, he rolls his dress shirt to reveal his tattoos. He is trying to intimidate or remind me where he comes from. That he isn't some silver-spoon trust fund recipient. Ethan Carter used to be a trained assassin for the Mafia. He made his money and invested it after contracting with Edgar Castellano to clean his money and create businesses all over the world so the government wouldn't be the wiser. Ethan is skilled at hiding his tracks and hides them well. He was too busy with his Mafia business dealings and didn't protect his wife like he should. Rumor has it they put a hit out on her. Not even his father could have saved her.

Slouching in my chair, not intimidated, I ask him, "What

do you want with Briana? Whatever it is, I'll pay you to get her out of it. She isn't some stripper whore you're used to." I tell him icily.

He gives me a smirk. "Do you think I would consider bringing a stripper whore to my home and let her lie in my bed? Briana is not a whore or a stripper but a very special woman."

My lip curls in a snarl at the mention of her in his home and in his bed. Fucking asshole.

"There is a difference between you and me, Mr. Carter, and that huge difference is that I don't pay for pussy."

He bellows in laughter. He holds his chin and eyes me with a determined stare. "Let's get one thing straight. There is one woman I have loved, and that is my dead wife. No one mattered more to me in this world, and I sure as hell didn't pay for her pussy. My arrangement with Briana is met with great care. She has a darkness that appeals to me. She feeds my own loss and pain. I respect her, and I like her."

I scoff. "Yeah, by using her struggles against her to feed your sick, twisted fantasy." Now I'm pissed. I sit up and snarl, "You sick fuck. Let her go. She doesn't deserve to be treated like a piece of meat," I say, my voice laced with steel. This asshole is trying my patience, but this is not the man you pound with your fist to get the message across. This man has an endgame.

"Get one thing straight. I don't treat her like a piece of meat. You obviously didn't treat her like you should have, or she would not be dancing or taking me in a back room."

"You motherfucker. I should get up and pound your face until you stop breathing."

He brushes off my threat, places an iPad on the desk, and turns it so I can see something that looks like a document. "What the fuck is that?" I ask.

"I'm showing you my agreement with her because we both run in the same circles and know the same individuals. I know her best friend is with Nate Phoenix, and he is your good friend. I don't want any problems. It's not good for business, and I don't want her childhood friend to worry that some mysterious billionaire is taking advantage of her best friend. That would cause Briana to be stressed, and if my sources are correct, Giselle is the only person she has left. Her drug-addicted mother doesn't count."

"Why should you give a fuck about her?"

"Because… I have fallen for her and I'll do anything for her."

Jealousy grips me. Rage fills inside me, waiting to erupt.

"Briana has a problem, as I'm sure you noticed at the club. She is a victim of trauma, and according to a well-known psychiatrist I have entrusted with her personal issues, Briana has PTSD and is a rape victim. She has extensive trauma, and it is not from one encounter. It's from a series of encounters. She probably doesn't sleep much."

Frowning, I look at the iPad to read the document. His words echo in my head. He highlighted the parts he knows I'm interested in.

"When reading the document, note it details what I expect of her when we meet. Oral from both parties, but no penetration except from my tongue. No anal, bondage, third-party, no hitting, slapping. She is adamant about not sleeping over at my house. She has never stayed the night. I'm not telling you this because I'm gloating. My agreement with Briana also states as a requirement that she will not take anyone else as a client in the VIP of Equinox. I'm her first and only client. My agreement with her was no kissing on the lips for a month and no other women. There is a week and a half left of the agreement. I have provided a generous mode of transportation. I have also agreed to pay extra for her studies so she doesn't have to worry about paying rent or food. She is also required to appear publicly with me on one occasion. She has already accompanied me to a fundraiser."

My rage is boiling, imagining her pleasuring this asshole. Imagine Briana coming apart on his tongue instead of mine. Serves me right for letting her go. What did I expect, that she would not be fucking someone else? It goes both ways, but like I said, I'm a selfish asshole. Now, I'm a jealous, selfish asshole. Briana has been battling something dark. Something most wouldn't be able to handle.

"The psychiatrist also told me she has adapted to this type of life because of events that occurred in her past. She has been coping with it since it happened."

"What events? What are you talking about? I know she wasn't raised in a house with a white picket fence. Her drug-addicted mother is in jail, her father could be anyone, and she was raped and beaten. I took care of it."

"You and your associates have looked out for her and her best friend. It is a little deeper than that. I also need you to be aware that her mother is being released on good behavior, and my guess is she will contact Briana and ask for handouts. It also doesn't take a genius to figure out that her mother will most likely end up back where she started or around the same scumbags. Hence, bringing Briana back to where it all began worsens her condition."

Looking at the device, I keep reading every part and the amount he is paying her.

My heart constricts at the realization that I abandoned her. Now Ethan Carter has her in his sights.

He slides a file across his desk and says, "I took the liberty of getting a copy of the request you sent from the guy we use." He points to the file. "Those are the medical records you requested. At the age of seventeen, when rumors were circulating about her first boyfriend when he took her virginity and went around town telling people she was a whore like her mother. Apparently, her mother's associates took notice and brutally raped her. Repeatedly."

With nervous fingers, I open the file and read the medical

records of her assault, her surgery to repair the damage, and medications given to prevent STDs and pregnancy. Everything was given to a rape victim on several occasions. Jesus Christ.

"I'm afraid there was more than one of those pieces of shit," he says, using the same words I threw at him. "My sources have found their location and will soon have the details with their names and addresses. I'm sure you would like to handle this since you tried coming to me. I am personally involved, but the same result will occur."

My eyes flash in dark anger I was too stupid and blind to see. My anger is more directed toward myself than this asshole.

Composing myself and keeping my cool, I know I can only direct the anger toward myself. I have no choice but to be a little civil.

"I appreciate you finding everything out on their whereabouts."

He shakes his head. "I didn't do it for me. I did it for her. She trusts you somewhat, but I'm trying to ensure she is… comfortable. She deserves that."

In trying to help Briana, this asshole is trying to make a point that he pleasures her. Even if I appreciate the shortcut in his giving me the information, I could find it through the same sources. He will soon realize who Briana belongs to and whose bed she prefers to sleep in.

"Are there any questions you have for me?"

"Yes. I want to know how much you spent on the gifts you gave her so I can wire you the money."

He chuckles. "No need. If she ever needs anything, she knows who to ask."

My teeth clench because he keeps pushing me to snap. "I'm going to take care of those pricks my way. The vehicle, she will give it back, or I'll simply pay for it."

He begins to get annoyed because his knuckles are turning

white when he grips the desk. "Taking care of those assholes is enough. The car and the gifts are hers to keep."

I bolt from my chair and lean across his desk with a snarl. "Then I'll fucking burn it all. I don't give a fuck about whatever agreement you have. Whatever sick fantasy you have with her ends now. Don't go near her," I warn him.

He gets close, and we are eye to eye, squaring off. "Or what?"

"I will break your fucking face, you pathetic piece of shit. Do you think she would even let you touch her if it weren't because you offered her money or something she desperately needed? She wouldn't let you touch her. Stop using her to replace your dead wife."

"You mention my dead wife again, and I will end you."

I give him a sarcastic smirk. "Struck a nerve, huh? Do you think she would want to be with you knowing she lives in the shadow of your dead wife? I don't know about you, but that's fucked up. Then, you are declaring that you have fallen for Briana. Mentioning your wife was never to insult her memory but to point out the fact that you are using my girl for your selfish replacement. A body to fill the void. If you care about her in the true sense and not trying to fix a girl with a broken soul for your own selfishness, then let her go. If you want the money back, you know I'm good for it, but leave her alone. She is not for you and doesn't deserve to be used."

"I'm not using her." I push myself off his desk and out of his face.

"Yeah, keep telling yourself that. Stay away from her, Ethan, or I'll make good on my promise and rearrange your fucking face," I warn him, walking toward the elevator and pushing the button.

CHAPTER TEN

Briana

"Are you ready for your set?" Marcus asks.

"Yes, Marcus. I'm ready."

"The MMA fighter you had the lap dance with last week is at the same table with one other guest. He paid the membership fee. I'm letting you know. I'm sorry I couldn't refuse him because of other circumstances."

I take a deep breath. Great, I tell myself. I know what circumstances he is talking about. The Mafia kind. Jaden pulled his rank and stance with his underground associates.

"Thank you, Marcus. I understand."

"Do you know him personally?"

Straightening the robe and leaning against the wall behind the stage, ready to be introduced on the floor, I look up at Marcus and say, "He is my ex-boyfriend. If you want to call it that. He ended our relationship right before he decided to go pro. I didn't fit in his future"—I make quotations with my fingers—"that's how I ended up back where I started."

His face falls, and it's replaced with a frown. I shrugged my shoulders, and then he gave me a smirk. "Then I guess you should give him a show."

I give him a grin. "Yeah, I should. Make 'The Destroyer' uncomfortable."

"More like hard as fuck, honey," Monica, one of the other dancers, says, overhearing our conversation.

I snort. "More like pissed off. He can get a little temperamental," I tell her.

"Sit in his lap and give them all a show," she says, giving me a wink.

"Maybe I will. Fuck him."

Marcus chuckles. "Serves him right. He will never expect it in a place like this."

"Make sure you make him really hard. I can't wait to see it," Monica says.

The sound of the DJ introducing me through the loudspeakers is my cue to head out on stage. "Equinox brings you their own queen of darkness, Coco."

When I peeked through the curtain, I saw Jaden seated with Brian. The poor guy will have a heart attack. I was going to just dance my normal routine but fuck it. It might piss him off, and he will go away.

Removing my robe, wearing the skimpiest lingerie with wicked little red bows and black mesh, the song "Fucked My Way to the Top" by Lana del Ray begins to play, and I walk leisurely to the middle pole.

When I grip the cold metal, I move my body, circling the pole and moving into a Superman move before landing on my feet.

Walking down the makeshift runway toward the farthest pole at the end of the stage like a supermodel in a fashion show, the music begins to pick up in tempo, and I drop to my knees to the beat of the song and lie on the floor near Jaden's table with my legs open in a straddle V pose with the pole between my thighs, blocking the view of my covered sex.

My eyes find him, and his gaze is full of lust trained on the mesh covering my pussy. Brian's eyes widened when I climbed the pole to the top and inverted my body with my legs open as wide as they could.

Jaden's gaze never leaves my body's movements. He watches me intently, like everyone else seated in the club. The song changes to "Cola" by Lana del Ray, and I slide down the pole slowly until my black platform heels hit the shiny black stage.

Giving Jaden a smirk, he raises his brow at the song's lyrics. His eyes scan the audience when I stepped off the stage. It is not customary for me to be on the floor with anyone, so some regulars open their mouths in shock. The straps of my bra are loose, and I slide them down slowly, making my way to where Jaden sits with his legs slightly parted, wearing black jeans and a simple white T-shirt with his bulging biceps, making my mouth water. He looks around, not believing I'm walking toward him with my breasts pushed up, making my nipples almost visible from the lining of the mesh.

I notice his chest rising and falling while his gaze caresses my almost naked form.

I stop in front of him, he looks up, and I straddle him on the chair. My hands slide over his shirt, feeling his muscled chest with my fingers. His muscles are hard like concrete. My hands and fingers slide up to his neck. He glances at my breasts, straining painfully against the see-through mesh of the teddy as the song changes to a slow tempo.

"Renegade" by Aaryan Shah plays, and with each lyric, I grind my pussy on the erection currently straining in his jeans. His hands find my waist, holding me steady as I arch my back, jutting my breasts painfully close to his face.

He places his face between my breasts, and my hands slide into the short strands of his hair. My pussy grinds on his cock over his jeans, and his gray eyes turn black as night as he looks up at me.

I lick my bottom lip, and his hold tightens.

He mouths "beautiful" silently with his lips. My head lowers, my lips hovering an inch over his, and I breathe in his exotic cologne.

Catcalls and whistles can be heard in the background. His eyes are molten, full of lust, but he knows the message I am sending him. *You can want me, but you can't have me.*

I get up and turn away from him like his thighs are on fire, and the darkness of smoke clouds my vision.

Climbing the stairs on the stage, I glide in the air, gripping the pole. The one person I thought could save me betrayed me, and all that is left is me and a room full of strangers.

CHAPTER ELEVEN

Briana

"The next day, I am at the center where I must complete my hours and residency requirements for the DPT program. Zavier Morales is the last patient requiring therapy I must complete on my own. He is considered a heartbreaker in the fighting world. He is cocky and sure of himself, like all single-combat fighters are. He has been behaving, but he loves to sneak in a comment here and there. Other than that, I have been making progress with his therapy, and he says he is ready, but my stomach clenches because his being ready means he will fight, and I want the best for all my patients.

He greets me when I walk up to the treadmill Zavier is warming up on. "Hey, Doc."

"Hello, Zavier. How are you feeling today? How's the knee?"

"I feel great. Can't wait until I get in the cage. Tearing my ACL is no joke. I'm back, and I have you to thank. Having only me for you to focus on has made a helluva difference."

"I'm glad to hear that, but it was the entire team of doctors, and FYI, I can't practice on my own as a doctor until I finish the required hours."

"So that means I still have a chance to ask you out before I'm officially your patient?"

"Uh-no. I'm not interested in going out with anyone." He looks over, and I watch him as his shirtless, muscled torso begins to reflect a sheen of sweat. Probably took off his shirt on purpose. He is so cocky and definitely a ladies' man. Having experience working at the club dancing, he is the least of my worries. I can handle flirting, and brushing it off is no big deal.

"Do you have a boyfriend?"

"I'm not discussing that with you." I brush his question off and ask, "Are you ready for therapy?"

He turns off the treadmill and follows me to the room where there is an exam table, and I can assess his knee and take notes on his progress. He sits on the table and watches my movements, and I can feel his eyes burning on my skin.

"Has anyone ever told you that you are very beautiful?"

"Has anyone told you that line is cheesy and a real turnoff?"

He grins. "So feisty. I like it."

I roll my eyes, place the file and pen down on the counter of the exam room, and move over to check his knee, making sure the door is wide open.

"I'm going to examine your knee before we head to the pool, and you start your therapy." He is wearing shorts, so it is easy to examine him. When I feel his knee to check, Zavier leans close and says softly, "I know you used to date Jaden' The Destroyer' Cyprus."

My hands freeze, and my head snaps up with wide eyes. "How did…"

He raises a hand, interrupting me. "It's no big deal. I check up on everyone. I'm attracted to you, obviously, and I Googled you, and there was this picture when he was managing Nate' The Reaper' Phoenix, and you were in it going to a gala on his arm."

My hands become clammy, and I wipe them on my uniform pants. I move to write on his open file, hoping he will drop the subject of Jaden, but he doesn't.

"What happened?"

"Nothing happened. We are just friends," I quip, not looking up. I keep writing my notes. When I look up, his brows are still raised in question.

"What?" He can probably see the hurt on my face because his eyes soften when my eyes lower and I look away.

"He hurt you, didn't he?"

I don't answer him and keep quiet. I move to wash my hands after examining his knee. I'm drying my hands when he says, "I fell in love once. It was three years before I turned pro, but she didn't believe in me. I guess, and she ended it." My eyes are on my hands as I dry them, listening to Zavier's story.

"I found out after I won my first fight. It was because she thought I wouldn't have money and would probably lose my first fight or end up a washed-up wannabe pro fighter who didn't make it. Her father has money and convinced her that being a combat fighter would not secure her future. Being with someone like me was only going to drag her down." He shrugs his shoulder. "It sucks when you love and care for someone, and they don't return the same sentiment."

I nod and give him a sad smile as I throw the balled-up paper towel in the trash bin. "Trust me, I know what you mean," I say.

I don't come from money; I never had a man love or care enough about me. I thought I did, but it was all a lie. If Zavier only knew of my past and what I have to do to make ends meet, he wouldn't flirt or call me beautiful unless it was for a quick fuck.

The tension in the air stretches, and he clears his throat and asks, "How about we go out as friends, and we go for drinks and some dancing? Maybe invite some friends so it won't seem like a date. What do you say?"

He gives me a cute grin and seems genuine in his invitation. I think about it for a minute and think of asking Giselle to come along with Nate. It would be harmless and give me a sense of normalcy. I haven't hung out with Giselle since Jaden and I broke up. She invited me to go out with her and Nate, but I felt I wasn't ready and needed to be alone. I also didn't want her asking me where I worked or where I was staying. My apartment looks like Halloween, and she would worry about me.

"I'll tell you what. I'll go if I can get my best friend to come along."

He gives me a smile, showing straight white teeth and his cheeks turning bright red.

"Really?"

"Yes, but you have to promise not to expect it to be more than just a couple of friends hanging out."

"Got it," he says. We exchanged numbers, and I told him I would call him if Giselle and Nate agreed to come along.

CHAPTER TWELVE

Briana

There is a resounding knock coming from the front door of my apartment. I'm scanning my room to find the bat I keep if some crazy person knocks on my door. I am well aware that working at a dance club half-naked can attract weirdos. Hence, I like riding the motorcycle if someone tries to follow me back home.

No one knows where I live, and I prefer to keep it that way. The knocking continues. I suddenly get nervous; I'm not expecting a visit from anyone. Taking a brave look through the peephole, I sigh in relief.

Opening the door, Jaden barges inside, crossing the threshold as I step back with a gasp with my hands gripping the bat. He raises a brow.

"Really? A bat." He chuckles.

"What do you want?" I snap and walk back to my room.

"Well, for starters, answering the door dressed in nothing but a T-shirt and a bat is not very effective against an intruder."

"I wouldn't have answered if you were someone else. How did you find me? No one knows where I live. Not even Giselle."

"I followed you. Obviously."

He walks through my apartment into my bedroom and

begins scanning my dark room with the black-painted walls, black furniture, and black sheets. Crossing my arms over my chest after putting down the bat, I face him at the foot of my bed.

"Black, huh?"

Rolling my eyes, I quirk a brow.

He smirks as he steps closer, looking down at me. His presence and cologne permeate my bedroom, making my stomach jump in anticipation. Biting my lip, his eyes track my reaction, and he lowers his head, his lips close to my ear. "Come with me. I need to talk to you outside."

"Not happening. Whatever you need to say, say it and get out."

He thinks he can come inside my apartment like nothing happened. Like he didn't throw me out of his life over his fighting career and his massage therapist. He can go fuck himself.

He tilts his head to the side. "You were always so feisty," he says, scratching his brow with his index finger. His full lips and angular jaw are so perfect you could draw a silhouette with the features of his face. He is breathtakingly masculine. All male, he could make any woman drop to her knees and worship him and his cock.

Jaden Cyprus's cock is perfect. I take a while to adjust to his length and impressive girth. Thinking about how he loved to take me against the shower wall of the old apartment has my nipples straining under my T-shirt at the memory.

He pushes me back so I'm lying over the sheets on the mattress, and my chest rises and falls. "What are you doing?

"Trust me. I'm not here to hurt you. I would never hurt you, Brie. It's me," he says, hovering over me, holding himself with his elbows caging me. My legs open wide to accommodate him between my legs. He lowers his head as he positions himself.

His gaze travels slowly up to my face, his lips close to my

ear, and he whispers, "I met with Ethan. He most likely has this place bugged. I can't discuss more now, but I need you to trust me. Remember my promise to you?"

He moves his face so he can look me directly into my eyes. I nod, letting him know I remember his promise that he would always protect me. My eyes flutter, holding back tears as I try to hold back a sob, remembering that promise he made while he was inside of me, making me his. Before he threw what we had, including my love, away.

Because he may have cared and wanted to protect me, but Jaden never told me he loved me. He never let me in. He closed a part of himself off from the world, including me, because I was never good enough to be his everything. It was a pity he felt for an abused woman. He just never knew how deep and sinister that abuse went. If he ever found out how bad and disgusting the things that they did when I was seventeen, I'm sure he would be disgusted with himself for even having sex with me.

In the three years I had to think about how he ended things, I realized it was for the best. I'm broken, and a man like Jaden need not be with trailer trash like me. He should be with a heiress or a model. Someone with a good social status without freakish nightmares. He could never love someone like me. Sometimes, we become the thing we hate the most. In my case, I had to dance for money like a stripper and let every rumor I fought back home come true. I had to let a man touch me for money because I was afraid I couldn't pay for my classes in time, and they would drop me from the program I had worked so hard to get into. I had to use my body to get myself out of the hole I put myself in.

No man would want a woman who was used and abused by the vilest humans or had to be a man's toy. Ethan having this place bugged wouldn't surprise me. If he has it bugged, I hope Ethan couldn't hear my screams from my nightmares. Every night since I was seventeen, I have had the same reoccurring nightmares, reliving the nights they came for me because my mother owed her drug dealers money. She was too strung out on drugs to notice. I was paying for a whole year's worth of my mother's debt because of the money she owed for the drugs she consumed.

Then I met Jaden; the first night I fell asleep in his arms, the nightmares stopped. I finally found peace, and I could sleep. The episodes of waking up in the corner of my bedroom, curled up in a ball, hoping they would stop touching me, or the burning sensation when I'm alone at night in my bed, reliving those moments of pain, wishing the torture would stop, it all stopped when he was with me at night holding me.

It was the safest place in the world for me to be, but where I would find solace at night in his arms, I found a whole new nightmare waiting for me the day he didn't want me in his life anymore. I was dealing with the nightmares every night before he came into my life until he became my protector during the day and at night.

A single tear escapes my eye at the reality of how, since then, I have been coping with the nightmares. The sleepless nights all alone, taking it one day at a time. He watches the tear leak down the side of my face. He leans close and slides his tongue out gently to lick my cheek, tasting it.

The scent of him reminded me of how it was when he would come home after a day at the gym. The memories come flooding my head of the rough sex. The way I let him take me however he wanted. Jaden always made sure he pleasured me before he got his release. Then, like a switch, he threw me and everything we shared away, leaving an empty, broken promise.

"Don't cry, baby. I hate to see you cry," he says against the skin of my cheek and moves to my ear again to whisper, "Come with me. Get everything you need and come with me for one night or however many nights you need. You need some sleep, baby. You can't keep doing this to yourself. Please come with me. I'll keep you safe. Always."

I sniff, and he looks down, taking my lips in his. The kiss is soft at first, but then I open and let him slide his tongue in, tracing the inside of my mouth. I whimper, and he slides his hands under my thin cotton T-shirt. He grinds his cock over the small fabric covering the slit of my pussy, and I mewl.

My hands caress the side of his ribs, and he shudders, pressing his chest over my breasts. His hands slide under my ass, lifting me to feel how hard I make him. His cock is throbbing against my clit.

Our tongues dance, a fire that grows like an inferno, and only our release will stop it from scorching us to ashes. He sucks my lips, and I suck his. He kisses me and sucks my neck. I arch, grinding my pussy over his needy cock, and I swear I'm about to go up in flames.

He pulls away from my lips and says softly, "Let's go."

I nod, still drunk from his touch, and slide my legs over the edge of the bed. He gets up and waits for me to pack my stuff in a duffel bag. He carries the large duffel bag when I go with him to sleep wherever he takes me.

My mind needs to be sharp in the morning when I head to the therapy center. If he is offering so I can get a good night's sleep, my psyche is telling me to go for it, but my heart is raising a red flag in warning. No intimacy. No promises. No sex.

My agreement with Ethan is not over. Kissing Jaden is as far as I'll go with him because of our pact when he found out Jack raped me and then beat me to watch him do it to my sweet, innocent friend Giselle.

I was always afraid of intimacy after I was raped. I feared a man's touch. The incident with Giselle made me relive everything again, and I was shattered. The only touch I had experienced before was Jace's, and it was awkward. I didn't even think I had an orgasm; I was so scared.

After the incident with Giselle and me, Jaden took the time to make me feel again. We made a kissing pact. A promise to only kiss each other. Always, no matter what. Jaden was my knight in shining armor. The man in my life above all others until he broke me.

Leaving it all behind, I had to be strong and continue to pull through and not give up on myself because God knows I wished they would just kill me after they raped me. There was a time I hoped they would just so I wouldn't feel the pain afterward and face the nightmares that plagued me in my sleep.

One thing about Jaden is that I still trust him not to physically hurt me. He may have broken me by shattering my heart and soul. But he would never physically hurt me. He looks savage and intimidating with his cocky demeanor, but he would never lay a finger on me.

Jaden never made me feel fear when I was with him. It's probably why it hurt so much when he kicked me out of his life. He was the only man that meant everything to me.

After getting dressed and locking up, I follow him to a blacked-out Range Rover in the parking lot. Looking at my bike and the Bentley parked in my designated parking spot, he says, "A man like Ethan has the Bentley tracked with GPS. He knows where you live, and he watches you. I will explain more inside the car."

"Okay."

I know Ethan watches me, and I expected he would track the Bentley, but it makes me feel safe. If Ethan was a monster, he would have shown his claws by now, but so far, he has kept true to the agreement, and I have kept mine.

Jaden places the bags inside the back, opens the door to the back passenger seat, and slides into the cabin of the luxurious SUV after me. Once inside, I noticed Brian, the young fighter at the gym, driving.

"Hey, Brie."

"Hello again."

"Nice performance."

Jaden punches him lightly on the shoulder. "Keep that shit to yourself. Smart-ass."

"My bad, Jaden. I have never seen dancing like that before. That was pure talent." Jaden gives him a murderous glare through the rearview mirror.

"Okay, I'm sorry. I'm rambling again," Brian says.

"Drive to the gym, and you can head home in your car."

"Gotcha."

Jaden holds my hand in his and sees that I'm cold. He grabs his hoodie, drapes it over my thighs, and puts an arm around me. My head rests on his shoulder, and he snuggles into me so close I can feel his heat and the scent of his exotic cologne.

After forty-five minutes, we pull into the parking lot at Jaden and Nate's MMA gym. Jaden gently slides me away from his body before jumping out of the car. He holds his hand out, and I slide mine in his.

After saying his goodbyes to Brian, he opened the front passenger door of the Rover and buckled me inside. He drives out to the main road, and I glance at him and ask, "Where are you taking me?"

"A place I should have taken you a long time ago."

I sigh. "Let me guess, a bigger apartment."

He chuckles sarcastically. "I deserve that. No. Not a bigger apartment. I want to ask you about Ethan Carter."

At the mention of Ethan, my cheeks flamed because of the things I had agreed to do with him.

"What about him?" I ask, trying to keep an even tone.

"I know I have no right to ask, but I want to know. Did you fuck him?"

The nerve to even ask me that when he has fucked God knows how many women.

"That's none of your business."

"Everything about you is my business," he snaps. He looks annoyed, and the way his knuckles turn white on the steering wheel lets me know he is trying to keep his composure.

Deciding not to play games, I answer truthfully. It doesn't matter.

"There was an agreement signed that detailed the sexual acts he would do to me and that I would do to him. No emotion. No expectation. No penetration except oral. I was to accompany him to one social event, but one thing led to another, and we had sex. Every materialistic item that was purchased was a gift given to me for his enjoyment. Nothing more."

"Who called you a whore?" he asks, his lip curling in a sneer.

"Trust me, Jaden. Back home, that is what everyone thinks of me except for Giselle. Trust me, you dodged a bullet by kicking me out three years ago. Can't say I blame you." I shrug. "The last thing a hardworking guy that has made something of himself needs is to be seen with a trailer trash whore like me."

He glances at me. "That was a mistake. I shouldn't have treated you like that, and I'm sorry. Don't say that because I've never thought about you."

I snort. "Maybe not to my face, but you sure didn't see me being part of your future. Hell, you didn't even flinch when you got rid of me. It doesn't matter if you didn't ever say it to my face. I'm just a pretty face and body that kept you company."

"You never had to dance for money while with me."

"So, what was I supposed to do when you kicked me out of your gym and your life in front of everyone? How was I supposed to survive and pay for school? You sure as shit moved your massage therapist into the apartment when I left, who happens to be a girl you had a sexual relationship with. If that wasn't a clear message, I don't know what is. Now, you ask me if I fucked Ethan Carter. How about all the women you have fucked for the past three years? You don't see me questioning your sexual relationships because, frankly, I know where I stand, Jaden. I also don't care who you fuck. Because you don't owe me anything. I'm surprised you are not with Janine at the apartment."

He winces because hearing it all laid out sounds awful. Betrayal. Abandonment. A guy that cut his girl off emotionally and let her leave, wanting nothing more to do with her. Then, he moves his ex-fuck into the same apartment with the same furniture in it. It was painful, and it hurts, and I don't think I have the strength to trust him like that ever again. Physically, I'm attracted to him. I mean, who isn't. The man is a complete badass and sexy as sin, but I'm not good enough for him. I'm damaged goods; if he ever truly found out how deep the damage is, he would drop me off at the nearest street corner.

Every guy I have ever been around that was not a rapist never wanted me for who I was. They don't know what I like or what my favorite color is. If I had a dream, what would be my favorite flavor of ice cream? The little things. Things that matter. Jaden didn't even know I had nightmares or that I would sleep in a ball in the corner of a dark room because it was how they would leave me when they were done. It meant it was over.

"I apologize, Brie. For everything I did that caused you pain, and it kills me inside that I wasn't there for you. You know I care about you." Here comes the pity party.

I sigh, try to make peace with him, and acknowledge the good things he has done for me. It wasn't his fault my mother sucks as a human or that she let guys rape me. He didn't have to buy me anything, but he did. "I want to thank you for everything you have done for me in the past. I won't sit here and not acknowledge the good things you have done for me."

"Has Ethan hurt you or made you do something you disagreed with?"

"Until now, no. He calls me his little toy."

Jaden glares at me. "You are nothing of his. He goes near you again, and I will rearrange his face. He has been warned. Whatever agreement you had is null and void as of now. You don't dance at the Equinox anymore. You have to finish your program at school, and that is what you should focus on."

"You can't tell me what I should do and not do. You are not my boyfriend or even a fling. Whatever we had was in the past. If you have a problem with where I work and how I'm doing things, then pull over, and I will get the fuck out and save you the trouble. I don't need anything from you."

"Fine, but if you think I will let you walk away, it won't happen. Giselle is worried about you. I'm worried about you. I know you haven't had a good night's sleep. I am curious to know how long. I'm trying to help you."

"Well, I don't need or want your help," I snap.

"Tough shit because you are going to get it. You need help and not the kind that involves a contract in a sex club to pay for school."

"Fuck you."

"Trust me. I plan on it."

I snort. "Touch me, and I will scratch your fucking eyes out. Who knows where your dick has been or rather what loose hole it crawled out of, fucking gross."

He smirks. "Are you jealous?"

"Why would I be jealous of a cage fighter that prefers to fuck random chicks after a win? Especially random girls who only know he exists because he is good-looking, fights, and is rich. I have enough personal problems, and the last thing I need is to catch a disease. I prefer to take my chances with

Ethan. At least he has been tested for every single venereal disease, and I'm not obligated to sit on his cock.

"It's probably too small anyway. That is probably why he made you sign an agreement."

I snicker. "Are you jealous? What if his dick is too big to fit inside my pussy and not small at all?"

Jaden glares at me before turning back to face the road. "If you don't want me to remind you about whose dick is bigger and can make you come four times in one night, then I suggest you keep comments about Ethan's cock to yourself. A billionaire that pays for pussy has a small dick in my book."

"Ha! You are definitely jealous of Ethan."

After the twenty-five-minute drive, we approach a modern gate surrounded by lush landscaping. "Where are we?" I ask. He presses a button on the car's visor, and a large black iron gate opens slowly.

He drives the car forward on a lighted path that opens to a secluded, sprawling modern mansion. The house looks like a resort rather than a home with all the white walls and glass. It reminds me of the house in the movie Sleeping with the Enemy, starring Julia Roberts. The mansion looks more like a glass house that looks open and exposed but secluded.

He presses another button, and there are seven garage doors to the right. The first one opens so he can park the Range Rover.

When I glance at him, he cuts the engine. He turns to me and says, "My home, beautiful. This is my home and I want you to stay with me."

Butterflies swarm in my stomach. The meaning behind him bringing me here is profound. Only Nate has been inside his home. He is a private person who must keep his demons chained so no one can see. No one knows how he lives or where he sleeps. When we were together three years ago, he would sleep over in the apartment most nights. Other times, he would leave after I fell asleep, and I would wake up to an empty bed.

Biting my lower lip, I swallow nervously. "You didn't have to bring me here."

He frowns. I avert my gaze and make no move to get out of the car. He should bring the person he wants to spend the rest of his life with here. He is not a damaged woman he doesn't see a future with who has an ugly past and a lot of baggage.

He jumps out of the car from the corner of my eye, silently opening the back to get my things. He disappears through a door that leads inside his house, his sanctuary, and a place I know I don't belong because that would mean he would see me. I'm not ready for him to see me or the demons that come for me at night. No one deserves to see my damage. It is ugly and would only warrant more pity. It would attract nothing other than a sense of shame, which is the last thing I want. It is bad enough I'm ashamed of where I came from, what was done how people view me, and what I've had to do to pay for food and a roof over my head.

Holding my purse, my phone vibrates from an incoming text.

Unlocking my phone, I see it is from Ethan. Great. What does he want? Jaden told me we agree void. It has been almost a month, and it is about to be over anyway. The only part that needs to be added is the rest of my tuition and fees for the last semester.

Ethan: Miss you.

Briana: No, you don't. You miss your wife. I am not your wife.

Ethan: I'm aware of that. You must think I'm crazy, but I miss you, Briana. Very much. I hope you are doing okay, and if you need me, I'm here.

Briana: No emotion. Remember? Please don't pity me. I need to give you back your car.

What is his problem? I figured he would want the car back. That could be it.

Ethan: It was a gift. I want you to have it.

Briana: I don't want it. It wasn't part of the agreement, and I don't want to feel I owe you for something I cannot afford and cannot pay you back.

Jaden appears in the doorway, eyeing me curiously, and I exit the car.

"Everything okay?" he asks.

Giving him a nervous grin, I brush it off. "Yeah, everything is fine. I have to get to school in the morning."

"You can take one of the cars. The keys are in that box." He points to a metal box with keys to different luxury vehicles hanging behind a glass window.

Yeah, it's not happening. Shrugging my shoulders, I tell him, "Sure, thank you."

"Follow me. I know it's late, so I will give you a tour of the house another time when we get home."

Home. It sounds nice, but this is different from my home. Looking at the interior of the impressive house, there are white walls and marble floors with wood accents. glass is used to divide the open interior space. It feels like you are outside. The downside of the house is that it feels empty and impersonal. Like a house, you would rent temporarily without memory of anyone living there. The pool can be seen from all angles of the house, with an outdoor gas fireplace and a glass screen. The pool's lights reflect the water against the glass like a mirror. My eyes travel to the second floor in awe. It overlooks the pool area and patio like a hidden oasis.

He turns to the right down a hallway, and at the end, double doors must lead to his master bedroom. He stops and opens a door to the left. "I thought you would be more comfortable in this room," he says, waving his hand to a room with a king-size bed and white sheets.

Everything is white, but the bedroom in my apartment is black. "There is a private bathroom through there with everything you need. If you need me, my bedroom is next door through the double doors."

"Thank you," I say, wringing my hands and looking around the room.

Funny how three years ago, I would have been honored and overjoyed to be invited to his house. Now, I couldn't care less. Jaden thinks he can help me, but it's too late. Living a life of solitude is what I have gotten used to. A dark room with dark thoughts and dark memories.

"If there is anything you need, beautiful. I'm right here." I turn my head to face him. "I appreciate you doing this for me, but I think it's too late for me, Jaden."

"No, it isn't. It's never too late," he says, getting closer. He tilts his head down and raises his index finger to caress my cheek softly. My eyes find him, and mine are blank because he frowns. "Please let me in," he whispers.

"There is nothing to see. It's dark, and the best thing for you and everyone is to leave me alone. You don't need my poison. You don't need someone like me. No one does."

He flinches at my words. "That is where you are wrong. Your best friend needs you. I need you. Let me take care of you for a while. Let me do that. Please."

Raising my chin up to look into his eyes, he leans his head down because Jaden is tall at six foot three to my five foot two and massive. His arms are much bigger than before, and his thighs are hard, solid muscle. Big but lean from when I last saw him three years ago.

At the club, I didn't want to acknowledge how much I was

attracted to him. But my body secretly aches for him to touch me. He asked me to stay for a while, and I let my guard down. But what happens after he finds I take up too much of his time? He will kick me out, and I'll be lost again. That can't happen. Ever.

He was always my safe haven, the man who fought for me when I was hurt. He fought alongside his best friend for Giselle and me, keeping us safe from the monster that tried to destroy us. Jaden was the man that kept me going.

After I left, I was lost with nowhere to go except to the place that I thought I would never set foot in again, a dance club. Dancing for money, lost in the dark with no sense of belonging because he didn't want me. He liked what he has now, and that doesn't include me.

"I'll stay for the night. Please don't change your routine for me. It's all I ask, and I will stay out of your way as much as possible."

His lips caress the top of my ear. "I want you in my bed and my space beside me. You think you can do that?"

The silence stretches as my mind decides for my body, standing still and unmoving, listening to his words.

God, he smells so good. Closing my eyes, my body says yes, but my soul screams in dark agony, and my heart hurts. Shutting down in my silence as I call inside, knowing when I fall asleep, the demons in my memories will come and collect.

"I can't, Jaden. I can't go through this again with you. I-I'm sorry," I say, turning away and running into the bathroom next to the room, closing the door and locking it.

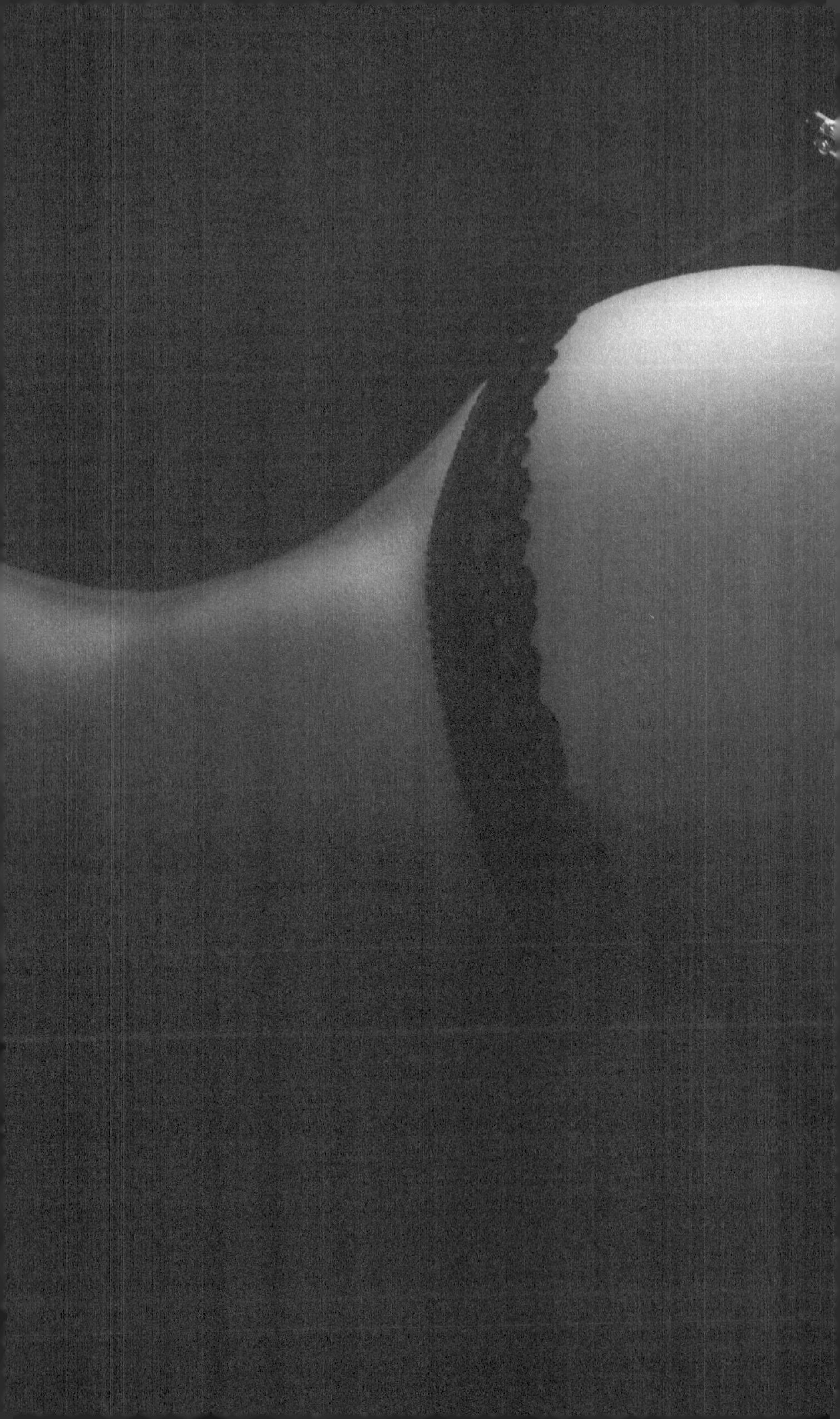

CHAPTER THIRTEEN

Jaden

Looking at the closed door of the bathroom Briana ran into before locking it, I run my fingers through the strands of my hair. The sound of the water runs, and I at least know she is taking a hot bath.

The way she gazes at me with so much hurt and sorrow, the pain she hides within, it's so great it crushes me to see it. There is nothing I wouldn't do to make it go away. I'm not expecting her to forgive me or to run with open arms.

The vibration of her phone catches my attention on the bed, and I'm not one to snoop, but it vibrates a second time, the screen lighting up with a notification. When I pick it up, it's a text from Ethan. Motherfucker.

Ethan: You must have figured out by now that I told Jaden Cyprus about our agreement, and I know it was wrong of me to invade your privacy. He must have contacted you by now, and I'm sorry. I did it because I care deeply for you, and he came concerned and didn't want you to worry or, even worse, your best friend, Giselle. I know I told you no emotion, but I fell for you the moment I saw you. When you dance, it's the most beautiful thing I have ever seen. I knew I had to have you any way I could. The way you came undone on my lips was the most beautiful gift you have given me. I miss you, Briana.

I dropped the phone like it burned my hand. That son of a bitch. I told him to leave her alone. I leave the room like there is fire on my ass. The only person I have to blame is myself because if I hadn't let her go, none of this would have happened except because I didn't know she was hiding something. I never noticed it because she slept like an angel in my arms, and I was at peace.

We were at peace, and I threw it away because I'm a coward who doesn't know how to love the woman who loved me so effortlessly. I snuffed the remaining light in her beautiful eyes.

After a cold shower, I lie in my bed and listen. Hoping that tonight she can sleep in peace. Trying to stay awake, I dose off twice, but I slap myself to keep my eyes open, hoping she comes to her senses and lies with me in my bed.

After a while, I peeked at my phone and noticed it was two in the morning. Satisfied that she should be asleep, I close my eyes, hoping my demons spare me tonight.

Darkness consumes me, and hands are trying to hold me back from reaching a bed with whimpering sounds. When I try to see what is on the bed, it's dark, and the only light is coming from a small twin-size mattress; the smell of putrid urine and cigarettes.

I'm trying to see the naked form on the bed, but hands keep holding me back, clawing and scratching me; I can't speak, I can't scream. I can only hear the whimpering of pain and agony mixed with a wicked laugh. My eyes try to see the figure on the bed, but when I'm suddenly let go, a voice I can't recognize says, "You want to see what we have done to her? Do you think you can save her? No one can save her. She has to pay her debt with the only thing she is good for." I'm thrown forward, staggering to my feet, and what I see has me screaming. The form on the bed is Briana, badly beaten and bloody. Her legs are full of angry hand marks and dirty with blood and urine. Her face is unrecognizable bruises mar her delicate skin, and it is clear she has been violated. Her head lolls to the side, whimpering in pain, coming in and out of consciousness. No, no, no, baby! I scream, but nothing comes out.

I jolt awake, arms are wrapped around me. "Shh. Shh. It's okay." Briana holds me as I sit upright; the door to my room is open, and she keeps me on the bed. "It's okay. I'm here. I'm right here," she says softly.

My eyes are burning, and my throat is raw. My hands touch her soft ones. I grab her and place her on my lap, checking her arms, face, and legs. When I'm satisfied that she is okay, I touch her face with my fingers. "I had a bad dream, and they hurt you. They hurt you really bad. Who hurt you?"

Her eyes were wide, and then I noticed she never fell asleep. She is wide awake, and when I look at my nightstand, I see my phone and the picture frame are not there. They must have fallen when I thrashed my arms in my sleep. She notices and moves, placing her feet over the edge of the bed to retrieve my phone. She finds it and hands it to me; when I check the time, it is 3:34 a.m.

She picks up the picture, and her eyes find mine when she turns it over. The light from the screen of the phone and the glass floor-to-ceiling window leading directly to the pool casts an illuminating glow in the bedroom. She looks down at the framed photograph, and her brow furrows as she recognizes herself in the picture.

The picture was taken when she wasn't looking. It is of her smiling after I made a joke. I remember that day. It was the day I realized I made her smile.

Our gazes meet, and the energy in the room crackles like an electric charge. She gently places the frame back on the nightstand and notices it's the only picture in the room. The only picture in the entire house is sitting on my nightstand, and it is of Briana.

"Who hurt you? I need a name," I ask her.

" It changes nothing. You have done enough for me. You can't risk your career or your future for me. I'm sorry, but I can't tell you."

"I'm going to find out, Brie. When I do, not even the devil can help them."

I mean every word. Whoever they are, death will come knocking, and it won't be quick. It will be painful. A pain that will be inflicted ten times worse than the pain she has endured in all the time she has suffered combined. Nothing, and no one can stop me.

She shivers, and I raise the blanket off my bed so she can crawl under it. She slides in next to me, and I begin peeling off her sleep shorts and top. Sliding my boxers down my thighs, we remove our clothes until we are both naked in my bed so I can hold her, skin to skin.

When we were together, we never slept with clothes on and always slept naked. We could feel the heat of our skin and the smell of each other's scent while I silently prayed sleep would come and find me. Now, I realize she was silently praying for the same thing. Holding her to my chest, I inhale her vanilla scent until sleep finally claims us both.

CHAPTER FOURTEEN

Jaden

I'm hitting the bag at the gym, pissed off that she left before I woke up. She took none of the cars I offered her from the garage. Her bag was gone, so she left, intending not to return. I checked the cameras and saw she left in an Uber at seven a.m. She was heading to school like she told me she would.

"What's up, brother?" Nate asks. The sweat slides down my bare chest.

"Nothing, I'm good."

"How's the shoulder?"

"The pain comes and goes. Depends on how hard I hit and train on it. Janine will stop by later for a few hours to relieve the tension."

He shakes his head, clearly not agreeing.

"How is Brie? Heard you snatched her from her apartment like a thief in the night."

"I asked, and I didn't kidnap her." I shrug. "That fucker Ethan probably is watching her or has her place bugged. You know he is a control freak."

Nate raises his brow. "That is some creepy shit. Why the fuck would he be watching her?"

"The fucker has this weird thing for her. Probably a lack of pussy and a small dick. I don't know, but I'm about to make good on my promise and gouge his fucking eyes out and rearrange his face."

Nate chortles. "That bad, huh?"

My eyes glare at him after I hit the bag with a combo and a roundhouse kick.

"He kept texting her last night. I didn't go through her phone, but it lit up, and he told her that I knew about their arrangement and that he missed her. Fucking creep. First, he is claiming he loves his dead wife, and then, professing that he misses Brie like a lovesick fool."

Nate grins. "Maybe he does really miss her. He gave her a quarter-million-dollar Bentley."

"That she left at her apartment along with her motorcycle. She didn't take any of the cars I offered last night to get around."

Nate pinches his brow in confusion. "Where was she staying exactly?

"Where do you think she stayed, my house."

Nate whistles. "Your house, huh? Giselle is going to be thrilled when she finds out. Why are you in such a grouchy mood? You got her in your house, which is a fucking miracle because only I have ever been invited."

My nostrils flare after I kick the bag with another combo. "She's fucked up, Nate. Like really fucked up. She's been through something worse than I ever thought possible. Some really fucked up shit."

My eyes sting when I think back to the medical records I read detailing what they did to her. How they left her. That is probably why I had the nightmare with the vivid image of her on the bed. It was the same bed in the trailer with the same smell except for the smell of urine. It was real like the image was placed there for me to see whatever memories she was battling, but what was weird was it was mixed with my own demons. Evil and disgusting. My eyes water when I imagine her whimpering.

Her eyes are haunted by something so dark, something so evil. She has been hiding it, and I was too stupid and self-absorbed to notice. A tear I haven't shed since I was a kid slides down my face, and I sniff, wiping it away with my forearm like sweat.

Nate notices before the other guys sparring in the cage look this way. He pulls me in for a brotherly hug, not caring that I'm drenched and crying like a bitch for my girl. Her soul and spirit are broken, and the love she had for me is gone because I killed it.

"It's all good, brother. I got your back. Whatever you need, I got you. You know that. Anything for you and Brie," he says.

After he pulls away, I nod and raise my head to the ceiling of the fifteen-thousand-square-foot gym. Breathing in and out slowly, trying to control the emotion clogging my throat.

"Thanks, brother," I croak, puffing air out of my mouth.

"Where is she?"

"She took an Uber to school this morning. She left before I woke up."

He checks his phone. "It is almost five. She will probably go visit Giselle and catch up with her BFF. I'll let you know when she shows. I will head to the office and catch up on the promo for your next fight. It's a series of three fights, the last being Zavier Morales for the title."

An hour, Janine shows up. "Hey, Champ. Ready for me?"

My eyebrow quirks, and Brian scratches his chin, eyeing her with disinterest. She is trying to make an impression with her tight uniform, which is about a size too small. Probably wears it like that on purpose. I don't know why I even slept with her before. She does nothing for me now and was a lousy lay. No attraction. It must have been an itch I needed to scratch, and she was just there and willing.

"Just the shoulder today, and that is all. Got it?"

"Whatever you say, Champ. I'll do whatever you want," Janine says with an innuendo, giving me a wink.

Brian purses his lips, and I roll my eyes. "Let's get this over with. My shoulder is killing me," I tell her.

She stands next to me, a little too close. She places her hand on my throbbing shoulder, and if things can't get any worse, the front door of the gym opens, and Brie walks in. Fuck. My. Life. The woman looks like a fucking wet dream with her simple white T-shirt stretched over her beautiful breasts with her skintight skinny jeans and Converse sneakers. Her hair piled high in a messy bun of platinum locks. Her sun-kissed skin flushed from the sun with her oversized bag on her shoulder.

Her gaze is locked on me, then slides to Janine with her hand on my shoulder. When I look at Janine and Brie, Brie's expression is blank. No emotion. My stomach clenches because three years ago, it was jealousy and hurt I now recognize. Now it's nothing. No anger, no jealousy, no hurt. Just nothing.

I shrugged my shoulder, trying to prevent Janine's hand from touching me, but she didn't budge.

"Isn't that your ex-girlfriend?" Janine asks.

Brian coughs, and Jake clears his throat. Brie ignores her. She clearly heard Janine ask a dumb question. Brie's attention turns to Charles sitting out front. Charles glances over, giving Janine a glare. He never liked Janine working here and hardly even acknowledges her. This is my fault and my own doing.

"Hello, gorgeous," Charlie says, greeting Brie.

"Hey, Charlie," she says, giving him a friendly hug.

"Are you going to dance at the studio? The Champ has therapy and then he should be done."

"That's okay, Charlie. I just stopped by to say hi.

The old man gets red in the cheeks, and Nate leaves the office. Nate looks over and surveys the scenario with a grim expression. He gives me a death glare and shakes his head when he sees the smirk Janine is sporting.

Nate walks up to Brie and hugs her but murmurs something in her ear. She nods and waves at Charlie. "I gotta get going, but I'll be at the studio."

"You're going to practice?"

"Yep. Got to help Giselle out with something," she says without a backward glance. Fuck. Taking a deep sigh, I mumble. "Let's get this over with."

We walk to the back room, leaving the door open. "Are you guys back together?"

I give Janine a glare, not answering her question regarding Brie. "I don't think that is any of your business, Janine," I snap.

"I didn't mean to…"

I interrupt her as I sit on the chair, not bothering with the massage table in the back of the gym. "You didn't mean to what?"

"I just thought that when you told me to come here and help you by giving you massage therapy sessions, that it was more. You took me out to lunch that day, ending it with her. Then you let me move into the apartment when she left."

Moving out of her grasp, I give her a murderous glare. "Are you fucking kidding me right now? There has never been anything going on between you and me, Janine. We were never anything. We had sex, but that was it. I intended to give you a job you needed and an apartment you were looking to rent. It had nothing to do with me trying to be with you. I told you the last time you tried to kiss me that this is strictly work and nothing more. I'm not trying to be an asshole, but I don't know how clear I need to be."

She looks down at her sneakers with embarrassment. "I'm sorry; I was hoping that maybe you would change your mind and, in time, you would consider giving us a chance."

I snort. "I have never given you any reason to think there would be. I'm not interested in a relationship with you."

"How about sex?"

"No, Janine."

"Is it because of her?"

I know she is referring to Brie, and I need to clarify this. My head was in the wrong place. Rising from the chair, looking down at a woman I have no feelings for and had no feelings for, I tell her what needs to be said so she doesn't think I'm leading her on.

"Janine, I don't want any personal relationship with you. The only person I want in my bed, and I would do anything for, just walked out that door thinking the worst of me."

She nods with an expression of a woman with a dent to their ego from a guy they desperately want. She takes a deep breath and asks, "What does she have that I don't, huh? She strips and dances for money. Everyone knows that."

My lip curls in a snarl at the mention of Brie dancing for money. Brie's words come back to my head when she said people think of her as a whore that dances for money. A shameful thing for a woman. A woman who must do whatever she must to survive is fearless. It takes guts and balls to not care what people think and do it anyway. Even if it kills you as a woman inside. A double standard in my book because men have no issues entertaining it. Hell, a billionaire fell for my girl because of it.

Snatching my shirt and pulling it over my head, I look down into her face and give her a piece of my mind. "Brie is beautiful inside and out. Even in darkness, her beauty shines, and every man that looks at her can see it. She dances for money but not by choice. I will tell you that when she strips all her clothes off, she is getting ready to slide next to me in my bed. If it were up to me, preferably on my cock." I move around her to walk out, but I turn around as she watches me by the door with wide eyes and her mouth hanging open.

"Oh, and by the way, her dancing is what caught my attention besides her amazingness. She doesn't beg me to fuck her, it's more like I'm the one begging. If you can't accept that she is the one I want to be with, I want nothing to do with you. I think it's best you resign in writing and leave it with Nate. If you decide to stay on, it would be for the other fighter's benefit because this is the last time I'll let you give me a massage. If you make Brie uncomfortable for any reason, you're gone," I warn.

When I walk out to the main floor of the gym, Brian and Nick give me a nod, lifting their chins. "Set her straight yet?" Nick asks, talking about Janine.

"Yeah, if she gives any of you trouble, just say the word, and she is gone. I don't need drama in the gym."

"For sure, brother," Brian says, rubbing the back of his neck with his gloves still on from sparring in the cage with Nick.

"Spit it out," I snap, getting annoyed.

He drops his hand and sighs. "None of my business, but Brie didn't look happy when she left for the dance studio. I wouldn't blame her. Who would want to see one of the reasons their relationship went up in flames still next to her man with her hand on him after three years? Especially if that someone had sex with her man before her."

"Yeah, that was fucked up. It was bad timing. We all know nothing is going on between you and Janine. It was just… messed up. I felt bad for Brie." Nick chimes in.

My nostrils flare, mad at myself. My fists clench at my sides, knowing I keep fucking up with Brie. I turn to the guys. "Then what should I have done? I already set Janine straight."

Nick scoffs, "Doesn't matter now. You let her go. Again. You never went after her. Let someone else take care of her if you don't want her."

Giving them both a cold glare. "Anyone touches her, and

I'll gouge their fucking eyes out and stuff them down their throat," I growl.

"That is what I thought. I figured you let her go because you were just being a selfish, conceited asshole that is used to women throwing their panties at you, begging for your cock. Except Brie. I hope you realize that any man would give their left nut to be with her, and here you are, acting like a fucking idiot. Let's just hope you are lucky, and she gives you a second chance because, brother, you will definitely need luck, God, the devil, and a holy prayer for her to even fall for you again," Brian says.

"When did you get so good at giving advice?" I ask him, crossing my arms over my chest. He watches behind me as Janine walks out of the gym, and I don't acknowledge her, relieved she doesn't look my way. Thank God.

"When I see a beautiful girl like that, I will die to have her attention, but then I see this asshole billionaire MMA fighter making mistake after mistake when it comes to her." Pinching my eyes together because I hate it when he is right. "You are really bad at this, aren't you? Have you asked her out on a date? The movies? Theme Park? Give her something she wanted on her birthday that she never had? I hear she didn't have the best life from the wrong side of the tracks and has a dark past. Has anyone ever done anything like that for her? It's not always Bentleys and Porsches, you know," Brian says.

My eyes snap to meet his, giving him a hard stare and he shrugs his shoulders. "Just saying," Brian says defensively.

"I have to agree with Brian on this one, Jaden," Nick says.

"I asked her out the other day and she turned me down," I answer.

The door opens, and the inner-city kids who train in the gym from the foster program waltz in. "Hey, Champ. I passed to say hi to Miss Giselle and saw my future girlfriend dancing on that tall metal pole, which was amaaazing. The way she can twist her body like that is pure art," Joey says excitedly.

He started here a year ago. He is fifteen years old with shitty parents and an ego as big as mine.

Brian snorts as the kid makes his way over. "Get in line, kid. That girl is spoken for," Brian tells him.

"Really? By whom?" He looks around and tries to see if there are any new fighters. "The only girl I know is spoken for is Miss Giselle, Nate's future wife."

Nate proposed six months before my breakup with Brie. They are waiting for the right time to get married, and they have put off the wedding because of Brie and me.

Jake walks up, having listened to the conversation. "By the Champ," Jake says.

"You? Nah. You don't have a girlfriend. At your last fight, you were banging that ring bunny, or did you forget I was told to tag along by the social worker to handle my 'anger issues,'" he makes silent quotes with his fingers.

Shit. I forgot about that. "That was before I found her again. We used to be together," I tell Joey.

He shakes his finger at me. "That means I still have a chance because Giselle told me she was visiting her and helping her with some new moves." He wiggles his eyebrows.

Jesus fucking Christ. Teenage hormones. Before I shut Joey's wild imagination down, Charlie walks up after he hears about Brie dancing. He slaps me on the shoulder.

"Brie is dancing, and I'm going to see what new moves she is teaching Giselle. The woman has talent just like Giselle, and if that young man is impressed, then I have to take a look. She dances like it is art, not like those cheesy places. Brie is like a daughter to me," Charles says.

Joey looks nervous and says, "Yeah, but she was dancing a little differently when I left. It was… distinctive. I'm not sure you want to see that. I liked it, but you look more into the classical stuff Miss Giselle teaches."

Walking after Charles, the guys follow me outside the gym and toward Giselle's studio. I don't care if Jake, Nick, and

Brian see her dance. They have seen her at the club, and ~~right now,~~ I only care for the woman in that studio dancing God knows how. The kid looked mesmerized by what he saw, and now I'm curious.

Inside the studio, Giselle has tears streaming down her face as she watches her best friend dancing in a black bodysuit with glitter fishnet tights, black platform heels, and black wings attached to her back. She is upside down in a V, like she is weightless.

"Giselle?" I ask softly.

She sniffs, but her eyes are trained on her friend as silent tears stream down like rivers over her ballerina slippers. "I used to dance like that when...," she trails off. "Ultraviolence," by Lana del Ray, plays in the studio. She dances like one is watching. No eye contact with anyone. No glances to acknowledge us all standing here watching her. It is haunting. Like we are watching a ghost that appeared. "Dark Side" by Bishop Briggs.

Charles gives me a sad expression. He empathizes with her pain. We all do. To see her like this breaks me.

She slides upside down without her hands, only her legs keeping her suspended in the air as the wings open like a creature in a dark fantasy.

Nate walks in and hugs Giselle, wiping her tears. He glances my way after he sees Brie, and he closes his eyes. Dancing is a language few understand, but we do. Brie is in a dark pain, sinister and insidious.

Goosebumps travel over my flesh at how she dances like a creature trapped in a gilded cage after being hunted. She dances on the floor-to-ceiling pole, pushing the limit. Defying gravity. It's like watching a show from Cirque du Soleil. I bet she could give them all a run for their money. Like that night on the motorcycle. Pushing and pushing. Stretching the limit.

When she finally places her heels on the ground, the song changes to "Hurts Like Hell" by Fleurie. It's the last song because she always does three songs and I've always watched her when she dances.

How did I not see it? But I know the answer was because she loved me, and it was all she had.

The song picks up, and she climbs to the top, everyone's head following her every movement. She glides on the pole, and she looks beautiful. Ethan's words creep into my mind. Hating him for acknowledging her, for wanting her, for falling for her.

Envying him because I have never experienced love or what love should feel like. I have never loved a woman. Not even my own mother. Briana is the only woman I've felt something for or even cared for.

The music ends, and she walks over, taking off the wings and sliding her arms around Giselle, hugging her tight. "I love you. Don't cry. I was trying to show you my routine at Equinox, is all," she says to her.

"It's beautiful. I miss you so much," Giselle says to Briana, leaving out the elephant in the room. The pain. She doesn't tell her everyone feels her pain.

Briana grins. "I miss you, too. My ballerina of light."

Briana looks at Nate, quirking a brow. "When are you going to marry my best friend? I've been waiting," she says, tapping her platform heel with her hands on her hips.

She glances my way, feeling my eyes boring into her body, slowly caressing her curves. When my eyes reach her face. I silently call her over with my finger, but she looks back up at Nate, waiting for her answer.

"We were waiting until you came back," he tells her.

"I'm here. It's not like I left for another planet," she says teasingly.

He smiles, getting a friendly dose of Brie.

"Good, now you can help me plan," Giselle says, relieved.

The guys smile when I glance behind me, and I catch her

gaze again when I turn around. She slowly walks over like a beautiful cover model.

"Yes?" she asks.

"Are you ready to go?"

Her lips form a grim line. "I'm going to wait for Giselle. She agreed to give me a ride home. I saw that you were busy and didn't want to interrupt."

"It's fine. I understand."

I feel deflated that she wants to return to her apartment and not stay with me. I can't blame her. What the fuck did I expect when she saw Janine touching me? I'm surprised she doesn't tell me to go fuck myself. Because I deserve it for not running after her, but I didn't, and it's too late now.

I'm about to leave after the guys start filing out of the studio, but I turn back around and ask before I chicken out like a pussy. "I can take you home. If you want."

"No, I'm good. Thank you."

CHAPTER FIFTEEN

Jaden

"The next day, Nate and Giselle leave for the night, and it's just us guys locking up. I overhear Crew, one of the new fighters who joined the gym, telling Nick that the bus for the kids has left with Joey and the other teens.

Brie finally agrees to let me take her home but stops by Charles's desk as he locks up and waits until I'm done. I keep glancing at Crew because he occasionally reflects in Brie's direction but then looks away. She doesn't notice. Her attention is on Charles as he shows her where the old man plans to go fishing.

I head to the office to lock up and retrieve my gym bag. When I head out, turning off the lights, I see that Crew is too close to Brie, and she looks uncomfortable. Charles says something to him, but Crew looks down at the old man with a scowl.

Walking closer with a snarl on my face, I catch what Crew is saying to Charles. "Come on, Charles. There is no way he is interested in her. First of all, I've never seen her here, and let's not forget he was just fucking some random in the locker room after his last fight, and let's not forget some girl he used to bang works for him here at the gym giving him massage sessions."

She stiffens when his last words leave his mouth and turns her back. Charles looks worriedly at her, but at that moment, Crew steps up behind Brie and whispers something, and I see red. She tries to move away, but he grabs her and pulls her close to his front, and she struggles to free herself. I see red because that motherfucker is dead.

"Come here, sweetheart. I'm not going to hurt you," he tells her as I run up to him.

"Leave me alone," she snaps, trying to move away.

The guys all stop in the gym as I'm running toward them, now wishing the gym wasn't so fucking big. They run quickly in the same direction, realizing Brie is in trouble.

"Get the fuck off her!" I roar.

She flinches when Crew grabs her arms tighter, holding her.

I'm coming, baby. When he sees me charging after him, he releases Brie. I quickly grab him in a chokehold and take him down. He struggles and tries to fight back, but I'm quicker, bigger, and stronger.

"What the fuck, Jaden?" he sputters, trying to breathe.

"You touched my girl, asshole. She said to leave her alone, you piece of shit. Do you think you can touch her? I'm going to fucking kill you," I say through clenched teeth, squeezing him tighter.

"Yo, Jaden. You're going to kill him," Jake says, his eyes wide, seeing I will not let up.

"Yeah, dude. Let him up." I let him go because the fucker was turning blue.

He gasps for air. He gets up after I get up and lunges after me.

I step back, square up, and land a single punch square in his jaw, and it lights out. He drops to the floor like a sack of shit. Knocked the fuck out.

"Throw him the fuck out. He sets foot in my gym again, and I'll kill him," I say through a fit of rage. "No one touches her. Got it?" I roar. My chest is heaving, the rage coming out of me in full force.

"We got it. We'll take care of him," Nick says.

I look around and find Brie shaking, her knees to her chest and her face hidden, sitting on the floor. My heart breaks to see her scared and terrified.

I pick her up and carry her, heading to the locker room. "It's okay, baby. I have you. I'm here. I promise no one will ever hurt you," I tell her softly, kissing her temple. She hides her face in the crook of my shoulder, and I push open the locker room door and head to the shower.

I take my shirt off after turning on the shower, let the steam heat up the shower area, and peel my shorts down my legs. She is looking away, shivering, wringing her hands. I remove her shoes and all her clothes until we are both naked. I pick her up and walk us both under the spray of water, trying to get her to calm down. She is in shock.

She looks at me, and I walk with her in my arms until her back is against the wall and her legs are wrapped around my waist. The water is dripping down our bodies, and my gaze travels over her beautiful, perky breasts and pink nipples. She is still shaking, but her eyes are trained on me. My head lowers, and my tongue slides over her nipple, wrapping my lips around the pink bud and sucking gently. A gasp leaves her mouth, and her back arches as the spray of water sluices down my back. Her body is seeking the pleasure it needs to feel warm and safe.

"I want to be inside you. The only one inside you," I rasp against her skin between each kiss I place on her breast. My cock is painfully hard, wanting nothing more than to slide into her where it belongs, but not tonight and never like this.

"Tell me you want me, Briana. Tell me you want me to

suck your sweet pussy. Tell me, baby. I need you to tell me so I can slide my tongue and suck that sweet cunt."

I never use her full name, but when I ask her permission, I want it clear. I'll never force her. I'll never take her silence as permission. Ever. If she will have me again, I will never let her go.

"Yes, Jaden. Please," she pleads breathlessly.

I let her slide down the length of my body and then get on my knees because she is the only woman I would kneel for. I slide my fingers between the folds of her tight cunt, making sure she is wet. Her tight bud is swollen and aching to be sucked, but I'm careful with her. I've always been careful with her, building her up before taking her hard. Call it instinct; deep down, I knew I needed to be. I always felt it with Briana. I am rough but gentle with her unless she asks me to take her a certain way. When I wanted to be rough, she would never protest. If I wanted to tie her hands, she let me.

My biggest fear is for me to hurt her physically. If I hurt her having sex, I would never forgive myself for being rough with her. That asshole touched her, the look of terror on her face sent me reeling, and I need to erase it. I will erase the feeling and do anything to keep her safe.

Her breathing picks up as I slide my tongue and suck her pussy, twirling and stroking her, holding one leg over my shoulder. Her fingers slide into my hair, and she moans in pleasure. Her pussy is slick with arousal on my tongue, and the taste of her is addicting. She is so sweet.

She arches her back against the wall, and she moans loud when my tongue swirls and flicks her clit over and over, rubbing on the spot that I know drives her crazy. The beautiful sounds coming out of her mouth echo in the locker room. I know whoever is inside the gym can hear her moans, but I don't care. Let them hear. How Briana is mine and always will be mine.

"Did he hurt you? Please tell me if he hurt you," I rasp

between each flick of my tongue inside her sweet heat, trying to erase any memory or trigger that caused her to shiver in fear.

"I was scared when he grabbed me, but then you came," she says, holding my face between her bare pussy.

"I promise, baby. I'll always protect you. Always," I say against her sweet lips, meaning every word.

Sliding my hands under her ass, holding her, I suck and flick my tongue in a rhythm. She moans with each flick—with each suck. I watch her head tilt back in pleasure.

"Yes, Jaden. Right there," she says between a breath and a moan.

Her pussy tightens around my tongue, clenching as I wait to taste her sweet cum on my tongue. A couple of flicks more, and finally, my angel falls so I can catch her in an earth-shattering orgasm. Her cry of pleasure is the sweetest music to my ears. My balls tighten, and when I'm sure she has gotten her fill. I fist my cock, fucking myself in my hand as I spill streams of cum, coming so hard I groan with my face against her bare pussy, sucking her clit inside my mouth until I drink all of her.

"You taste so good, fuck," I say breathlessly. I gently lower her leg, making sure she can stand on the tiles and her knees don't give out. We wash each other with shower gel until we rinse each other clean. I dry her first with a fluffy white towel. I reach out of the towel warmer before drying myself.

Hand her my hoodie so she can wear it with her sneakers. She pulls it over her head, and I smile, inwardly loving how she looks wearing my clothes.

Placing our soiled clothes inside my gym bag, I ask her, "Are you okay, Brie? I know you were scared, but I want to know if you feel better after I… after the shower." I'm afraid to say it because I hope she doesn't feel I took advantage of her because she was scared. She already thinks the worst of me.

She ties her wet hair in a messy bun. "I am grateful for you saving me from that asshole back there."

"I'm sorry. This was bad timing, and I never meant it to get this far. I didn't bring you inside the locker room to take advantage of you. You were shivering, and I wanted to comfort you."

She stops in her tracks before leaving the locker room. Her eyes widen with a glare.

"I know it didn't mean anything, but thank you?"

"I didn't mean it that way." I quip.

My mouth opens and closes, not knowing what to say. I don't regret touching her or pleasuring her with my tongue, but I kind of feel like I took advantage of her when she was scared and vulnerable and it's eating me inside. The seconds tick by when I stay silent. She closes her eyes and then opens them.

"I would like you to take me to my home, please."

"Not until I know that you are okay."

"Fine." She turns around, and I grip her wrist but not so tight it would hurt her.

"Let me go," she says, snatching her wrist from my hand.

I look down at her beautiful face. "Brie, I'm sorry. I didn't mean to hurt you or make it sound that way. I can't take you home right now. You need to stay with me."

"I don't want to stay with you. You need to leave me alone and let me go."

"No, I can't. It's not safe for you to be alone. You don't sleep when you're alone, and it's unhealthy."

She laughs sarcastically. "You know what's not healthy, being around you. Being around a man who only looks at me with pity. That right there isn't healthy. Stop trying to be my fucking savior. I'm not saying I don't appreciate you and everything you have done for me, but you need to stop feeling sorry for me. I don't want your money, help with sleeping at night, and I sure as hell don't need a pity fuck."

I flinch at her words, cutting me deep. I have nothing to say to her because I don't know how I feel except that I care so much for her and need her. My promise to keep her safe was broken when I let her go, and I know I don't deserve a second of her time.

She walks out, and I'm walking right behind her. Jake, Brian, and Nick are waiting by the front.

"Charles left after we assured him it was okay to go. He said to call him to let him know how Brie was doing," Nick says.

I nod. All three pairs of eyes move to where Brie is standing with her bag over her shoulder in only my oversized hoodie and Converse sneakers.

"Let me ask you guys something. How did you end up at Equinox?"

Jake, Brian, and Nick look at me nervously. Fuck. My stomach clenches, knowing where she is going with her question.

Jake swallows nervously. "I know someone who is a member and got an invite for Jaden after his last fight to celebrate," Jake says. My eyes close. I know she will figure out that we were there by chance, a coincidence.

She bites her lip with her teeth, chewing on it, and then says, "I see."

I was never looking for her.

She turns, her eyes are dark and haunted, mixed with anger and hurt. Fuck, how could I get it so wrong with her? She smirks but it scares me because she is shutting down from me and pulling away.

"If you were never invited, you never would have known I was there. You should have just enjoyed the show and left me alone. It wasn't like you were looking for me or anything," she says, walking away.

"Where are you going?" I ask.

She whirls around and faces me once again. "To my apartment, alone."

"You can't sleep alone."

She snickers sarcastically. "I have been sleeping alone. Dealing with my own shit before you and after you. Stop acting like you give a shit and don't feel sorry for me. I'm doing you a favor and staying away from you. You have a fight card with three fights ahead of you that you have to train for, and you don't need me in the way," she says, looking down at her phone and typing away.

After ten minutes, a black Merc pulls up outside with a driver holding open the door.

My face contorts in anger because the only person she could have messaged with a fucking driver is Ethan Carter.

"You called him?" I growl.

She glares at me. "Yeah, I called him. I needed a ride home because I obviously don't have a car and cannot call an Uber because it's late. So yeah, I called him. Now get out of my way."

She moves to leave, and I block her exit. She stops up short and stares at me. "Get out of my way, Jaden."

"No. I'm not letting you leave. I'm taking you home. My home. Where you belong."

Giving her my back, I open the front door to the gym and speak loud enough for the driver to hear. "She doesn't need a ride. Tell your boss I'm taking her to my house, where she will be in my bed. Preferably, naked."

"Jaden, what the hell?" she barks, trying to reach the car pushing me out of the way, but the driver is on the phone, relaying my message.

The driver looks at me speaking on his phone. "My boss says that she would have to tell him herself," the driver says.

Looking at Brie, I give her a hard stare. "Tell him, Brie. Because if you don't, I will go where Ethan is, and it won't end well."

She sees I mean every word and I'm not backing down.

"Fine," she says through clenched teeth, looking to her phone and typing quickly, sending Ethan the message.

After five minutes, the driver gets in the car and drives off.

My finger lifts her chin so she can look at me. "Don't you ever call him to come and get you or for anything else? If you need money, a car, a motorcycle, whatever you need. You ask me. Do you understand?"

Her beautiful eyes glitter from the reflection of the light coming from the gym. The guys are finishing locking up. They stand outside the gym's front entrance to wait for my instruction.

Fishing the keys for my Zenvo out of my pocket, I hand them to her. "Here, you're driving."

She looks at the keys. "You are letting me drive your precious car?"

"Yes, my girl can drive my car. Now get in. I'm hungry, and you need to eat."

Brian stands there with a smirk. "What?" I say, opening the passenger side door, looking his way.

"You are really letting her drive your car?" Brian asks.

"Yeah, why?"

"Brother, you hardly let anyone sit in that car," Jake says.

"Briana can drive or ride whatever she wants as long as it's mine."

They chuckle. "We took care of Crew and sent him on his way when you two were busy," Brian says.

"Good. If anyone ever questions my relationship with Briana, you tell them she is mine. Anyone who puts their hands on her is done."

"We got it, Champ. We know she's your girl. We won't let anyone hurt her," Nick says.

CHAPTER SIXTEEN

Jaden

She drives out of the parking lot, trying not to floor the car, changing gears, and I'm impressed she drives the vehicle well.

"We can go wherever you want, but just note that the fights have been announced, and the media will take notice. I want to talk and air out our differences."

"There is nothing to air out, Jaden."

"Keep telling yourself that. I'm sorry for what happened with Crew back there. You don't have to worry about him. He won't be allowed back in the gym or around our camp. Are you okay?"

She sighs. "Yeah. I'm good. He surprised me, and I never expected him to be so aggressive. I was more startled by your quick reflex in how you took him down."

I grin. "You never have to worry about someone hurting you, Briana. Not with me."

"I told Ethan what happened."

My head tilts to the side, and I quirk a brow. "Which part?"

She gives me a smirk. "The part that mattered."

I scoff. "The only part that mattered was me fucking you

with my tongue and the taste of your pussy when you came. The second part was when I almost killed Crew with my bare hands. Make sure you don't leave anything out."

"I never figured you were the jealous type."

"When it comes to you, there is no such thing as jealousy. More like possession. The faster you understand that, the better."

"I don't belong to anyone, Jaden. I'm not an object."

"No, you are not an object. I don't think of you as an object. I think of you as mine."

Getting comfortable in the passenger side, not used to sitting and being driven in my sports car, I tell her how I feel about us. I will open up to her like I should have done the six months we were officially together. My feelings for her have run deep because she's the one woman I have allowed to be around. She respected my wishes and never pressed me about what I was doing or where I was going.

She had every right to question me about Janine three years ago, and I was a total asshole, and she deserves better, but the attraction I feel and always felt is still strong, and I will act on it.

It is hard to find someone in your life who cares about you and can love you as a person and not what you have or judge you where you came from. Especially when you have this strong connection to each other. I will just try a different approach. I want to start over if she gives us a chance. Give me a second chance.

This time, slower. I clear my throat and glance at her profile, admiring how she looks without makeup and dressed in my hoodie. She is still the most beautiful woman I have ever laid eyes on. Briana always reminded me of a platinum Barbie or a pinup doll. She's a knockout and would stop traffic with her looks. She has that effect on people.

"What happened back there? I wanted it, but at the same time, I know that asshole touching you triggered bad memories, and I wanted my memory to be the last one you remembered."

She grips the steering wheel as she maneuvers the car effortlessly toward different fast-food places until she parks in the parking lot at the Cookout. Barbecue is her favorite food, and I can't blame her. The smell coming from the place is heaven.

I continue as she places the Zenvo in the park and shifts in her seat toward me. "When I asked how you were feeling, I feared taking advantage of the moment. That I acted out because you were vulnerable."

Her eyes find mine as she bites her lip. I keep asking her what has been bugging me in the back of my mind because whatever her answer is that would determine how I will move forward. How will I handle the push and pull I feel toward her.

"I know I have asked this, but I will ask you again. The reason is that you were quick to call him, and I'm not going to be dishonest and tell you it doesn't bother me because it does. Do you love him, Briana?"

She knows I'm referring to Ethan. The tension in the luxury cabin of the car ignites, and it's almost stifling. She places a loose tendril of blonde hair behind her ear and answers the burning question as I wait, taking a deep breath.

"No, Jaden. Like I have said before, I am not in love with Ethan Carter. Whatever happened between us was based on a written contract in exchange for money toward finishing my program. He saw an opportunity for whatever personal reason, and he took it, and so did I. There was—"

I raise a hand, interrupting her. "I'm not judging you. I am part of the blame for putting you in that position. I wasn't there for you like I promised I always would be. I'm aware of what transpired, and believe me, I offered to pay the money back, but he refused."

"What?" Her eyes flash in anger. "Why? You had no right, Jaden."

"You heard me. I went to see him, told him to leave you alone, and offered to pay back whatever he gave you to terminate the agreement. You are not a whore or an escort for hire. I had to ask if you loved him because I'll walk away if you do. I care that much about you, Briana."

Her eyes turn glassy, but she looks away. I'm wondering what is going on inside her pretty head.

After a few agonizing seconds, she asks, "What now?"

I smile and slide my fingers through hers. "Let's sit down and eat, and I will tell you." We ordered food and sat down outside on the outdoor seating. Some people recognize me and take pictures and videos whispering my cage name, "The Destroyer," but other than that, they leave us alone.

Grabbing a napkin, I get up from my seat, walk up to the order window, and borrow a pen, watching the girl blush in front as she hands me the pen. The sign from the road behind me displaying my face and my opponents with bright lights can't be missed. It's obvious I'm the same guy painted on the billboard sign. Scribbling something on the napkin, I hand back the pen, walk back toward the outdoor table, and take a seat across from Briana while she rolls her eyes upward, clearly enjoying the food.

"What's that?" she asks between bites of her pulled pork sandwich. She leans slightly, looking at the napkin to what I wrote. It reads, Please go on a date with me? 702-555-0341. It is the same thing I wrote to her in the diner when Nate and I first realized Briana and Giselle worked there after we saw them dance that night at the Porcelain Dollhouse in South Dakota.

When she looks up, she grins, remembering that day. "Are you asking me out, Jaden 'The Destroyer' Cyprus?" she asks, teasing me.

"Yes?" Hell, yes." My ego set aside, I would ask her out like a teenage schoolboy.

She slides her tongue over her lips, licking the barbecue sauce from her mouth, and my cock strains in my pants, wanting to slide inside her wet heat. I shift in my chair, trying to calm my raging hard-on, wishing it was my cock she was licking.

"It depends. Where are you planning on taking me?"

"I'm planning on taking you to dinner and a movie."

She quirks a brow. "That would be a first. I have never been on a formal date before. Not like that." She wipes her mouth and takes a sip from the plastic straw of her drink.

"I would like to take you on many dates if you agree. I wrote my number on that napkin because you probably don't have it saved in your new phone, even after I texted you. Sometimes, writing it on paper makes it seem genuine."

"You're right. I don't have your number saved, but you have mine. Funny, I don't remember giving you my new number when I saw you at the club."

"I have my ways," I say, giving her a grin. "I want to taste your skin and find those hidden secrets you keep." My eyes flick to hers, and she stares into my own, seeking. Searching.

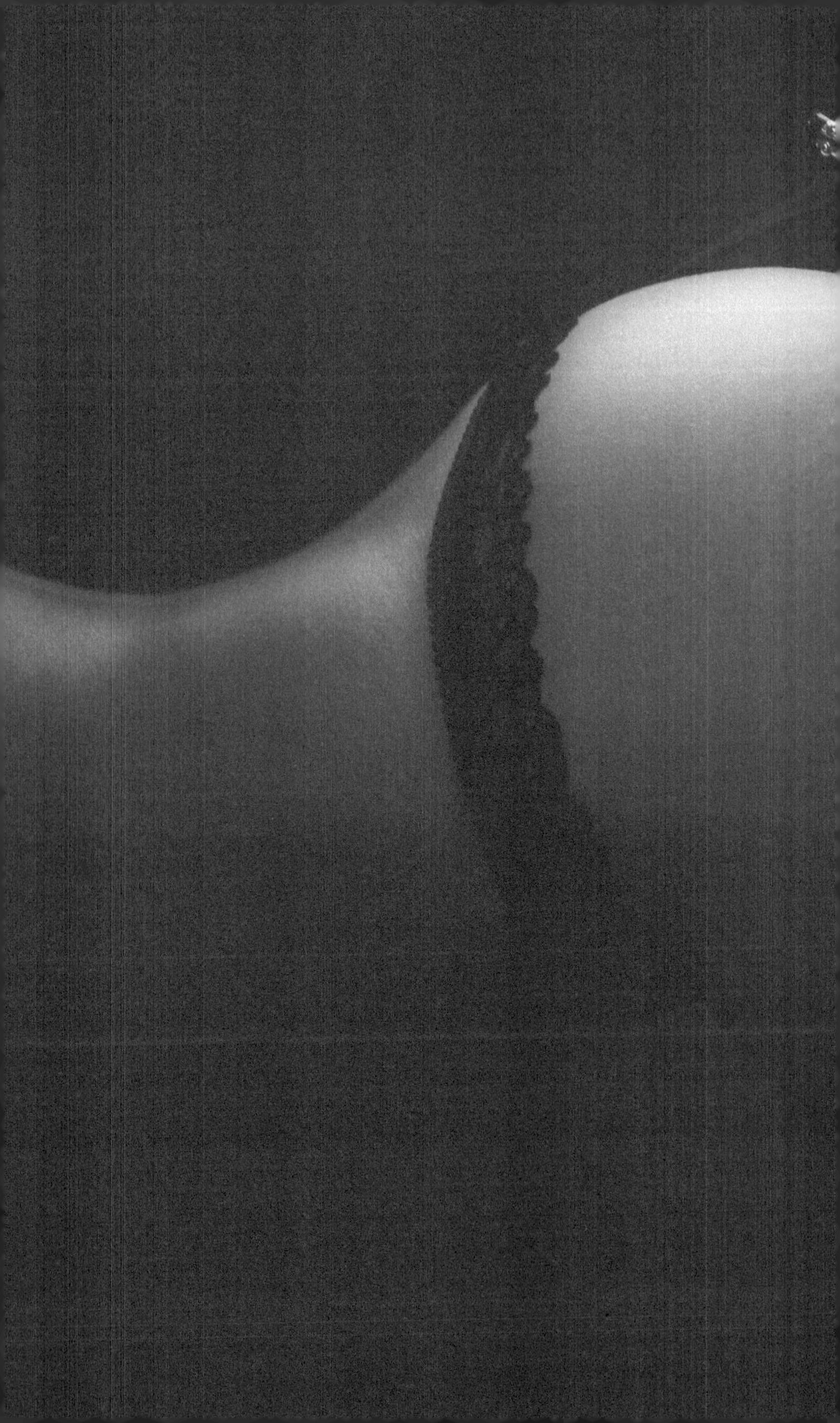

CHAPTER SEVENTEEN

Briana

My eyes bore into his, searching for what he wanted. Why now? He had the chance to do all the things when we were together. We never went on dates. Jaden is the type of man that gets straight to the point. He likes you physically, he fucks. That is basically it. If he wants you around, he'll buy you shit.

We have a connection. That much is obvious. We both come from a dark past with evil secrets most people would run away from once they discover what haunts us. I realize it is what draws me to him. The convenience of never telling him what they did.

I'm surprised he went down on me in the shower. According to Ethan, Jaden knows some of the damage that was done, and my worst fear is that he would risk everything to seek revenge on those who have broken me. Those who left me almost fighting for my life when I was dragged and left to die one night at a clinic in another town. Where I lied about my age and who I was. Where I hardly remembered what happened the first and second time until the nightmares began. Giving me bits and pieces of what happened those nights of torture.

The mind sometimes can block out the trauma, but sometimes it likes to choose certain scenes as a reminder, like a kaleidoscope of images for you to see.

The hospital took pictures, but everything was swept under the rug. I found them in my chart and brought them before I left that day. It was partly because I was ashamed and decided I wouldn't give them any information. There were no names to be given for fear they would make good on their promises and kill me.

If the authorities knew I was really seventeen, they would have taken me away and sent me into the foster care system. The two men besides Jack weren't old. They were maybe the same age as Jaden or even younger. They promised to kill me if I told anyone, and I believed them.

When I paid my mother's debt, she turned to Jack for meth and started the cycle all over again. When I left my mother's trailer, I learned to pole dance and landed two jobs. One is in the diner, and one is at the Porcelain Dollhouse.

Giselle's parents died in an accident, and she came from New York heartbroken. She was my only friend since we were kids. Her parents were everything. They were the best parents anyone could ask for, they were a kind, loving couple who loved their daughter so much. Sometimes, they would give me food and a warm place to stay when needed. It hurt to see them pass, and it hurt most to see Giselle lose the best parents in the world. They are the only people I consider family.

After everything that has happened, Jaden is back in my life and wants to take me out on a date. How do I answer that? He hurt me and broke my heart. The guy I thought was my savior dismissed me like a one-night stand.

When Jace, the guy I gave my virginity to in high school, found out I was dancing at the Porcelain Dollhouse, he actually tried to ask me out and plead for forgiveness.

I remember how Jace was ashamed of me because of my mother and where I came from. That is why I don't tell people about my parents or where I'm from. He spread awful rumors I was an easy lay but then felt guilty for spreading a lie and apologized. He pleaded for me to forgive him, and I did, but I couldn't stand looking at him because he was part of the reason I was being raped.

Then Jaden showed up with Nate at the Porcelain Dollhouse and swept me off my feet. For me, it was like love at first sight. He was my everything until he wasn't.

Taking a deep breath and looking down at the table with my hands fidgeting, I ask, "Have you ever been in love, Jaden?"

He frowns, pinching his brows together, and still looks handsome. The man is sexy. His arms bulge as he bends them, placing his elbows on the table. I hold my breath, waiting for his answer. Maybe I'm waiting for him to finally tell me the words I have longed to hear from him or that at least he can fall in love.

He looks away, and my stomach bottoms when he says, "I don't know. I've never felt love for anyone before. I have never had a mother's love or father's love, only their hate toward me. If you asked me if I could identify what love is, I wouldn't be able to give you an answer."

My stomach squeezes because it is sad to know you couldn't identify what love is or if you can even feel it. I learned what love was through Giselle and her parents. That was love. Two people could love and care for each other in marriage and pass the love on to their child. How Nate and Giselle love each other. That is what I longed to feel with Jaden. Love is what I felt for him three years ago. Now that he is honest with me, I was right for giving him what he wanted and quietly walking out of his life. Now I know the truth. When I was busy loving him, he never loved me back.

It makes sense now. When you don't love someone, it is easy to let that person go. It is why he let me go and never looked for me or called. Jaden didn't love me then, and he doesn't love me now.

I swallow the lump lodged deep in my throat. My hands are in my lap, clammy with sweat because I know I have to turn him down. I need to look out for myself; deep in my heart, I deserve someone to love me.

I'm tired of being hurt and don't want to explore something I know he cannot give me. If he couldn't see the love I had for him when we were together, then there is no point. Being friends is the only thing I can offer him, and it's a friendship that involves not staying in his house or sleeping in his bed. I'm making a terrible mistake in letting him touch me intimately as much as I crave it, and the physical attraction is there but I'm selling myself short, as the saying goes.

Placing my hand on his arm, he looks up, and I give him a wry smile. Licking my lips and swallowing, I let him down gently. "I'm sorry, Jaden, but I can't go out with you." Looking at the billboard announcing his next three fights, I know I'm doing what is best for him and what is best for me. "You have three big fights coming up. You need to be in the gym training, not wasting your time with me."

His lips form a thin line, and I know it's not what he wants to hear. His finger taps impatiently on the table. "Why?" he asks.

"Because I'm not part of your life. I never was. You can have sex with whomever you want and won't have to worry about me getting upset or feeling guilty about it."

"I want to have sex with you and only you."

I scoff. "It is highly unlikely after your last fight and your next one. I can't give you that part of me anymore."

He wipes a hand over his face and stares down at me. I hate disappointing him but can't risk him rejecting me again. He can't love me, and maybe if I was incapable of loving him or wanted someone to love me in return, I could say yes. But I can't. I cried too many nights because of him, alone in my dark room. The pain of Jaden breaking my heart was too much, and I wouldn't be able to survive it a second time.

I had to start over, and it reminded me of when I left my mother's trailer alone with nothing. It was my fault for depending on him and believing in his promises. He has done much for me and cared for me for a while. He doesn't owe me anything. He should be living his dream. A dream he has earned. He doesn't need my baggage dragging him down. He was honest with me about his feelings; now I need to be honest.

"Look, I don't want to throw that in your face, but you must stop acting like you wanted me. For three years"—I put up three fingers emphasizing how long it's been since we broke up—"you have managed to be undefeated and fight as a pro fighter without me. You never reached out after you let me go, and I understand now. It was hard for me. I was alone, striving to finish school and dancing for a buck. I had to lie to my best friend so she wouldn't feel sorry for me because I just wanted her to be happy with the man she loved. Three years, Jaden."

"I'm sorry," he says with a grimace.

"It's not your fault, it is my fault. You can't help the way you feel. You just said you don't know what love is or if you ever felt it. It means you never loved me, and I'm okay with that. It answers a lot of questions I wanted answers to."

"What questions, Brie? I'm trying to make things right between us."

"I know that, but this is the best way."

"I can't let you go."

I tilt my head, holding back the tears. "You already let me go. I slept in a motel until I could make enough in a week dancing to get an apartment after I left. While you were living your dream, I was dealing with my demons alone in the dark. You didn't come looking for me to see if I was okay; now I know why. Leaving with Janine to lunch that day at the gym when you asked me to leave that hurt, Jaden. It was mean and cruel but it was your way of ending things, and I respected it."

I'm tired of putting myself out there. I may never get over him, but I cannot fall to his feet because he wants me on his terms. He doesn't get to choose, and he sure as hell will not get to decide. He may have a dark past I know nothing about, and I appreciate him showing me he cares by bringing me into his home. His sanctuary. But caring for someone is not the same from loving them. My heart has been put through the fucking grinder and I'm tired.

"You were never a distraction. I told you I was sorry, and I made a mistake."

"And I have accepted your apology and I totally understand. I know you care about me, but you can't risk yourself defending me. The last thing I need is for you to risk your title or career because of me."

"Why do you keep saying that?" he says through clenched teeth.

"Because I'm not worth anything to anyone and you made it very clear I wasn't worth shit to you," I quip, rising from my chair, leaving the key to his Zenvo and money for my meal under the fountain drink, leaving the napkin with his number on it on the table.

"What are you doing?" he asks as I walk away to an awaiting Uber. "Where are you going, Brie?" He quickly gets up from his chair.

I stop and turn around with my hand on the rear passenger door of the white Toyota Corolla before opening it. "To my apartment, and don't worry about me sleeping. I've been dealing with my shit alone for a while," I say as I slide into the car, watching him place his hands over his head as he watches the car drive away.

I'm sure he hadn't noticed me ordering an Uber, but it was my plan while he went to grab a napkin. What happened in the locker room should have never happened, and it was pure need mixed with lust stemming from a bad situation that triggered me. In his honesty, how he feels toward love hurts, but knowing they cannot love you back is better. He has protected me and has never hurt me physically, but what he has never done with his fists, he has done with his words.

When I left his house that morning, I took my bag with me and took them to my apartment before heading out to the clinic where I would treat my first patient and combat fighter, Xavier "The Sergeant" Morales. My focus is on my career, and Giselle agreed to hang out when he invited me out as friends this Friday. I need a change of pace and some fresh air.

It is the beginning of my career; I just hope they can offer me a payment plan when I go there tomorrow so I need not depend only on dancing at Equinox until I fulfill my requirements. I was recently awarded my title of doctor by completing all the course requirements and hours required in my core program, but I still have to complete Xavier's therapy at the clinic, which is dubbed clinical hours. Then, I have to find a permanent position, so I am permanently leaving dancing at Equinox behind.

I was so excited to hear that I had finally earned the title of Doctor of Physical Therapy. I did it. When I called Giselle, she was so excited. That is when she agreed to hang out with me and celebrate, including my new friend/patient. She assured me Nate didn't mind and that Nate, Jaden, and the team would be busy training until we planned to go out late on a Friday night.

After thirty minutes, the Uber dropped me off, I entered my apartment, and got ready for tomorrow. I text Ethan to ask him if he has my apartment bugged like Jaden suggested.

> Briana: If you have my apartment bugged.
> That is creepy.

> Ethan Carter: I don't, but I have GPS on the
> Bentley for your safety.

Briana: Fair enough.

Ethan is an attractive man. There is no doubt about that with his chiseled physique, tattoos all over his body, the dark Mafia thing going on, but not my type, and the fact a woman must compete with a dead wife. Double pass.

Ethan Carter: Are you okay? I'm displeased with the incident involving Mr. Crew.

Briana: What are you going to do? Hang him? Chinese torture?

Ethan: Maybe?

Briana: Fine. Whatever.

Ethan: Was his tongue better than mine?

You have to be fucking kidding me. I should have never told him everything, but I was still reeling from what happened, so I assured him Jaden would take care of Crew and my needs afterward. I was honest because of our agreement. I was okay if he wanted to end the arrangement, but he said he understood.

Briana: I will not answer that. It is none of your business.

Ethan: That is where you are wrong. You are my business.

Briana: If your wife was still alive and walked into a room. Would you choose me? Would we still have an agreement?

Setting my phone down on my nightstand, I know I hit a hard spot, mentioning his wife. I did it so he would back off. I make sure I remove my clothes in the bathroom to take a shower. He didn't respond as quickly as before and I know the answer. How easily he can say he is falling for me when he pledges his undying love to his dead wife. It would be heart-wrenching to fall for a man who will always be in love with a ghost and would choose that love if given the chance. You would always be second in his feelings, living in the shadow of a dead woman, knowing he will always be hers.

When I return to my room, I peek at my phone to see if I received an answer from Ethan. No answer. Just as I thought, I'm a substitute for what he is missing. I have no feelings for him. Whatever I did was transactional and never would have happened if… I was with Jaden. I would never look at someone else if we were still together because I was so in love with him.

Double-checking that my apartment is locked and I have my bat, I return to my room and get ready to go to bed, waiting for the memories to come and haunt me with a vengeance.

Sitting up on my bed, I look at the darkness of my walls, the black sheets of my bed, and the black furniture, and envy the dead woman probably buried in the black dirt of the cemetery. I don't envy her for being dead, but I envy her for having someone who would do anything to have her back.

CHAPTER EIGHTEEN

Jaden

I have been training nonstop since the night she left in the Uber at the fast-food place. I have tried to text and call her for the past two days, but she doesn't answer. I'm moody and pissed off because she has been avoiding me. I was tempted to show up at her house again but decided against it. She made it clear she didn't want me to take her out or to have sex. My ego took a blow, but I can only blame myself for ending it with her. When I had her in my arms, full of her love, I was too stupid and blind to see it. I hurt her, and I know it is not going to be easy trying to win her back and asking her for forgiveness.

"What's up, brother?" Nate asks.

"Nothing."

"Is it because of Brie?"

My head snaps in his direction at the mention of the woman plaguing my thoughts. I haven't been able to sleep, so instead, I take my grumpy ass to the gym and just train for my upcoming fight.

My nostrils flared, and I let out a deep sigh. "Yeah. She isn't taking my calls or accepting my invitations to take her out. I don't know what else to do. She won't talk to me and told me to let her go."

Nate rubs the back of his neck with his hand, and his lips thin. He looks up at me with a frown.

"What?"

He shakes his head and powers on the big flat-screen T.V. on the main wall of the gym to the latest news gossip channel highlighting the fundraiser's attendees. The flashes of the camera can be seen as a black Phantom pulls up, and the door opens to the mysterious billionaire; no one has dirt on them because he is a controlling dick, Ethan Carter. He suddenly holds his hand out, and a small, delicate hand slides into his. My heart begins to hammer as a wave of rage and jealousy hits me with the force of a blow.

Briana smiles at him, and Ethan pulls her toward him. His hand is placed on the small of her back, and she is wearing a beautiful emerald mini dress with a deep cut showcasing her delicate breasts that leave little to the imagination. She looks breathtaking, her platinum waist-length hair cascading down to her back. She stops and fixes a button on his suit jacket, and the look he gives her is of a man that looks at a woman he just thoroughly fucked.

Looking at her, I can see her expression. The look on her face is of a ravished woman, and it is the same look she would give me when… I would take her against the wall in the apartment. The headline on the T.V. reads, "Billionaire Ethan Carter has a new love interest."

"What the fuck?" I roar.

"Yo, is that Briana?" Nick asks, pointing to the screen.

"Yep," Giselle says, coming up next to Nate.

"You knew about this?" I ask Giselle.

"I know she has an agreement to accompany him to an outing. She is single. She can date and go out with whomever she wants."

"You know what I mean, Giselle. Did you know all this time that she fucked him?"

"She…"

I snap, interrupting her, "Look at her face." I place my hands on my head, trying to control my fury. I lower my tone because it is not her fault or anyone else's but mine. I know Briana told me when I asked if she slept with him, but to see it on T.V. plain as day. I can tell, and it fucking hurts. "I know that look on her face. It's the same look she has after..."

Giselle scoffs. "Oh please, Jaden. If she did or didn't, that is none of your business. How many women have you fucked after you tossed her out of your life? The night you saw her at the club by chance, when you realized how she has been scraping by, trying to make something of herself all on her own. You had a title fight, and we all know what Jaden Cyprus does after a fight; he fucks a ring bunny. So, stop crying when a girl goes and has consensual sex with someone else."

I know what she is saying is true. Briana isn't cheating, and Ethan isn't married. His wife died, and Briana is gorgeous; any man is lucky to have a beautiful, smart girl he can love unconditionally. She is right. There is nothing wrong with a young woman like Briana, who has been through so much to date and have sex with a good-looking man who is obviously under her spell. The problem, she is fucking the wrong man. The man she is supposed to be fucking is me. I'm the man who is supposed to be putting that look on her face every chance I get. She doesn't want me, but I know she doesn't love him. That tells me I still have a chance.

"He is wrong for her," I blurt in frustration.

Nate, Nick, and now Brian stand watching me with a look of surprise at my outburst.

"At least she is getting some," Giselle mumbles.

Nate raises his brows and chortles.

"You are not helping," I scold Nate.

"I warned you that day you hurt Brie and ended it with her. I'm with Giselle on this one."

I blow a puff of air out of my mouth. My rage is beginning to burn through my veins like an inferno. Crazy thoughts of kicking Ethan Carter's ass and chopping off his dick cross my mind. I know that will not have Briana running back into my arms, but a guy can hope, right?

"What do you suggest I do?" I ask Giselle.

She places her finger over her lips in thought. Her eyes find mine and she says, "Show her you care about her. Remind her of the good times you two shared. Get to know her on a level no man has ever done. Make an effort, Jaden. You are going to have to crawl to win Briana back. It is not going to be easy. I'm her best friend and I know how Briana thinks. She is convinced you don't need her in your life. Briana doesn't stay where she isn't loved."

Giselle looks at the screen, replaying the clip of Briana and Ethan arriving at the fundraiser. "That man is in love with his dead wife and Briana knows that he couldn't love her the same way. Even if he falls for Briana because everything in life is possible. It would be pointless."

"How do you know that?" I ask.

Her gaze finds mine, and all the guys hold their breaths, listening intently to Giselle. She tilts her head, and her eyes go soft when she talks about her best friend, whom she loves and adores like a sister. "Because no one can compete with a girl's deepest love. No greater love can compete with just one day of her loving you."

My chest tightens from Giselle's words when she described the love I had from the most important woman in my life. Like a fucking idiot, I let her go. She must feel like I betrayed her, that my promises had an expiration date. The day I told her to go and not set foot in my gym, the things I said that day replay in my mind, and I feel disgusted with myself. I left with Janine to lunch to push her away because I thought I was doing the right thing.

Everyone thinks I'm the best fighter in my prime with an

undefeated title, but I'm a coward because I didn't fight for the one girl who loved me for who I was.

"I'm going to win her back. I'll do anything for her."

"Then you better start groveling because that guy she is with up there just found out the diamond he has is priceless, if you know what I mean," Brian says.

"Fuck him. All he is going to do is put a target on her head. People like him have a lot of enemies, and he thinks he isn't endangering her by parading Briana out in the open. If anything, I have to protect her."

"What do you mean?" Giselle asks with a frown.

Looking around to ensure it is only us and no one is eavesdropping on our conversation, I lower my voice and tell Giselle how we are involved with Ethan Carter.

"We have ties with the Mafia. Nate and I used to run with them and are partners in many of their business operations. Nate and I love MMA, but it is not what we always did. I run all their tech and firewalls, surveillance, you name it."

Giselle looks at Nate. "I know you told me something, or rather that you run in darker circles, but the fucking Mafia, Nate?"

"I know it sounds bad, but we aren't as deep as Ethan because we chose this life and are always in the limelight. Jaden and I always wanted to fight. It is how we got out of it. We have had to do things we aren't proud of, but we don't come from rich families. We came from the foster care system and ended up on the streets. We have no parents, no lineage, we have nothing, Giselle. We have to make it out there; sometimes, we have to deal with bad people to make it ahead. Ethan Carter is part of the Mafia and is considered a Mafia king because he directly deals with them, and his father is a leader, and what Jaden is saying is that he thinks Briana is now in danger."

She gives me a fierce look of determination and says,

"You have to do something. I'm not going to sit here while he puts my best friend in danger."

"I'm on it. Trust me, nothing will happen to her. You have my word."

CHAPTER NINETEEN

Briana

I lie down, my head hitting the pillow with a thud, and my cell phone rings. When I look at who is calling, it's Jaden.

I answer the call, closing my eyes. "Hello?"

"Open the door," he growls.

I sit up, bolting from the bed in my simple white T-shirt and lace panties. "What?"

"If you don't want me to get in your apartment my way, I suggest you open the door."

I end the call and hurriedly open the front door. Jaden is standing there, filling the open doorway with his broad frame, looking sinfully attractive with his shirt stretching across his chest and his sweats hanging low on his waist. He raises a brow as he catches me ogling him.

"Please don't give me another excuse. Why do you answer the door dressed like that?"

My eyes lower to my bare thighs. The hem of my white T-shirt barely covers the band of my panties. When I look up, he moves inside, closing the front door with a thud and flick of the bolt.

I cross my arms across my braless breasts, trying to cover my hard nipples from his gaze. His eyes flicker over my arms. "I don't invite men inside my apartment."

"The only man invited inside this apartment better be me," he quips.

I lift my chin in a challenge. "Or what?" I snap.

He dropped the strap of his gym bag, which I hadn't realized was hanging on his shoulder because I was too busy admiring his perfect chest and bulging muscles I wanted wrapped around my body.

He lifts me, and my legs wrap around his waist as he walks us back to my bed. "Or I will have to kill each and every man that comes through that door to touch you"—his eyes lower to my chest—"no one gets to touch you," he says, holding me against his body with both hands on my bare ass.

My panties barely cover the cheeks of my ass, and the lace does little to conceal my skin underneath. My hands are wrapped around his neck. The clean ocean-scented cologne he is wearing smells like an exotic place I want to get lost in. My eyes trace his chiseled jaw, straight nose, and gray eyes. His light-brown hair up close looks messy, like he has been running his fingers through it in frustration.

It only makes him look sexier; it would be a lie if I said I didn't want him. My pussy is contacting the skin exposed just above the waistband of his sweats, giving off a scorching heat. He must feel it because he hesitates to place me on the bed with my back on the mattress. His eyes are full of lust mixed with a deep need I recognize.

He wants to fuck me. He wants to fuck me so bad. But I can't let it happen because that is all it will ever be, just sex. Sex with Jaden has always been achingly hot. Since the first time he touched me, he made me feel safe. I could safely explore my sexuality with him. Being with Jaden let me explore sex in a new way, and I wasn't frightened. He always replaced the bad memories of the men who violated me with the memories a woman craves. He would never force me to do something I didn't want.

He must feel the heat between my legs. I should push him

off. I should stop whatever this is because I cannot complicate his life and mine. Jaden can be determined, dangerous, and very possessive.

His eyes are trained on my lips, moving slowly to where I'm spread open against his lower stomach. "Tell me, Briana, why your pussy is hot and wet, pleading for me to slide my cock inside it?"

He slides me down to where his cock is, tenting his sweatpants. My eyes close, loving the feeling when he runs the tip of the head down my slit with only my panties and his sweats between us. He rubs his cock on my clit. Then he grinds his hips. I feel the tip of his dick slide and push inside. My eyes widen when he rolls his hips. My hands grip his muscular shoulders and dig my ass into the mattress.

"I want you," he whispers.

"I know you do."

"Then what's the problem?"

"I-I..."

He slides his hands over my arms in a caress, but I flinch when he reaches the sore spot that caused a bruise when Crew grabbed me.

His brows knit in confusion, and then he looks at the spot his hand touched. He notices the angry bruise forming on my arm when he lifts his hand. Anger takes over his features.

"Brie?"

"Yeah," I whisper.

"Does it hurt?"

"Only when you touch it."

I sigh and look up into his handsome face, full of anger. "Jaden, please don't do anything that will get you in trouble because of me. It's bad enough I have to watch you fight."

"You've watched me fight?" he asks, shocked that I would still watch his fights after everything.

I nod, confessing that I have watched him fight, and each blow he took was like air leaving my lungs, and I struggled to breathe. I wanted to walk into the cage and claw his opponent for every blow he inflicted on Jaden. But Jaden won all his fights.

"I watched your first three fights and couldn't stomach watching anymore."

He frowns. "Why?"

"Because every punch landed, every blow to your body was like taking my air, knowing it was hurting you. Giselle would tell me horror stories about Nate after he would fight. The pain the first few nights after a fight. The blood dripping out of his mouth. The swollen cuts and the pain he would go through to take a shower. The struggle to eat with all the cuts and bruises. I could imagine the pain you went through, and the worst part, I wasn't there to help you. I wasn't there to take care of you, and it hurt, but what hurt the most was that you didn't want me."

A lonely tear escapes my cheek, and I try not to let myself cry in front of him? He doesn't love me, and it hurts so fucking much.

He leans down and kisses the wet track on my cheek and neck. "I'm sorry, baby. I hate when you cry, but I promise I won't get hurt. I know what I'm doing, and no matter what, I will always protect you. My promise to you will always stand. You are safe with me, and I will do anything for you." He rasps against my neck.

He gathers me in his arms and pulls the black comforter. Before sleep claimed me from the heat of his embrace, I last remember him whispering in my ear, "I'm not going anywhere."

CHAPTER TWENTY

Briana

It's a Friday night. Giselle and I sit at our table for our girls' night out with Zavier. It's been so long I haven't hung out. I am still waiting to hear from Ethan after my last text, but I have learned we sometimes understand more with silence.

"So, when are you going to finally get married?" I ask her after the waiter brings us our cocktails.

She smiles. "I think I am going to wait a little while longer. Maybe I'll set a date when Jaden finishes the last three fights he has lined up. His shoulder has been killing him."

My brow furrows in concern for Jaden. Zavier glances at me but spots one of his buddies from his camp. "Go ahead, it's cool. Giselle is my ride tonight."

I'd haggled with Giselle to pick me up to hang out, and I told her we would meet Zavier. He is one of the fighters on Jaden's fight card, but he confided in me that he will not fight. The meeting with the head doctors advised him it was too soon for him to fight an opponent like Jaden. I was so relieved Zavier agreed, and it gave me the added bonus of not feeling like I was betraying Nate and Jaden by being friends with Zavier.

Jaden also has issues with his shoulder; the last thing he needs is a shoulder injury to hinder him from fighting. His title and everything he's worked for are on the line.

"Is he okay? What he needs is proper therapy so he can avoid an injury. He trains nonstop and doesn't rest."

"He is stubborn, and Nate is tired of telling him the same thing, but Jaden is persistent. He is also pissed about you and Ethan."

Giselle rants about me being around Ethan, saying it is dangerous because of his underground dealings. She has a point, but I assured her there is nothing between Ethan and me.

"Why is he pissed?"

Giselle smirks. "He knows you fucked him. You can tell when you two arrived at the fundraiser." She gives me a toothy grin and gives me a playful shove. "The camera doesn't lie. It was clear he fucked the shit out of you right before you arrived that night. You guys couldn't wait until after?"

I sip the cocktail and swallow with a grimace. "It was more like I was horny, pissed off, and sat on his cock."

"Jesus, Brie. Really?"

I nod. "I was pissed off, and my head was all over the place. At the time, I was alone. Then pictures of Jaden with random girls after every fight popped into my head. I was angry at myself and with him, and I took it out on having sex with Ethan. It was an opportunity to blow off steam, and I took it. It was before Jaden showed up at the club. You know it takes a while for the media to air stuff on TV."

"I'm sure he was happy to oblige."

Waving my hand, I tell her, "It didn't mean anything. It was just sex."

Giselle giggles. "Was it good?"

My eyes light up. "It was crazy and rough, but nothing

compared to Jaden. Don't get me wrong, Ethan is hot as hell, but Jaden knows what I need. I have to tell Ethan what I want and how I want it, not with Jaden. I never had to give him instructions.

"Just be careful. Jaden wants you back, Brie. He wants you in his life and will go to war with Ethan if he has to. Let's just hope Ethan gets the memo and it was a one-time thing."

"Ethan loves his dead wife, and I'm not in love with him. There is nothing to worry about. The poor guy just needed to get laid, and so did I. Before that, I hadn't had sex in the three years since Jaden. While Jaden has fucked God knows how many women. He wasn't worried about me when his dick was getting wet. He can stick his jealousy up his ass."

"I know you will make this difficult for Jaden, and it serves him right. Just remember… Jaden doesn't like to lose, and he never gives up without a fight."

Giselle's phone rings, interrupting our conversation. She picks up, and her brows draw together. Her eyes find mine, and she replies, "Okay, we will be right there." She hangs up.

"What happened?"

"That was Nate. He said he was at the gym with Jaden, and he hurt his shoulder. His fight is this weekend. Brie, he is in a lot of pain."

"Shit. Let's go," I say, sliding out of the booth.

I take out my phone and call Zavier, looking around at the lounge. He said he saw one of his buddies from camp on the other side of the lounge.

My eyes are scanning for him everywhere. He picks up on the fourth ring. "Hello?"

"Zavier, it's Briana. Listen, I have to go with Giselle. She has an emergency."

"Is everything okay? Do you need my help?" My eyes soften at how sweet he is.

"Nothing we can't handle. Are you good? I'm so sorry I had to leave so suddenly."

"It is all good. Is Giselle okay to drive?"

Scanning the table, I see barely touched-out cocktails. "We didn't even finish the first one. We are good."

"Okay, but you have to promise for us to hang out again. I want you to meet my friend at camp."

I smile. "You got it, Zavier."

"See you soon, beautiful," he says, and the call disconnects.

I glance at Giselle, and she is on the phone again. "Where?" she asks.

She places the phone in her back pocket and tells me, "Nate says to meet him at the gym."

"I'm going. I can help him. Besides, he needs me right now. They were there for us when we needed them."

She smiles. "You still care about him."

I sigh as we walk toward her Bentley after paying for our two cocktails. "He was my first and only love, Giselle. I will always care about Jaden, even if we are not together. If he gets hurt, I will be there for him and help him however I can. Just like I would do for you and Nate. You guys are my only family. I have no one else."

A tear rolled down Giselle's cheek. "That is why I love you. You are the best friend and sister I could ever have asked for."

We arrive at the gym, and I see that the guys are still inside and haven't left, but my eyes find a familiar silver car that belongs to Janine. I'm annoyed because he called her for help instead of me, but then I realize only Giselle knows I'm a physical therapist. He doesn't know I have to complete the therapy with one combat fighter at the center, and I'm done.

My heels clack on the gym floor, mixed with Giselle's foot-steps. We are both dressed in minidresses with our hair and makeup done.

Nick is the first to spot us approaching. "Wow. You girls look beautiful," he says.

A blush creeps in my cheeks, knowing we look out of place in an MMA gym full of hot-blooded alpha males.

"Where is he?"

"He is in the back with Nate, Brian, and Janine."

He looks at me with concern when he mentions Janine, but I shrug it off. I didn't come here like a jealous ex to reprimand him. I'm just here to offer him my help as a professional and as a friend. Jaden has fought and killed for me. I owe him that much.

Giselle follows me to the back, and when I reach the open door, I can see Jaden with his shirt off and his face turned away from Janine with a scowl. He looks uncomfortable with Janine's hands on his shoulder. She isn't helping him by massaging the area causing him pain.

When he sees me standing in the doorway, he tries to get up, shrugging Janine away from him, but his face grimaces in pain. Janine's hand freezes but doesn't remove her hand from his shoulder, and I want to claw her eyes out but remain calm.

"What are you doing here? Are you okay? Do you need me?" He grimaces as he sits up on the table. "I'm a little fucked up right now, but I will do my best to kick their ass."

I give him a grin. "I'm here because Nate called Giselle. I heard you are in pain, and I came to help."

The corner of his lip lifts in a grin. "You're here because of me?"

"Of course, now tell me, where exactly does it hurt?"

I watch his throat as he swallows and motions near his joint and rotator cup. I quickly make notes in my head. He needs therapy, range of motion exercises and rest between his workouts. The problem is that he has a fight in three days and can't back out at the last minute. The only thing I can offer him is a steroid shot because pain medication is not an option before a fight. Not the painkillers allowed before a fight.

He doesn't have time. I can order him a steroid shot since

I have my license, but he cannot train until he fights for it to work and give him relief.

Giselle watches me with a knowing look. She knows I can help him. She slides her arm through Nate's and looks at him with adoration.

"Brie's got this. Everything is going to be fine," Giselle says.

Nate looks between me and Giselle with curiosity.

"Okay, Champ. I need you to get up and walk to the punching bag."

Janine steps back and rolls her eyes. I wish I could punch her in the face, but I keep calm and handle this like I would at the center.

Jaden doesn't hesitate and does what I ask without protesting.

I'm relieved he doesn't question me or resist. We all follow him toward the punching bag by the mirrors. The guys wait with confusion and a mix of surprise on their faces.

"Hold the bag for him," I instruct, and Brian quickly volunteers and holds the bag while everyone watches patiently for my next instruction.

Jaden looks at me from head to toe with appreciation but tries not to stare.

"I want you to slowly, without hurting yourself, move to strike the bag and pause when you feel the pain. I need to know exactly where it hurts when you strike your opponent. Then I'll know how I can alleviate the pain."

"How would you know?" he asks.

I quirk a brow. "Trust me, baby, I'll know."

He gives me a sexy smirk. He caresses my cheek with his index finger before he takes a boxer's stance. With his arms up, I notice he is putting more effort into his left shoulder. When he turns with his hips to strike, slowly, he rotates his wrist to connect with the bag, and right before he lands the punch, he grimaces in pain. My chest constricts at the pain he is in when he freezes, his arm in position.

"Right there. It hurts like a motherfucker right at this point," he says, struggling through the pain.

I quickly move and feel the tension on his joint near his shoulder. It must be swollen and inflamed.

"Okay, relax."

He grips his shoulder, and I know it hurts. It's been too long.

"Giselle, hand me my phone and get the number to the closest twenty-four-hour pharmacy."

Giselle doesn't hesitate and gives me the phone with the number. I unlock my smartphone and punch in the number for the pharmacy to speak to the head pharmacist.

Jaden looks at me curiously, placing his hand over his left shoulder. The phone rings, and the head pharmacist is on the line.

"Hello, yes, this is Dr. Briana Jameson. I'm a physical therapist. Yes... hi... I need an urgent prescription filled for my patient. I need a corticosteroid shot and muscle relaxant you have on hand." I rattled Jaden's birth date and my medical license number and settled the dosage with the pharmacist. The look on Jaden's face is of shock. I can hear whispers and mumbled conversations behind me.

When I get off the phone. Everyone stares at me like I'm a unicorn, except for Giselle. She has a knowing smile that screams *my best friend is badass.*

"You're a doctor?" Jaden asks.

"Yeah, I was celebrating with Giselle and a friend tonight. I was just given my title and license to practice physical therapy. I just have a patient at the center whose treatment I need to complete and then pay the remainder of my fee when I'm done. After I find a permanent position, I can quit the club. That is my plan so far. We were hanging out tonight, and then Nate called...you know the rest." I clear my throat, going back to my professional voice. "We need to pick up the meds I ordered for you from the pharmacy so I can administer the shot. After I give it to you, you can't train until the day of the fight. It will reduce the swelling, but it won't be effective if you keep aggravating the area."

I chew on my lip and look at the guys. I'm not used to giving him orders, but I'm only trying to help him.

"You're a fucking doctor. That is…badass. You're smart, huh?" Brian says.

"I'm not smart, just determined. I worked hard. No sleep, and I studied a lot."

"You're the smartest and bravest woman I know. I'm proud of you and want to thank you for what you just did," Jaden says.

There is an audible gasp behind him, and when I look over, Janine is glaring at me. "She hasn't done anything. She just ordered some drugs because she can."

"Get out!" I roar, pointing to the exit of the gym.

She places her hands on her hips. "Or what?"

"Or I'll drag your ass out of here, and I'll have your dead body thrown in a ditch somewhere. Trust me, no one will miss a desperate masseuse with the sole purpose of delivering happy endings after every session."

"But you listen to a whore that dances for money and fucks rich men."

I laugh sarcastically. "Aww, Janine. You sound jealous. You're a little concerned about my pussy and who it fucks," I snarl, standing inches from her and lowering my voice. "This is how it is going to go down. You are going to find someplace else to work. You will move out of Jaden's apartment and not set foot in this gym or around Jaden. Do you understand me?"

Janine looks at Jaden and then at Nate.

"You heard my girl. She doesn't want you here. I told you if you made her feel uncomfortable, you were gone. There is nothing between us and stop trying to make it seem like we were fucking. I have never touched you since I met Brie. Even after Brie, I never touched you. I felt bad because you cried when you pleaded with me that you needed a job and a place to stay. You rent the apartment as a tenant and work here as an employee. I have had to put up with your sexual advances and innuendos, and I have told you over and over that I want nothing with you in a nice way, but you obviously don't get it. I made a mistake hiring you. It was one...a long time ago, and it was wrong; I made a terrible mistake that day and regret every minute."

With tears in her eyes, she looks mortified and storms out of the gym.

Nate lets out a puff of air. "Good riddance. It is about time."

Giselle scoffs. "For real, I hate that girl. What the fuck were you thinking, Jaden?"

Jaden swipes his hand over his face, keeping his shoulder in place.

"I have no idea. I'm sorry, I should have never agreed for her to work here."

Jaden cups my cheek. "I'm sorry for disrespecting you. I'm sorry for everything I put you through. You were right to question me that day, and I was wrong for speaking to you like that. I should have never let you walk out that door. I should have stopped you and apologized. I should have fought for us. I'm an asshole, and I don't deserve your forgiveness. I don't deserve you, Briana."

"It is in the past. We need to go to the pharmacy to pick up the medication, and you need your rest before your fight."

"Come with me?" he asks with a pleading look.

I sigh, knowing I can't resist him when he asks me for help. "Okay," I agree.

I know he is asking me to stay with him. I obviously have to give him the steroid shot.

The way he blurted out his apology and the fact he never

had sex with Janine after I settled something inside me. Almost. He cleared up any doubt about Janine brewing in my mind whenever she was here. That day played out in my mind repeatedly after I left. The hurt I felt but also the niggling feeling of him cheating on me with Janine.

He still tossed me out of his life, but it wasn't because he cheated. It doesn't mean I'll take him back with open arms and forgive me easily.

If Jaden wants me back, he will have to prove it.

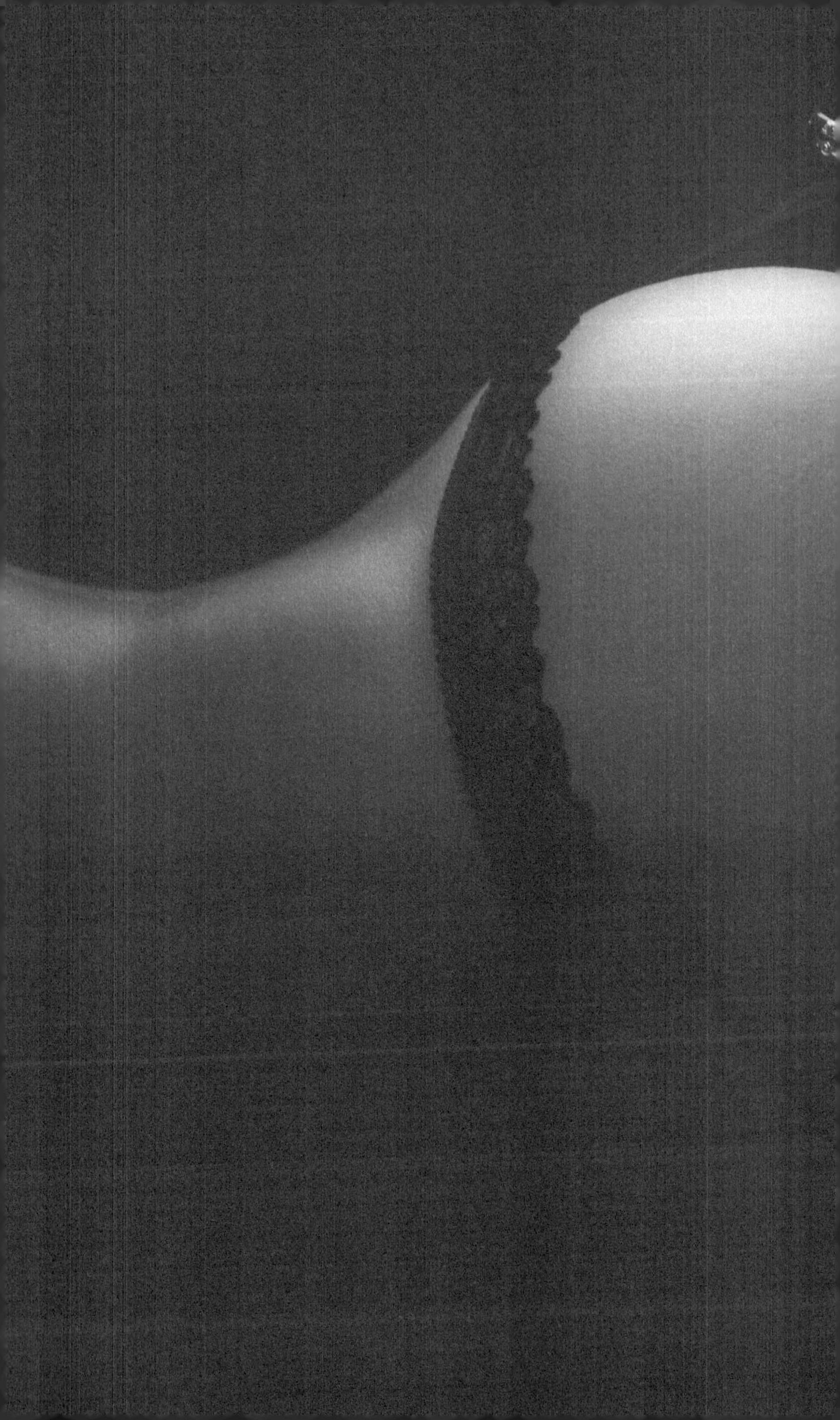

CHAPTER TWENTY ONE

Jaden

She gives me the shot and the relief instantaneous. I want to devour her in my bed at how incredible she is. I want to claim her and make her forget about being in the arms of another man. I want to possess her and make her mine all over again. But I have to take it slow because, underneath her exterior, there is trauma and pain, and it haunts her. It is her demons I want to destroy.

When she walks out of the bathroom and stands next to my bed naked, I move over to make room.

She slides in, her vanilla scent hits me, and I close my eyes, remembering how her smell was everywhere. I could still smell her intoxicating scent when I would drop her off in my car.

She lies on my right side so I don't strain my left shoulder. She also placed a shoulder brace on after the shot, and it helped keep it in place.

"Thank you for what you did for me just now. I feel so much better. You were brilliant, and I would like you to take care of me from now on. If you want. No pressure. It would be great to have you on my team. The guys saw how brilliant you were in a tough situation, and you would be an important part of our camp."

"Are you trying to hire me, Jaden Cyprus?" she teases.

Giving her a grin, I caress her arm with my finger. "Yes,

Dr. Briana Jameson, I am offering you a job to be on my team and as my personal therapist. Under one condition."

She snorts. "I haven't even accepted, and you're giving me conditions?"

"Yes. I need you to move in with me and stop seeing Ethan Carter. It is important because there is one other aspect I need you to agree on if you decide to accept my offer."

"Now, I'm curious," she says with a smirk.

My finger finds her erect nipple and circles the straining bud under the crisp white sheets. Her sudden intake of breath lets me know she likes it.

"After every fight, you know I have a need." I swallow, hoping she agrees to what I will ask her. Why, it must be her and no other. I need her to understand my needs. "I want you on the exam table in my holding room, holding the edge with your pussy wet and ready for me to sink my hard cock inside you. It has to be you."

She stays silent, lost in her thoughts. After a few minutes of silence, she sighs and says, "You want to fuck me in your holding room after every fight? How?"

She knows I like dominance in the bedroom. She knows I can be gentle, or I can be rough. She is asking because I feel she wants to be prepared so she is not surprised when I come for her.

She knows I've taken random girls after a fight, and she can only imagine it's not vanilla sex. It's rough, hard fucking.

I would never hurt her or force myself on her. I have made it clear that I would die before hurting her.

"Hard. I'm going to fuck that sweet, tight cunt hard and fast. Raw. No condom. I'm going to fill that sweet pussy with my cum. Sometimes, I'm going to take that ass. I'm going to pound into you until you forget your name and only remember mine. Your pussy will be swollen and used by me… and only me"—I twirl my finger over her nipple—"I will make sure you have your pleasure as always. Your thighs will be drenched. Cum dripping down your thighs, so I suggest you dress accordingly."

Her breaths are coming out short and fast. Her nipples are hard like twin peaks, and I bet if I slid my finger between the folds of her pussy, she would be ready and wet. My fingers would come out of her tight hole drenched, pleading for me to take her.

"Jaden?"

"Yes."

"If I say no to the sex, would you take another?"

I know she means a ring bunny. Fuck no. I would never choose a random girl if she denied me right now.

"No. I would jerk off at the thought of your pussy milking my cock. It would suck because I would rather have you."

"I'll think about it. You will know my decision on the day of the fight," she says.

Being a jealous pussy, I ask, "Is it because of him?"

Her fingers caress my chest, and my head tilts to watch her dainty fingers rasp on my skin.

"No, it is not because of him. I have no feelings for Ethan. I'm sorry if you think that because I slept with him."

"You don't have to apologize. You don't owe me an explanation. If I hadn't let you go, you would never have had to go back to dancing, and you would have never even met Ethan. That is all on me.

"I know this sounds crazy, but I'm glad you did. I'm achieving my dream on my own. I wanted you part of that journey, but I understand you had your dream and goals."

"That is no excuse for hurting you, Briana. I broke my promise to you and regret it every day. The only thing I can do is prove to you that I want you in my life. I know you are dealing with something deep inside, baby, and I want to be there for you. There is nothing I want more than to own the darkest part of your soul and be present in your nightmares... I'll kill them all."

She snuggles close to me and holds me tight. "I don't trust you with my heart, but I feel safe with you, Jaden. That part is real."

"I will do anything to be the one you trust with everything. I took you for granted and hurt you deeply; for that, I am truly sorry. Please let me prove to you how much you mean to me. Can you do that?"

I know she is not ready to tell me who the guys were that hurt her. The ones that raped her.

Ethan is using our shared connections to gather the information. Briana is not aware, but her mother is getting out of jail, and she will contact Briana for money. Knowing Briana, she will want a relationship with her mother now that she is sober and out of jail and will try to help her because that is who Briana is. I know her mom will bring her trouble somehow. I may be angry about Ethan with Briana, but I cannot blame the man. Briana is gorgeous. There isn't a man who wouldn't take the chance of being with her.

She made something of herself on her own.

She deserves happiness. Not judgment.

"Okay," she says, and I fall asleep, hoping to have her by my side.

<hr>

I wake up in the morning with Briana's silky blonde hair sprawled on my pillow. She is sound asleep. Moving my shoulder to test how sore it is, I am surprised that the pain is gone. The woman is a godsend. Whatever she gave me worked like magic.

Looking at her sleeping form, I admire how gorgeous she looks. Her soft, delicate skin, her leg entwined with mine, savoring the moment of having her in my bed.

The sun is bright in the blue sky. The pool reflects the water against the floor-to-ceiling windows. Having her in my house makes it feel like a home. When I'm alone, the only thing surrounding me is my past haunting me in my sleep.

The bad memories reminded me of the depraved things they did to me. How my mother and father would let junkies molest me as payment for drugs. The unwanted hands touching my body, the way they would grab me at night, forcing me to strip naked and watch men masturbate as they watched me.

I was just five years old when it started. It lasted until I was twelve when they finally took me away. The school called social services because of the beatings I received. My malnourished body was more visible when entering my teen years and I was going through puberty. It was obvious at that point I was being abused.

I never uttered a word of how they molested me.

I was ashamed.

It was bad enough I was made fun of at school because of the way I looked and my bedraggled appearance. When I met Nate, he came from a similar background, and we made a pact. We planned to remain friends, but instead, we formed a brotherhood. We were inseparable, and we still are. Nate is family, and so are the other fighters in my gym. They are the only family we have.

Giselle and Briana are the only women in our lives, and we plan on keeping it that way. I have to prove to Briana she belongs with me, and I'll do anything to show her that this is home. I can understand that she doesn't want to tell me the details of her abuse because I'm the same way. We are more alike than I would have thought.

The last of the flowers are placed neatly in my bedroom. I nod at the courier as she walks softly out my bedroom door.

I called a florist, who assured me they could do this before Briana woke up. She must have been exhausted from last night. We stayed talking until three in the morning.

I want her to be surprised when she sees all the flowers.

I bought a bouquet of flowers, marking every day I was not with her for the past three years. I bought different kinds in different colors. Basically, I bought all the flowers they had on hand. I didn't know which ones were her favorite, but I hope to find out. I'll buy her the ones she likes. It also shows me what her favorite color is.

I caress her face and place a gentle kiss on her cheek. Her eyes flutter open, and she smiles. She stretches her limbs like a cat and gasps when she realizes the bed is full of rose petals.

The contrast of red rose petals all over the white linen sheet and the scent of all the beautiful flowers engulf the room. The sun shining through the glass windows and doors makes the bedroom look magical.

Her hands fly to her mouth in shock. "Oh my god, Jaden!"

I give her my best smile as I sit on the bed, holding her between my legs.

"Do you like it?" I say softly.

"Yes! It's beautiful. Look at all the flowers and the beautiful colors in different shapes and sizes. How did you—"

"You were sound asleep, and I wanted you to wake up with a smile. I wanted you to see how the rest of your life with me by your side will be."

Tears glisten on her lashes, and at first, I've fucked up and made her sad, but then I realize they are happy tears.

"A bouquet of flowers for every day we weren't together for the last three years. One thousand ninety-five bouquets of flowers."

"No one has ever given me so many flowers before." She looks around. "They're beautiful. The white lilies are my favorite."

"The white lilies are your favorite," I repeat, taking notes.

"Yes. My favorite flowers are definitely the lilies. That is why my favorite color is white. The lilies represent the opposite of me," she says and sniffs. She wipes her face as she gets up from the bed, places one under her nose, and inhales. "The lilies represent purity and majesty. They represent virginity and what is pure. I'm the opposite because I'm tarnished and damaged. My hope is one day, the lily can restore my departed soul. My apartment is painted black because that is how I feel inside, dark and damaged. The lily reminds me that I still have a chance."

Briana thinks she isn't pure. Those fucking monsters took that from her. I will kill those bastards. I will buy every goddamn lily if that would make her happy.

"Now I know what flowers to buy you. White lilies. And Briana?"

"Yes?"

We are both naked. I wipe a tear from her cheek. "To me, you're pure and not damaged." I place a soft peck on her cheek and whisper. "You are the purest person I know. The darkness is just a cloud on a rainy day, and I am the sun that will bring you light."

She smiles, her eyes shining bright as she wraps her arms around my neck and says, "Thank you."

I made a promise to myself to remind her how beautiful she was.

CHAPTER TWENTY TWO

Briana

It is fight night. The past three days have been a dream. Jaden has slept with me in the bed and has abstained from having sex. He told me he doesn't have sex a week before a fight.

Ethan has been a ghost since the last text. He must be feeling guilty over his dead wife. Besides, our agreement had an expiration date. It's over.

The black Escalade shows up outside the gate of Jaden's home. Only Nate is allowed to approach the iron gate in one of the SUVs. Brian is driving and Giselle is in the back, waiting for me and Jaden to slide in.

"How are you feeling?" Giselle asks Jaden.

"I'm great. Briana has worked her magic. No pain. I know it is temporary, andI hope she will accept my offer for her to work at the gym and be part of the team."

Giselle looks at me and we both share a silent message. We'll talk about it later.

Nate hands me a hoodie, I thank him and my gaze finds Jaden's with a smile.

"In case you get cold, I had it made just for you," Jaden says, "It is white instead of black, now that I know your favorite color is white."

Giselle gives me a grin and then smiles warmly at Jaden. She knows he is trying and so do I.

He ordered takeout for me to the house these past three days and watched movies. He knows I love Marylin Monroe, and my favorite food is barbecue chicken. His favorite color is black, but I didn't want to make him feel bad and tell him I already knew that.

There is nothing I don't know about Jaden except his past. I don't know what his demons are, but he doesn't know what mine are either. In time, I might be able to tell him, but I am still guarded.

I'm afraid to bare my innermost secrets, afraid he will look at me with disgust.

When we reach the venue, it is at capacity. I squint from the flash of the cameras. Paparazzi asking questions. People are screaming our names.

I'm wearing a tank top dress and designer sneakers Jaden insisted I wear. He ordered new clothes from the boutique in one of the Las Vegas hotels three days ago, including the one I'm currently wearing for the event tonight.

When some of the paparazzi recognize me, they ask about my relationship with Ethan and how I am involved with Jaden.

I'm grateful he ignores the comments and questions about our relationship. He tells them to watch the fight. The media has dubbed me the powerful mystery woman who has the most eligible bachelors under her spell.

There is so much attention on Jaden and me, they chant my name next to "The Destroyer," Jaden's cage name.

We take our seats, Giselle is sitting to my right while Nate, Brian, and Jaden are in the holding room waiting to make their entrance. I'm nervous and cold and thankful for the hoodie I have on my lap. I want to put the hoodie on but don't want to miss Jaden making his debut entrance to the cage.

He's in the zone, his body is in great shape compared to the other fighter.

According to the stats on the prompter, Jaden has a longer reach and is an inch taller. Jaden is also massive in size compared to his opponent but all I can think about is his injury.

The lights dim as Jaden is introduced to the cage with his intro song "Gatti" by JACKBOYS and Pop Smoke blaring from the speakers. The crowd goes wild as their favorite heavyweight MMA fighter makes his entrance.

After being cleared by the doctor, I shiver nervously as he prepares mentally to fight in the cage.

The crowd screams and shouts. Giselle squeezes my hand, reassuring me because she knows I'm nervous for Jaden. Jaden looks over and makes his way over to where we are seated, and my eyes widen. His mouthpiece is in his mouth so he can't talk.

He motions for me to put the hoodie on. I do, pulling it over my head as I stand. I can see him smiling when my head slides through the hoodie. When I look at his mouthpiece, it reads, Coco, my stage name.

He looks at the hoodie and points so the camera can showcase our exchange when I look at the screen. His hand caresses my face, and the back of the hoodie reads in bold black lettering: Property of The Destroyer. He gives me a wink and walks to enter the cage.

The crowd goes wild. Goose bumps snake my spine. Butterflies swarm in my stomach from both the fear of Jaden being hit or injuring his shoulder and then after, when I'll let him fuck me in the locker room after the fight.

The ding of the bell signals the beginning of the first round. Jaden wastes no time landing blow after blow. He is impressive and a total athlete.

In the second round, he sends a kick to his opponent's face. The expressions on the judge's faces are of shock when

Jaden's kick lands on his opponent, clean in the face, knocking him out cold. Jaden steps back and jumps over the fence of the cage. My hands cover my mouth as they try to get the guy to sit up.

Jaden is like an animal, making silent hand gestures across his neck. He finds my gaze and he grins with his left eye swollen from a blow to the face. He jumps down and removes his mouthpiece before he is interviewed and officially announced the winner by knockout. He motions for me and Giselle to come inside the cage with his team.

"Briana!" he calls out.

I get up and make my way inside the cage with Giselle in tow. He motions for me to stand next to him.

The commentator holds the mic in front of him and says through the mic echoing in the arena, "Jaden 'The Destroyer' Cyprus, how does it feel to remain undefeated? Who is the lovely lady everyone is talking about? What is the secret to your success?"

Jaden grabs my hand and squeezes when he leans to answer the commentator. "It feels great. I owe it to my brother and best friend Nate 'The Reaper' Phoenix, his fiancée Giselle, and my boys in the gym, they know who they are. They train with me day in and day out. My secret is family, determination, and surrounding yourself with people who love and support you. This lovely lady is none other than my secret weapon. The only woman who has my attention and is part of my family, Dr. Briana Jameson." He turns his head and looks at me while he speaks through the mic. "Thank you for everything, baby. This victory happened because of your talent and you always believing in me, and for that, I'm devoted to you." My chest squeezes.

There commentator pulls the mic and says, "There you have it, and by way of TKO, now the still undefeated heavyweight champion, Jaden 'The Destroyer' Cyprus!"

I can't stop staring at him for what he said to the world.

The crowd goes wild, Jaden, Nate, Giselle, and Briana walk ahead, and I follow behind Jaden toward the doctor. I walk ahead toward the back and head to Jaden's personal holding room while the doctor clears him to leave. He doesn't notice me walking ahead because the doctor is shining the light in his eyes.

Once inside the room, I strip but leave my sneakers and black lace thong on. I hold on to the exam table in the middle of the room, knowing Jaden is the only one that will come through the closed door. My long hair slides to the side over my shoulder and I wait like a submissive. My ass is in the air with my legs spread wide, bent over, waiting for him.

I suck in a deep breath as I hear the door handle turning and pray that it is Jaden and not someone else.

When I look over my shoulder, Jaden stands leaning on the closed door. His eyes find mine and the look of lust mixed with need bleeds off him in waves, causing my pussy to clench and drip with anticipation.

He steps forward, slides his hands across my waist, and holds me in place. His finger hooks my panties and tears them in one swift tug. He slides a finger from my clit to my ass.

"Jesus, you are drenched. Are you sure, Briana?"

I nod, but he shakes his head. "I need your words, baby. Do you want me to slide my cock in your pussy, and take you my way?"

"Yes," I croak.

I want him to fuck me. I need him to claim me. The need to feel his impressive cock inside my pussy is overwhelming.

He removes his cup and slides his shorts down. He quickly walks over to the showers and washes off.

He walks back to stand behind me with his cock springing free like a steel rod. I look forward, bracing myself for the hard fuck I am going to receive. I can imagine the adrenaline he must need to release but I don't fear him. He would never hurt. I trust him.

The head of his cock is at the mouth of my pussy and he inches forward. I gasp at how thick his dick is as it stretches me open.

"This pussy belongs to me. I'm claiming it. Do you understand?"

"Yes," I say breathlessly.

"If you are unsure, you will understand when I'm finished."

He slams into me, and my stomach hits the cushion of the exam table. The tips of my sneakers lift from the floor. Holy shit! I feel like I'm suspended in the air. His body keeping me pinned to the exam table as he shoves his cock inside my wet, throbbing pussy. He assaults me with such enormous force that the table slides across the concrete floor. My pussy throbs and grips his dick in a vise while he is driving inside my folds.

"Fuck me, Jaden," I whisper.

He grabs a handful of my blonde hair, causing my head to tilt back as he pounds into me harder and faster. His finger makes its way into my mouth, and I suck it. It is his way of ensuring I was with him all the way. He knows what I like in bed.

He keeps fucking me deeper, to the deepest part of me. A place no other has gone. The only thing you can hear in the room is his deep groans as he thrusts inside me and my raspy moans. He is close to coming and so am I.

It's hard.

Quick.

In one last thrust, his hot cum spills inside my pussy .

"God, yes," I cry out.

He pulls out, mixing his cum all over my puckered hole and true to his word, he uses his cum to slide his finger inside my ass, stretching me slowly.

"Relax and take it. I am going to go slow at first so I don't hurt you. Once you adjust to my size, I'm going to pound into this sweet ass like I promised, and you are going to come. I promise you I will make you come while I fill your ass with my cum. Your pussy is dripping with my cum already. I'm going to fill you with the scent of me." He snakes his hand around and cups my pussy. "This is mine. Who do you belong to?"

"You."

"That's right, you and this pussy belong to me."

He pulls my hair and wraps his arm around me so that his fingers coated with his cum rub over my nipples.

It is so erotic and filthy my pussy clenches but can grasp nothing inside it, only the pressure of his cock filling my ass.

"I'm going to dirty you, my princess," he says, "There isn't going to be a place on your body where I haven't licked or sucked."

My aching core throbs with each word that he utters. The tip of his cock is at the entrance of my ass and he slides in and out slowly. His other hand slides toward my clit and he rubs and pinches it. With each moan that escapes my lips, he slides his cock deeper inch by inch until he is balls deep inside my ass. He continues to rub and play with my clit and it feels so good.

I can't take it anymore and want him to fuck me in my ass.

"Jaden, fuck me," I gasp. "Please." He chuckles while he grips the globes of my ass and begins to pound into me like an animal. I writhe and moan, pushing against him. "Yes," I scream.

The slapping of his thighs against my ass is fast and sounds like someone is clapping. He keeps pounding into me. "You feel amazing," he growls. "I can't get enough of you. You have the best pussy and ass I have ever fucked."

He keeps pounding into me and his words cause an ache to build inside of me like an inferno, bringing me to a mind-blowing ecstasy. I come hard. The feeling of his hot cum fills my ass. His cock spasms inside me like a marking to his claim.

We are both spent and exhausted. He pulls out from me and carefully flips me around so my legs are spread-eagled on the edge of the exam table. My pussy and ass dripping with his cum tickles my skin as it slides down my thighs and the crack of my ass.

He looks down and whispers, "Beautiful."

He cleans his cock in the shower and returns, placing his hands on either side of the table as he leans in position, placing the head of his cock at the entrance of my pussy. My eyes widen because I don't think I can come a third time, but he quickly proves me wrong. He slides the tip of his cock inside my swollen pussy and we both groan.

My pussy is swollen and tender with a mixture of pleasure and a delicious burn. He slides in slowly, building me up. My legs grip the sides of his hips. His face is inches from mine.

I can see the slight cut under his left eye already forming an angry bruise on his beautiful, handsome face. His lips are swollen so I don't dare kiss him for fear of hurting him.

He leans close to my breasts and bends his head to lick my nipples. I cry out at how good it feels to have him bare and raw inside me, mixed with the sensation of his tongue on my skin.

"You like my big dick inside you, baby?"

"Yes," I say breathlessly, leaning on my elbows as he watches his cock disappear inside my pussy.

My body is tender and a bundle of nerves. He grips my thighs and begins to move faster. His cock is amazingly hard and erect, like he hadn't just come two times already. The man is like a machine, but it always was like this when we were together. It was hot, raw, aching sex, like an erupting volcano. Jaden fucking me is explosive, like pulling the trigger and the gun going off. It was never gentle, but he never hurt me either.

Grabbing his biceps, I hold on as he increases his speed and my back arches as a wave of my orgasm rises through my body.

"Come for me, baby. I can feel that tight pussy milking my

cock. That's it, give me that pussy," he says, grinding his dick inside me while causing friction on my clit. He kisses my neck and whispers close to my ear, "I love being between your legs, deep inside that wet, hot cunt."

Fuck if that doesn't do it. I come and I come hard. My pussy soaks his dick and he groans as hot cum spills inside me. I rotate my hips, grinding in a rhythm until my orgasm fades and I'm spent.

He slowly pulls out and cleans me the best he can. I'm full of his cum as he promised I would be. I pull the tank dress then the hoodie over my body but when I slide my legs down to stand, my legs buckle.

I can't walk.

He rushes to my side. "I got you, baby," he says, as he carries me like a bride before I fall.

I grip his neck, careful not to touch his face. He opens the door and calls to Brian to get his bag and my purse. Giselle and Nate have already left and it's just Brian, Jaden and me.

"You think you can walk once we reach the back exit?"

I nod and when he tries to help me stand, my legs buckle again, like Bambi.

"Jesus, is she okay?" Brian asks.

Jaden gives him a smirk. "It's been a while. She needs to get used to me again."

"Ha-ha. Very funny," I mock.

He gives me a peck with the side of his mouth that is not cut or swollen.

Brian drives us to the Palms Casino Resort hotel located on the Las Vegas Strip. When he pulls up front, more flashes from the cameras assault us. I finally have feeling in my legs and I'm able to walk.

We reach the Empathy Suite, and it is magnificent. I have never stayed in one of the most impressive two-story sky villas in all of Las Vegas before.

"Wow!" I say, impressed with the accommodation and the remarkable view looking out the window. "This is impressive."

"I wanted the best to celebrate the win with my girl. If it wasn't for you, I wouldn't have won. You were there for me when I was hurt and in pain. You were brilliant and you fixed me so I could fight and keep living my dream. I honestly thought my winning streak was over. If you only knew how much that means to me. I would be honored to have you on my team. Please consider it."

Giving him a smile, I nod. "I have and I accept. I just need to finish therapy with a combat fighter and I can join the team."

He tilts his head. "I know you keep mentioning this fighter. What is his name?"

"Zavier Morales. He goes by The—"

"The Sergeant," he finishes, interrupting me. My brow furrows.

"I know who he is because he is the third fighter going against me in my third fight for my title."

"I'm so sorry, Jaden. I know I should have told you before but he was assigned to me by my superior and I was part of the team that has been working with him and now they have entrusted me to finish his therapy. I didn't know in the beginning but off the record, he isn't going to fight you. It was discussed in the last meeting with the team of therapists and his camp."

Jaden walks up to me and tilts my chin. "It's okay, baby. I'm not mad. This is not your fault. Is it true he is withdrawing?"

"It will be announced in a week. I thought they would have let you and Nate know by now. I have to give him therapy sessions in the pool and then sign off on the report so they can clear him. Obviously for him to fight, but it won't be in time for him to adequately train."

"When you give him therapy, what do you wear?"

"Are you serious?"

"I'm dead serious," he says through clenched teeth. "I'm not mad at you and I know you are doing your job but if that asshole makes a pass at you. I will kill him in the cage and out of it. He so much as touches you in an unwanted manner, I'll make sure to kick his ass, title be damned. Understand?"

I nod, reassuring him with a smile. "We are friends and he knows we used to be together. He was at the lounge with me and Giselle. He is totally cool."

Jaden gives me a glare but takes a deep breath and remains calm. "Fine. I'm sorry I overreacted. I'm just being an overprotective, jealous jerk. I get it."

I head to the bathroom to freshen up.

When I'm in the bathroom, My phone rings with the distinctive ringtone of an incoming call. I hear it ring one more time but then I hear Jaden's voice.

"What, asshole?" he snaps when he answers. My eyes widen and I am about to put my clothes on to see who is calling, that has Jaden so pissed but his next words have me frozen in place with my ear to the door and my grip on the handle.

"Briana can't come to the phone right now. She is currently recovering from having my cock inside her pussy and ass. What the fuck can I do for you?"

I gasp at his crazy behavior. I know it is Ethan on the other line because Jaden places my phone on speaker, and I can hear Ethan's voice.

"I have nothing to say to you. I obviously called Briana to make sure she is safe."

Jaden snorts. "Was this before or after you decided to put her in danger, putting a target on her head by being associated with you? You may not give a fuck, but I do. I warned you if you touched her, I would gouge your fucking eyes out, you pathetic piece of shit. You preyed on her weakness and exploited her by using it to your advantage. I know what you did. You went to the club to find yourself a girl that you consider a whore to play with and use her because your investors feel you are unstable because you cannot cope after the death of your dead wife."

That piece of shit used me? Well, I knew he had a purpose but to risk my life? I know Ethan is in the Mafia and has enemies but I never thought he would use me as collateral damage or as a pawn.

"It wasn't like that and you know it."

"Oh please, what part? Men like you do not care about women that dance at a club. There is only one woman that you care about and you failed because she is in a box six feet under. She is dead because you put her in harm's way, and she paid the price. The life you lead has consequences. I am not going to sit here and let you drag an innocent woman that I care about into danger or end up dead because you care only about yourself. I see right through your facade and your crap, Carter. Remember, I know everything there is to know about you and your business dealings. It's not like we haven't done business before. You knew what she meant to me and that didn't stop you. Did it?"

"You're right. I saw the opportunity to have her, and I took it. It is not my fault she was there, that falls solely on you, Cyprus. You know what they say, one man's trash is another man's treasure. It wasn't like you sent a search party looking for her."

What Ethan says stings at the reminder of how Jaden tossed me away and wasn't looking for me. It also stings at how Ethan is using me. He thought so little of me. Jaden's right, Ethan bought a whore for his selfish purpose with deadly consequences. The car and the agreement to handle all of my problems was a smoke screen. He had me believe that it would benefit me to deal with one VIP instead of having to figure out a way to pay for my school or, worse, have to take on more than one client.

In all reality, it wouldn't benefit him for me to be with

anyone else, so he could convince his investors he is mentally stable by making it seem he is able to move on with another woman. What are two hundred thousand dollars and a Bentley to Carter when he must have millions on the line? The rage boiling inside me has me wanting to break the mirror looking at my reflection. How could I have been so stupid and blindsided?

"Fuck you. You showed me her medical records in the hope I would back off and be disgusted with her like she is damaged goods. News flash, asshole," Jaden roars. "I am damaged goods. I am glad I fucked up your little plan and the world knows she is mine. She doesn't belong to you, Carte. She never did. If you are worried that someone might hurt her or come after her because of you, you better fix it because if not, I will pull rank and gut you like a fish. Remember what happened to the last asshole that fucked with Briana."

"Yeah, we'll see, Cyprus. Don't underestimate me. I'll take care of it but not for you. I'm doing it for her. I fucked up and I'll own up to it. I admit I didn't give a shit at first about her and thought she was just another stripper with a dark past and shitty upbringing. I want to apologize to her. My intention was not to hurt her or put her in danger. I'm honestly worried about her."

"Yeah, I can tell," Jaden says sarcastically. "Leave her alone and don't call her again, Carter." The room goes silent, indicating the call is disconnected.

Angry hot tears slide down my cheeks as I look at myself in the mirror, hating myself. Hating that I let myself be used in a way that would have put everything I was working toward on the line for nothing. What if some rival Mafia assholes put a bullet in my head because of Ethan Carter. Then what? I would be dead, and no one would have given a shit except maybe Giselle.

Jaden never loved me. He made it clear he was incapable of love. He wasn't even looking for me and was fine living his life without me. My stupid decisions could have cost me every-thing, including my own life. It hurts to think I mean so little to people. That my life means nothing. That I'm worthless.

Who would want a woman like me anyway? I don't even know who my father is and my mother is a drug addict. She didn't care I was raped repeatedly by drug dealers so she could get her next fix. No one wanted to be my friend except Giselle.

I'm trailer trash. It is no surprise I ended up being a pole dancer for money. Everyone knows where I came from and there is no escaping my past. People dig up the information you want to keep hidden and then use it to their advantage and it is sickening. I should feel ashamed but I don't.

Jaden wants to know who hurt me. Probably because he feels sorry for me. Jaden does have a heart, but I have to remind myself that he doesn't love me.

I turn on the shower until it's scalding hot and let my tears slide down my cheeks. I want to feel independent and have a career, meet a nice guy and fall in love. Maybe have a family of my own.

The bathroom door is shoved open and startles me. Jaden strips and enters the shower. I look down avoiding his gaze. He tilts my chin up with his finger.

"Don't cry. You have nothing to be ashamed of. I know you heard me talking to Carter. There is nothing to feel ashamed about. He used you and he knew what you meant to me. None of this situation is your fault. You are one of the bravest women I have ever met and I am an asshole for letting you go. It didn't stop you from achieving your dream and I am so proud of what you have accomplished. You did it all on your own."

I sniff. "I-I'm sorry for causing you any trouble. I should be taking care of you after your fight."

He shakes his head. "You have never caused me trouble and you being here with me is more than I could have asked for, baby… and you did take care of me. Now I'm going to take care of you."

He slides his finger gently down my chest, over my nipples and stomach. My thighs clench together.

He reaches for the shower gel and bathes me. He washes my hair and gently massages my scalp.

My eyes close, loving his hands all over my body as he rinses my skin. When his hands reach between my thighs to clean me, a whimper escapes my lips. I'm tender but he is gentle.

When he is done, I give him the same treatment with gentle strokes. I'm careful, not knowing if he was hit in a certain part of his body. My fingers feel every dip and bend of his muscles under my fingertips, reacquainting myself with his massive body.

CHAPTER TWENTY THREE

Jaden

After we shower, we lie on the bed facing each other and I'm captivated by her beauty. Watching the glow of her skin after a hot shower and her face devoid of all makeup. She is still one of the most gorgeous women I have ever laid eyes on. I have had my share of beautiful women, but Briana is by far the most beautiful. She is sexy and naughty. The darkness within her is haunting. I'm attracted to it like a bee to honey. She is smart and her body is perfection.

The dusty pink of her nipples, her tiny waist, and the dangerous curve of her ass drive me crazy.

In my mind, I've always thought I wasn't good enough for her and that she deserved better. She deserves a man that loves and worships her for the rest of her days. A man that understands her and assures her that she is the best thing to ever happen to him.

The last time I was in her apartment, I placed cameras inside. The thought crossed my mind when I told her Carter could have bugged her place. I waited until she fell asleep and checked. I was relieved to find that he didn't but instead placed a GPS in the car he gave her.

When I was alone in my house, I watched her like a creep, but I was curious about how she slept at night. I watched her heartbreaking screams that would come out of her lips at night. The way she would curl up in a ball in her dark room, pleading for the men that raped her to have mercy on her. For it stop.

I was torn and wanted to barge into her apartment and hold her. It was gut wrenching to see her having night terrors. Her demons assaulting her in her dreams. I sobbed like a pussy the first time I watched her, but I vowed to find those assholes that did that to her, robbing her dreams and leaving her with the memories of their torture.

It was daunting to see that we are alike in many ways. We both come from drug-addicted parents that abused us and let us be abused by the filthiest of human beings. The feeling of pain, hunger, and hopelessness is a norm from where we come from. We both know what it is to come from nothing and have no family to call our own.

"What are you thinking about?" she asks in a soft voice. Her beautiful blue eyes watching the expression on my face.

"I'm thinking about how lucky I am to be here with you, how much I have missed you. Admiring how beautiful you are."

Her cheeks blush and I love how it creeps up her neck to her cheeks. Her platinum-blonde hair is in soft waves framing her face. If I look deep enough, I see it lurking. What she tries to hide but I've seen it. When she decides to cut him loose, that is when she will snap. And when she snaps, I want her to know that I have her back. I want her to know that I care for her. It is just a matter of time before it happens.

She sighs and asks, "Why do you have nightmares?"

She asked me once, but I refused to tell her. She has never mentioned the nightmare the first night she stayed at my house. She shook me until I was awake, and her arms were cradling me like a baby.

It was the sweetest and most welcoming feeling to have her there assuring me that it wasn't real. But the dream I had that night was different. It was Briana they were hurting instead of me and the fear that gripped me had me thrashing, ready to kill whoever touched her. A fear that I know lurks deep inside me because the men that hurt her are still out there and they think they got away with what they did to her.

Her mother is out of jail, and it is only a matter of time before she contacts Briana for money. My sources tell me she is back doing drugs in the same trailer park. When her mother can't pay, she'll tell them that her daughter can pay them with either money or her body and they will come after her. Ethan and I know it.

When drug dealers think they can get paid, they will give her mother the hard stuff, the expensive stuff. Her mother is too far gone for rehab. She doesn't see Briana as a daughter. She sees her as a way to get her next fix without having the money to pay or work for it. Drug addicts will do anything for the next hit, and I know from experience the monsters they can become.

My gaze finds hers and I give her a piece of me that I have given no other. Not even Nate knows the details of my dark past, but for her, I'll do anything.

My fingers trace the side of her face and I begin, "My parents were drug addicts. They would beat me and deprive me of food because it would hinder them from buying drugs. They figured if they had to buy me food, they wouldn't have enough to buy drugs. So, they starved me as much as they could without killing me. I was made fun of at school because I smelled and was too skinny. I was malnourished and every time social services stepped in, the government checks would stop coming in from the state so my parents would clean up their act for a week and the state would send me back. It was a vicious cycle. When I was five, my parents decided to use me instead to fund their drug habit. They would bargain me to other drugs in exchange. Allow them to molest me, and in return, they would get their next fix. They would grab me when I was asleep and have me strip naked. It was men and women. They would touch me with their filthy hands and masturbate. When I would resist, it would get worse, and they would hold me down because they were stronger than me, so I couldn't fight back and had to endure it until the next time."

A tear slides down her cheek. "Five, Jaden." She tries to hold in the sobs as she imagines me as a little boy. I can see it in her eyes, the pain she feels reflecting from their depths.

"After that, it became a regular occurrence. As I got older, it became worse. They forced me to have oral sex and then the men would rape me or make me have sex with the women as they watched. All for twenty dollars' worth of drugs." Her tears are silently sliding down her cheeks and my heart breaks for her because I know she feels the pain. She, of all people, could imagine it.

"When I was twelve, I started to fight back because I was older and stronger. So, they backed off but the damage was done. I would have night terrors every night because they would grab me when I fell asleep. They would beat me until I gave up. They made sure not to hit me on my face or arms so the teachers at school couldn't see I was being abused. When I entered middle school, I needed to eat more because I was hitting puberty, but they wouldn't feed me or clothe me properly, so when the school finally noticed, they called social services again. I was so skinny I was beginning to have breathing problems. I was tired all the time and my clothes were dirty and I smelled. They took me away and sent me to foster care and I received medical attention for malnourishment. Then I met Nate, and we hit it off. You know the rest."

"That is horrible. I want to find your parents and kick their asses."

I smile. "Those asses were kicked in jail when the inmates found out they abused and prostituted their own son for drugs. They were eventually killed."

"Good riddance, pieces of shit," she snarls. She swipes a strand of hair from her face and snuggles deeper into the crisp white sheets of the bed. The humming sound of the air conditioner mixed with our freshly scented skin from our shower enveloping us in our own cocoon.

"I'm so sorry that happened to you. I'm happy that you made it out of that situation. That you and Nate found each other and have both become a success."

This is the closest I have felt with any woman and it scares me, but not enough that I wouldn't admit my innermost feelings.

"I have never told anyone what really happened to me. You are the first."

"I would never say a word. No one needs to know what happened. I wanted to know because it haunts you in your sleep and I was there to witness the agony that plagues you in your dreams. I wanted to see if there was anything I could do to make it go away."

"If you stay,"I admit.

"What?"

"When you sleep with me. They go away. The same way I know that when you sleep in my arms, they don't come for you. It's why I keep asking you to stay with me."

She swallows and says the words I have waited to hear. "Then, I'll stay with you."

CHAPTER TWENTY FOUR

Briana

The next day, Jaden left for the gym to help train the guys for their respective fights in their weight classes. He is not only a fighter but also runs an MMA gym with other fighters as well as young students from government programs with dreams to become pro fighters.

Nate and Jaden are also advocates to help eliminate bullying and child abuse. He wants to make a difference with his acquired wealth, and I feel proud just to be around him.

My cell phone pings with an incoming text message from Ethan.

> Ethan Carter: I'm sorry, Briana. If you are ever in trouble, you know you can call me. I also want to pay for the remaining balance of your tuition.

He is treating me like I'm a transaction. If I am ever in trouble? Really? If I'm dead, how could I call for help? My eyes find the key fob of the Bentley and the rage inside me erupts. There is only so much a girl can take. I'm tired of being a doormat.

A crazy thought enters my mind and I act on it. He is sorry. Yeah right. He is sorry that his plan with me didn't go his way. Jaden did me a favor and shed light on Ethan's little game.

Placing the plastic containers in the trunk of the Bentley, I make my way to Ethan Carter's office building.

When I see the tall glass building, I enter the parking lot and make sure I park away from other vehicles. I park the Bentley so it is visible from the windows of the tall office building. Knowing a man like Carter, he would have the best view from the top floor.

Opening the trunk, I reach and grab the container filled with gasoline.

The sun is shining bright and it is very hot. When I finish emptying the gasoline all over the car, I light a match and watch the flames. Ignoring the heat and people shouting that a car is on fire.

I make my way inside the building. When I reach the lobby, I make my way to an impeccably dressed woman sitting at a desk. She looks up at me warily but shrugs it off.

"I am here to see Ethan Carter. My name is Briana Jameson." I leave out my title as a doctor because it isn't official to me. Until I pay my debt to the school in full, I can't officially practice outside of the center.

"Is he expecting you? Do you have an appointment?" she asks and the way she is looking at me dressed in my leggings and motorcycle jacket, she is curious as to why I am here. If my instincts are correct, this woman sees me as a threat. Noticing her attire, she is not dressed to be a professional but to seduce any available man that would give her a glance.

"No. I do not."

She gives me a sarcastic smirk. "I am sorry but I cannot let you see him."

"Just tell him I am here."

Reluctantly, she walks over to the phone on her desk. The sound of her heels clicking on the black marble floor is the only sound in the reception area. She picks up the phone and in a low tone murmurs something but I cannot make out what she says.

Her head rises with shock and the look on my face as I tilt my head has her fuming. She slams the receiver down. Quack! Clearly, this woman doesn't like females having meetings with her boss.

"He will see you now."

"It is in his best interest that he does."

She walks over to an elevator and swipes a key card, and it opens. She waves her hand so I can proceed into the car with a sarcastic but curious expression.

When the elevator reaches his floor, a large office comes into view with floor-to-ceiling windows and a single wooden desk in the center. Ethan is standing leaning over his desk with his hands placed on the surface facing me.

My fingers slide over the smooth key fob to the Bentley burning below in his parking lot and the look of fury is etched on his face.

"Are you fucking crazy?" He says through clenched teeth.

"Maybe or I'm just a little unhinged," I say, shrugging my shoulders.

"They will think someone is trying to attack me."

"I don't give a fuck about who thinks whatever the fuck. The same way you didn't give a fuck about me. I heard what you said to Jaden over the phone when you called. I have a target on my back because of you. You think you can just come into my life and lie to me? You preyed on me and deceived me, you bastard," I say, my voice full of rage, throwing the key on his desk. "Here is the key to your fucking Bentley. If you want to send someone to kill me, go ahead. I don't give a fuck anymore."

I walk toward him until I'm close enough, and I smack him across his face. Thwack! He grabs my wrist and his nostrils flare. "I'm going to let that slide because I know you are angry. Don't you ever come up to me and hit me."

"Or what? You're gonna kill me? There is one thing you didn't factor in when you picked me out of the bunch. You may think I am a whore with a fucked-up upbringing that no man wants but here is the thing. I have nothing to lose. No family. No money. No husband. No children. Not even parents who would come looking for me. There is nothing to take from me that hasn't already been taken. To someone like you, I am worthless. Collateral damage. I see you no different than the monsters who raped me and left me to die."

I snatch my wrist from his grasp.

"I told you I was sorry. I made a mistake in deceiving you but I want you to know I have fallen for you and I won't let anything happen to you. You have my word."

"Maybe in your little Mafia world." I wave my hand around his impressive office. "But to me, it means nothing. I don't trust you. I don't want anything from you. I don't want your car or your money. I prefer to keep dancing on a fucking pole to get by then to take another dollar from you."

"You know he is incapable of loving you. You realize that, don't you?" He changes the subject and redirects it to Jaden because he knows how I feel about him. I regret telling him how much it hurt when Jaden let me go. He is telling me is something I already know. Something I have already accepted.

Giving him a hard stare, I tell him, "Where I come from, you cannot miss or hope for something you never had. It just makes it easier to accept things the way they are. I want to thank you for reminding me."

He flinches and I walk away from him toward the elevator. When I push the button and the doors open, I turn around once I step into the car.

He stands facing me with his hands inside his trouser pockets and watches me with an expression of defeat. "Remind you of what?"

Before the elevator doors close, I answer, "That I'm worth nothing."

When I reach the outside of the building, I quickly call an Uber to get to my apartment and grab my motorcycle and ride toward the gym.

There is a voice message from my mother that she is out of jail. I know it is just a matter of time before she owes money again to Daniel and Ben. They are the ones that run the streets in South Dakota and handle all the drug deals.

All the hard stuff is filtered and run by them. They are also the ones that raped me. They are coldhearted and filthy. They graduated high school when I was in seventh grade. They would come around the trailer park and sell drugs to my mother.

I was still a kid and they left me alone, but when I fell for Jace in high school, I gave him my *V*-card and then the rumors began about how the star football player was dating trailer trash. He was so worried about his image that he told everyone I was just an easy lay that would end up being a drug-addicted stripper. He made up lies and said that I begged him to have sex with me for money.

It wasn't long before Daniel and Ben got wind of the rumors. Football is a very popular sport in a small town, they would believe anything Jace would say and no one except Giselle believed me when I said the rumors were lies.

The night they left me to die, they were afraid I had told the authorities what had happened and left me alone.

I left when I turned eighteen and found a job dancing to support myself. I had no skills, no money, and everyone thought I was a drug addict and a whore like my mother. I realized that day with Jack that my mother was too far gone and only used me to get her fix. It was a mistake that Giselle and I paid for, and I vowed to never fall into that trap again.

Jaden and Nate just bought me time.

Jaden promised to protect me, but I quickly learned his

protection had an expiration date when I was left on my own. My only saving grace was that my mother was still incarcerated. There weren't many options for a girl like me.

Either way, Daniel and Ben have enough resources to come looking for me and if they think I can pay them with cash or my body, they will come after me to collect.

I need to be ready when they come for me.

CHAPTER TWENTY FIVE

Briana

After parking my motorcycle I enter the gym. I spot Jaden near the cage, coaching Nick and Brian as they spar.

Charlie spots me walking over and I wave at him but don't stop to talk like I usually do. When Jaden spots me, he signals for the guys to stop.

"Hey, is everything alright? Why are you riding instead of driving?"

"Because I don't have a car and the only way I can get around is my bike."

He frowns at me and then his gaze travels to where I'm watching the flat-screen TV behind him showing a breaking news report about a car lit on fire in front of billionaire Ethan Carter's building as the firefighters extinguish the flames.

"Where's the car?" he asks but I dodge the question.

"I need you to train me on how to defend myself."

He frowns and then gives me a cold, hard stare before he says, "No. I asked you a question. Where is the car, Briana?"

Rolling my eyes upward, Giselle and Nate walk up beside me as I point to the TV.

In slow motion, everyone, including Nick and Brian, turn to look the screen where the Bentley is a charred piece of aluminum.

"Are you fucking crazy?" Jaden yells.

"Brie, you didn't," Giselle says, shock clear in her voice.

"Well, I can tell you are pissed," Nate says.

I grimace, tilting my head. I look pointedly at Jaden. "Maybe." I pinch my fingers together. "Just a little bit." I drop my hand. "Train me."

"No," he snaps.

"Fine, then don't." I turn on my heel and walk away.

"Where the fuck do you think you're going, Briana?"

Ignoring him, I walk toward Giselle's studio, not wanting to freak my best friend out with my crazy behavior.

Sitting in Giselle's office, I exhale the breath I have been holding.

When she walks inside, she looks at me worriedly. "What's up, Brie? Are you okay?"

"I'm fine."

"No… you are not. I see that look in your eye and it's that same look you had when you left. Don't shut me out again. Please," she pleads.

"I'm not shutting you out, Giselle. I'm just… tired." I stare at the white drop-down ceiling. "I need Jaden to show me self-defense and he is being a dick about it."

"Why would you want to learn how to fight, Brie?"

Looking back at her in her cute little tutu and leotard, I smile at how pretty and delicate she looks. She is happy but I see that I make her sad. It hurts me deeply and feel like an awful friend.

"My mom got out," I blurt.

Giselle's eyes soften and it dawns on her. She understands why. I tell her about Ethan and why I lit the car on fire.

"Bastard. What an ass."

"Yeah, Jaden is probably trying to make sure he won't kill me for what I did."

Giselle shakes her head. "I don't think he would be that

stupid. Not with Jaden or Nate. Jaden would kill him. You know that, right?"

"Yeah, but he won't train me, and I refused to take another dime from Carter or borrow money to pay the school what I owe."

"I can give you the money, Brie."

"No, I don't want it. I'll work at Equinox until I can pay for it on my own. I have been doing it for three years, what is the difference if I do it a little while longer? It's not like I don't have rent to pay and other bills."

Jaden and Nate rush into Giselle's office, barging in. "Brie, are you okay?" Jaden asks.

"Yep, I'm just peachy. I am going to ask you one more time, train me."

He gives me a hard stare. "I can't train you, Briana. If someone is threatening you, you need to tell me."

"No one is threatening me. I just want you to train me in the basics. It's not too much to ask."

"No, and that is my final answer."

There is no getting through to his stubborn ass.

When I get up from the chair, he asks, "Where do you think you are going?"

Throwing up my hands. "My apartment. Where else?"

He runs a frustrated hand through his short hair. "I'll pick you up when I'm done here."

"Can't. Gotta work tonight."

"What do you mean work tonight?"

"The world revolves around money, Jaden. I obviously broke the agreement I had with Ethan by lighting the damn car on fire. I have these pesky little things called bills and I can't exactly look for work as a therapist until I complete the hours and pay what I owe to the school."

"If it's money you need, I will—"

"No." I shake my head and repeat the word. "No."

"Why are you being this way?"

Setting my lips in a grim line, my eyes find his. "I asked myself the same question when you kicked me out of your life. Then I asked the same question when I saw you on television with your latest hookup and I came up with the same answer every time. I wasn't important enough for you to have me around. The last thing I need is for you to play the hero for me right now."

When I try to walk out, while Jaden blocks my exit.

"I can't let you leave on that bike upset. I told you I was sorry for treating you like that. I will tell you every day if I have to but I can't let you dance at some club for money. You are mine. We—"

"Do you love me?" I know I'm pushing. Maybe Ethan's words are fucking with my head, but I want to push.

Something deep inside of me keeps pushing the limit and I am tired of hiding. I'm tired of wondering where I stand. If he can't tell me he loves me after all this time. The flowers and his nice gestures are all bullshit in my eyes. Pointless actions of affection with no meaning. He told me he doesn't know what love is, and he is probably incapable of it, but I want to hear him tell me how he feels about me. About us.

"What?" he asks like he didn't just hear me ask the words.

"You heard me. I asked you a simple question. Do you love me?"

From the corner of my eye, Giselle looks at Nate and bites her bottom lip.

Seconds tick by and I already know the answer. He doesn't have to say it. I already knew that Jaden Cyprus could never love me. My eyes get glassy but I quickly gather my composure because the only thing I have left is my pride.

"You know what? Don't bother answering that. I knew what the answer was before I asked."

The silence is so deafening you could hear a pin drop

inside the studio's office. He moves to let me pass through the doorway, but I turn and give Giselle a silent nod.

She gets it and probably is the only person in this world that understands me. It sucks to ask a question like that and not get the answer you hoped for. Hope is such a bitch, but it's the only thing you have left when you have nothing.

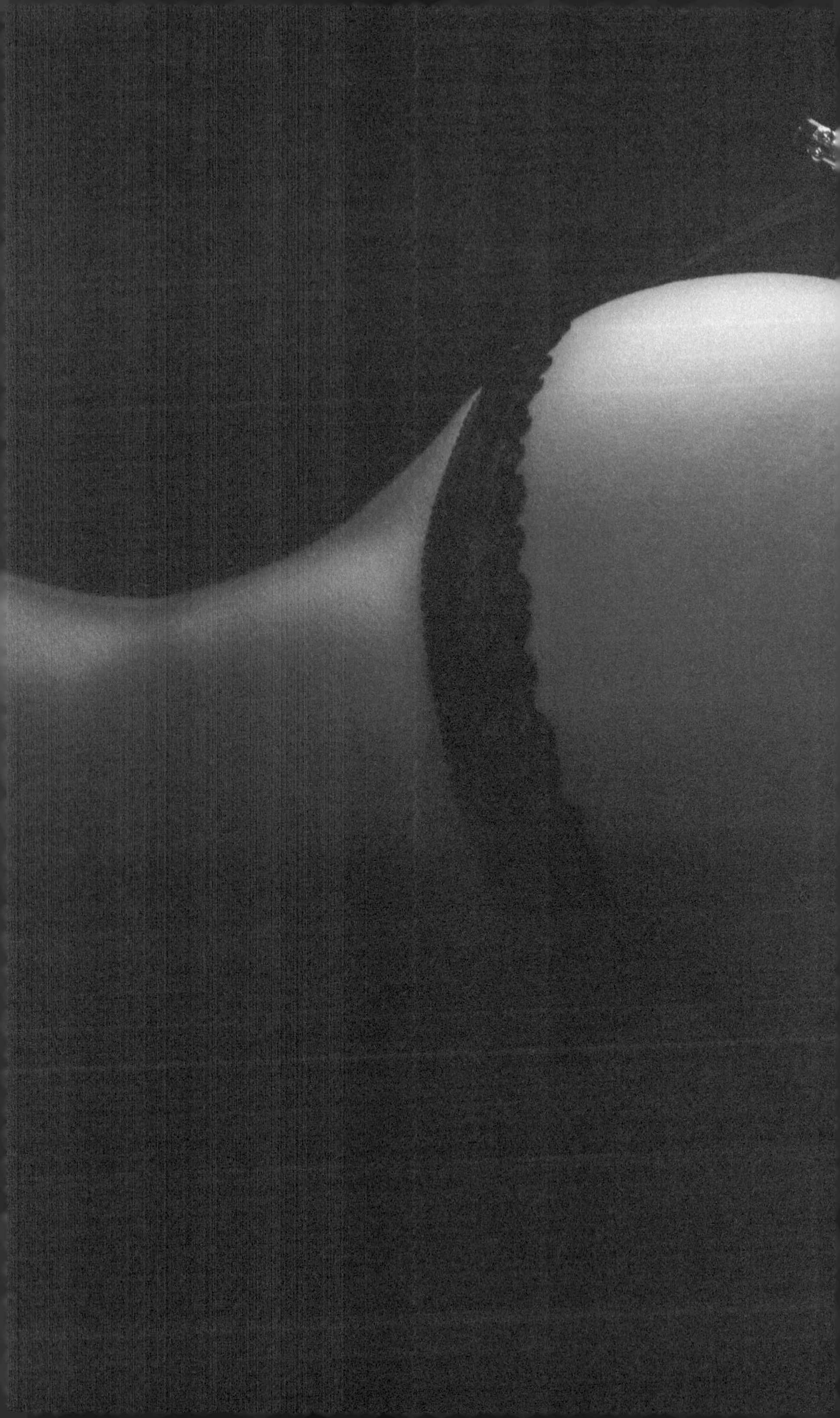

CHAPTER TWENTY SIX
Jaden

What the fuck? Everything was fine. We were fine and she went crazy on me.

"You need to let her go, Jaden," Nate says to me, walking back toward the gym after Briana sped off on her motorcycle.

That thing is a death trap.

"I can't, Nate. She needs me."

"No, she needs someone to love her and obviously you can't give her that. She is dealing with her shit and she is tired of people letting her down. Everyone has let her down. She feels she has no one except Giselle. She still feels guilty about what happened and blames herself. The only friend she knows that loves her, she failed. She has nightmares to remind her every night."

"She won't have nightmares if she sleeps in my arms."

Nate nods his head. "Yeah, until you toss her out on her ass, and it starts all over."

"What the fuck is that supposed to mean? I would do anything for her. I'll give her anything."

"Except what she wants the most, and it definitely isn't

your money. She wants you to love her, Jaden. She wants reassurance that you will be there for her. Always. If you can't be that for her and you can't love her, then you need to let her go and let someone else love her like she deserves."

We walked to the back and entered the office, where I had already placed a picture of all of us from my last fight when we were all in the cage with Brie by my side.

We were all smiling, and it was the best feeling in the world to know I have a family. She asked me if I loved her but I'm too much of a coward to understand the meaning of that word. I care about her so much. I have killed for her but something is not right and has her acting rash and unpredictable.

Inwardly, I smile about her lighting the Bentley on fire. Fucking prick deserves the show for deceiving her. I knew the minute he was in her life he was taking advantage of her.

"What do you plan to do?" Nate says, sitting in the office chair while I look at the photo, contemplating my next move.

My phone vibrates, letting me know Brie made it to her apartment. I have a tracking device on her phone and cameras inside her apartment. I placed the tracking device after my call with Ethan for her safety.

My head is spinning, playing out different scenarios. Why would Brie want me to train her in self-defense all of a sudden?

"Nate, call the South Dakota detention facility and ask if Briana's mother was released."

"On it."

After five minutes and a phone call later, we got our answer. Her mother was released. Briana is acting out in fear, and she is trying to prepare. But prepare for what?

"Ask Giselle to come over. I need to ask her something," I tell Nate.

He nods, shooting a text.

When Giselle enters the office, she closes the door. "What happened?"

I tell her about Briana's mother.

"She is afraid they will come for her."

"Who?" I ask.

She closes her eyes. "Her mother put Briana up as collateral in the past. Either with money or her body." My hands grip the edge of the desk but she continues, "We all thought it was just Jack, but we now know there were others. Her mother will tell them her daughter will pay. Especially when they see her around—"

"Billionaires," I finish for her.

"Exactly. Her becoming a doctor in physical therapy doesn't help either. She won't take my money and she feels like she has no one. She asked you for help and you turned her down. The situation with Ethan didn't help either. It's like her past and present are closing in on her and feels she only has herself that she can trust."

"It took balls to light that car on fire in broad daylight. Briana has some serious *cojones*," Nate says with a chortle.

"Yeah, my girl does have some serious balls."

"Why won't you teach her how to defend herself?" Giselle asks.

"Because she will use it and end up getting hurt. I know the feeling. Ask Nate.

When you are in a dark place, you want to arm yourself to survive. And sometimes, you want whatever you are trying to fight to come for you."

"Why? Why would she do that?" Giselle asks.

"To stop the pain. She lives in fear every night from what those monsters did to her. They raped her repeatedly and left her to die. They broke her. Then I fucked up and let her go because I thought I was too fucked up to deserve her. If you think I have a dark soul, Briana has a sinfully darker one.

When she goes to sleep, it is like *Nightmare On Elm Street* if you know what I mean."

"How do you know?" Giselle whispers.

Nate catches my gaze. "Show her."

Handing Giselle my phone with the recording of Briana's nightmares, we wait while she watches in horror. She closes her eyes, and the sounds of Briana's horrifying screams pierce the room, I have to turn the volume on my cell phone down. She watches her best friend scream, pleading for them to stop while she curls herself in a ball in the corner of her black room, sobbing until she falls asleep.

Silent tears fall like raindrops down Giselle's cheeks. She looks at Nate and then at me. "Freddy Kruger is like Disneyland compared to that shit," I say.

"Nate. She must think it's real every night," she says, sniffling.

"I know, baby. Jaden has talked to a therapist and has found a way to help her."

"How?"

"BDSM therapy with bondage."

She pinches her brows. "I have heard of that. It is like control and dominance but the submissive has to trust the person and feel safe and protected. She has to submit like she is a captive, and it reverses the mind from a past trauma. Like replacing it with another event that causes pleasure instead of pain and fear."

"Exactly. I plan to use that tactic with Briana," I tell her.

"She is pissed at you right now."

"I have to let her dance and do whatever she plans on doing, but I'll pursue her and convince her to come to my house, or I'll go do it at Equinox. Either way, I will get her back and help her."

"Okay. What about her mother and Ethan?"

Sucking my teeth, I stare at Briana smiling in the picture of all of us and say, "If they come for her, they die. Briana is mine and I protect what is mine. Ethan knows not to fuck with me. I'll cripple him and he knows it."

"Did you know she slapped him?"

I give her a grin. "She did?" Then the thought that he could have put his hands on her has me asking Giselle in a stern tone, "Did he touch her?"

She shakes her head. "No, he didn't," she says.

"Motherfucker knows the other leaders wouldn't interfere if we went after him. We are too important for their operations for them to get involved. The Mafia doesn't give a shit about domestic disputes either way," Nate says.

"I'm going to train the guys then head to Equinox."

"You're going to see her?" Giselle asks me.

"You know I'm a sucker for Briana dancing on a pole," I say, giving her a wink. "I'm going to have to install one for her in my house just for my pleasure."

"Making plans, Jaden?"

"I should ask you that question. I'm waiting for you two to tie the knot and make me an uncle already."

She giggles, a blush creeping up her cheeks as her gaze full of love reaches Nate.

"I'm going to close the door so you too can start making my nephew," I tease, and I know as soon as the door closes that is exactly what they are up to.

I enter Equinox as a member, and take a seat in front of the pole that Briana slid down on the last time I was here when she straddled my lap and had my dick almost bursting through my jeans. The lights dim and I catch the man in charge, remembering his name is Marcus.

I signal for him to come toward my table. When he reaches me, he nods. "Mr. Cyprus, it is a pleasure seeing you here. What can I do for you?"

"I want a VIP room with Coco tonight. I don't care what it costs."

He gives me a worried frown, he is about to give me an excuse but I lift my wrist and show him a tattooed mark in case he forgot. The mark that indicates I am with the Mafia. Ethan and Nate have the same mark.

His eyes widen and I raise my brow. "Is there a problem?"

"N-no, sir," he stammers. "I will arrange for it right away."

I nod. "Don't worry about Mr. Carter. He won't be requiring the VIP with Coco… ever," I tell him in a hard tone. His hands shake because he recognizes the tattoo on my wrist that indicates I have a higher rank than Ethan Carter.

Instead of owning a business and sitting behind a desk, Nate and I chose to live our dream and become pro-MMA fighters, but we provide an invaluable service to very powerful men in very powerful circles. We make things disappear. Information, money, people and we secure things, making them untraceable. No one fucks with us.

Marcus nods, motioning me toward the back hallway with red velvet carpet. The mahogany siding on the walls shines against the dim lighting, giving off a sex club vibe. He opens a door for me to enter the expansive room.

It is equipped with a bed, a dance pole, refreshments, and a tray with condoms, whips, and other items used for pleasure. The one item I am interested in is the blindfold.

"Thank you, please tell Coco that someone is waiting for her, but do not tell her under any circumstances it is me. I want it to be a surprise."

"Yes, Mr. Cyprus."

Placing the chair in front of the bed I want Briana to sit in, I grab the collar with the tethered chain and blindfold. This is her first session with me. The first thing I need is her trust and then I need her to submit to me and only me. There will be no other man she will ever trust *but* me. She will receive pleasure from me and only me.

After ten minutes, the door opens, and Briana appears in the doorway with a look of shock on her face. "What do you want?" she snaps.

Giving her a smirk, I say, "You are not happy to see me. Were you expecting someone else?"

"No. I was going to tell whoever it was to go fuck themselves."

I nod, scratching my chin. "Hmm, I see. Now that you know it is me, I need you to sit." I motion to the red velvet chair.

"No."

"I said, sit."

Her platform heels glitter against the lights as she walks over slowly. She is wearing a short robe outlining her breasts and is wearing those sexy pasty things that look good on her tits, covering her nipples.

"Take off the robe and sit."

"Why?"

Walking up to her, I lean down close to her ear. Even in her platform heels, I'm still taller than her. "Because I want that sweet pussy. I paid for it so sit in the fucking chair."

I don't mean it that way, but I will help her pay for whatever she needs however I can. Her eyes darken and narrow to slits.

Let the mind games begin.

I don't mean to be a dick to her, but it is the only way I can get her to agree. She sits reluctantly after she lets the robe slide off her soft skin from her delectable body. Fuck, she is beautiful.

I stand behind the chair and let my playlist by Aaryan Shah play through the room's speakers. She tilts her head to glare at me.

"Do you trust me, Briana?" I ask. Her chest rises and falls

with each breath. Her legs squeeze together and my eyes trace the white lace of her panties covering her bare pussy. My cock strains inside my black jeans. I remove my belt, shoes, socks, and shirt. "Answer me, Briana. Do you trust me?"

"Yes."

"Are you sure?"

"Yes," she says breathlessly.

"I'm going to place a blindfold on you now and the only thing you will be able to hear is the sound of the music and my voice. You are to follow my every command. Do you understand?" My voice lowers to a whisper behind her ear. "I'm not going to hurt you. All you will feel is pleasure but you have to trust me."

She sighs deeply, and her hands wring nervously on her lap as I place the blindfold over her eyes.

"Jaden?" she asks, squirming.

"I'm right here, baby. I would never hurt you. You know that, right?"

She nods.

"Words, Briana. I need your words."

"Yes, Jaden. I trust you. It's… dark and I'm scared."

My fingers trace over the pasties hiding the pink velvet skin of her nipples. I run my finger over one and then the other and her legs open instinctively. She arches her back, so her neck is exposed. I lower my mouth to the tender spot where her pulse beats. My lips feel the blood pumping underneath. Her smell of vanilla hits my senses and my cock strains painfully.

Closing my eyes, I love the thrill of knowing she trusts me to place the blindfold over her eyes, enveloping her in darkness. She doesn't understand the power she has over me.

"Do you know what you do to me, Briana? The power you have over me? I will do anything for you… anything." My fingers slide down her stomach to the triangle of lace between her legs. Her pussy lips strain against the white scrap of fabric.

"I'm going to place cuffs on both of your wrists," I tell her softly.

"Why?" she asks.

I chuckle. "Because I can. Because you will let me do whatever I want with you. There is something you want from me and I'm the only one that can give it to you."

"What do I want from you?" She says confused.

After I place the cuff with the tethered chain, she tries to test how far it goes by stretching it causing the chain rattle. "You want me to give you pleasure. You want me to fuck you so hard that you come undone and the only thing you remember is my cock inside your cunt. You want me to love you." My finger slides to the center of her core and she gasps, "I can only love you if you are truly mine in every sense of the word. The only way I can love you is if you give me your dreams, your nightmares, your screams. I want your body. I want your soul. I want it all, Briana. It is the only way I can be whole. It is the only way my pain stops." My tongue licks her neck up to her ear. She shudders when my tongue sucks the lobe of her ear and whisper, "I want all of you."

"Jaden, please," she says, writhing on the chair. Her hips roll as she grinds, seeking my finger to slip inside her wet pussy.

"You don't need these." My fingers bundle the lace in my hand, and rip them off her.

Her legs open. She is so wet the velvet chair is soaked from her arousal. I kneel in front of her and lift her legs over the armrests on each side. She leans back, her pussy is spread wide with her pink flesh. I lick and suck her pussy savagely.

"Yes, Jaden. Please… don't stop," she moans.

"What do you need?" I rasp against her lips.

"I need you to make me come."

"You come when I say you can." I lick and suck her swollen clit, I know her pussy so well. I know when she is about to come. She writhes and moans, the cuffs stretch the chain and she tries to reach for my head so she can push my face to the part of her that drives her crazy. I pull back, and she protests.

"Please, don't stop."

"I'll give you what you want. If you let me do what I want."

She is panting and pushing her hips forward, seeking my tongue. I smile and suck her pussy until she comes.

Rising to my feet, I pick her up out of the chair and lay her on the bed. I kneel and spread her legs wide so I can slide my jeans off and then my boxers.

Fisting my cock, I place the tip at her entrance and rub it against her swollen clit. She arches and pushes, seeking my dick to sink into her wet heat.

"Please, fuck me, Jaden. I can't take it anymore. I need you inside me."

"I thought you didn't want me here," I say playfully.

"I want you inside me."

"Why?" I play with her until she admits she wants this. Until she can't take it anymore and submits to me.

"Because… I need you."

"I will give you what you want when you give me what I want."

"What do you want?" she asks.

"I told you. I want everything. I want you in my bed so I can spank and fuck you."

"Then fucking do it," she says on a moan. I want you inside me."

I lower my head and lick her stomach all the way to the hollow part of her neck and slam into her hard until I'm balls deep.

"Oh god, yes. Your cock is so fucking big," she says, biting her lip. She stills for a minute to adjust to my size, and I squeeze my eyes closed as her tight cunt grips my cock.

"You feel so good, baby. Fuck. I love your pussy," I say,

taking a deep breath as I try to take it slow. This is about control and her submitting to me. I want all of her. She needs to know that she can trust me to give her everything she needs.

"Arrived" by Aaryan Shah plays. I slide in and out of her slowly, making love to her while she stays blindfolded with her hands cuffed above her head. I capture her lips with mine.

When I break the kiss, I tell her softly the words she needs to hear from me. The words that I was too much of a coward to say but feel deep inside of me. The way I truly feel about her. "I love you, Briana Jameson. All of you. I'm never going to let you go. Never." Moving inside of her, I feel the walls of her pussy tense and I know she is close. Her breathy moans escape her plump lips as I move inside her, and whisper, "I love you. I will always love you and I will wait until you can love me again. However long it takes." Grinding deeper, she falls apart and I fall right with her.

"Jaden." She says my name in a breathy moan as she comes. Her thighs grip my hips while she rides her release. Her pussy milks my cock and I spill myself deep inside her with a groan.

"I love you," I tell her again against her lips and continue to tell her my innermost feelings, assuring her that we have a bond between us that no one will ever break. "In the darkness of your dreams, you will find my voice with the whisper of my love, and you will know I am here. Always and forever. You don't need me to teach you to fight because I'll always be here to fight for you."

A single tear slides down her cheek and I lick it because I know it is her way to express what her mouth can't say, how much she needs me. I taste her voice on my lips. The voice that screams… she is mine.

CHAPTER TWENTY SEVEN

Briana

The next morning, my eyes flutter as I sense the bright sun streaming through the glass doors and windows. When I feel the side of the bed beside me, I'm greeted with the cold, crisp white sheets of Jaden's bed.

His room feels like I'm sleeping in a white cloud up in the sky. Compared to where I am used to sleeping in a dark room, Jaden sleeps in a square box of white light. We left the club shortly after we had sex and I submitted to him.

Taking a deep breath, I smell a familiar flower.

When I turn my head and look at his nightstand, I see a bouquet of white lilies and smile. He remembered.

I freshen up in his ultramodern bathroom and pad my way to the kitchen as the smell of coffee greets me but instead of Jaden, I find an older woman making breakfast.

She turns and smiles. "Good morning, Dr. Jameson. My name is Clara. Mr. Cyprus instructed me to make you breakfast or anything you would like. I usually only clean three times a week because his meals are pre-made, but he insisted I come in and cook for you now."

"Oh, there is no need to trouble yourself. Please call me

Brie. Dr. Jameson sounds too formal. Do you know where Jaden went?"

She smiles and motions toward the pool. Jaden's house looks like it is made entirely of glass. You can see everything from any point of the house except the bathrooms.

When I look over at the pool, Jaden is under the waterfall coming from the second story. It is breathtaking in the light of day to see the water cascading into the pool with Jaden and his shirtless body under the water as it sluices down his chiseled back.

"Brie? Brie?" I turn my head to look at Clara. She gives me a knowing look and heat creeps up my cheeks as she catches me openly staring at Jaden.

"I'm sorry, you were saying?" My cheeks must be beet red because she smiles warmly. She was calling my name, and I was too busy ogling Jaden in the pool.

"I was asking how you like your eggs, sweetheart?"

"Umm—scrambled. Please," I tell her and I see the way she effortlessly moves around the kitchen. I am quick to notice that she does not cook here often because the pan and everything she opens is brand new like it was just purchased.

Looking back over to where Jaden is in the pool, looking hot in his long board shorts with a body like it has been carved out of granite. His tattoos accentuate his arms and chest on his tanned skin, making my legs squeeze with need.

Last night, sex with Jaden was different. It was fear mixed with pleasure and it is an experience only Jaden can give me. He wants submission and control over my fears, it scares the shit out of me.

He looks over at me through the glass and gives me a wink catching me staring at him like a lovesick schoolgirl.

He pushes the glass and it slides forward. His house is a true work of art, like it was designed to hide nothing.

It is all white, glass and marble with a touch of birchwood accents in the kitchen and pool area. The second floor has a waterfall that overflows into the pool, creating a calming sound of flowing water.

"Did you sleep well?" he asks.

"I did." My bottom teeth catch my lip at the mention of last night in the club as he blindfolded me and tied me up. "I need to head home and change. I don't have any of my clothes." I wave my hand down my body, wearing his T-shirt and boxers I found in his drawers.

Ever since I met Jaden at the Porcelain Dollhouse in South Dakota and we hit it off, we have always slept naked. This house has no privacy and I'm surprised Clara didn't see me sleeping naked in the bed.

The smell of buttery scrambled eggs and buttered toast permeates the kitchen and the light sound of a plate hitting marble has me turning my head toward Clara.

She looks surprised, and I realize it's because of what I said. Her brow furrows and she looks at Jaden and then back.

"She hasn't seen it. She doesn't know," he says to her. My brows pinch and I look from Clara to Jaden, wondering what they're talking about. What don't I know? What haven't I seen?

"Eat and then I'll show you," he says before he turns toward the hallway to change out of his wet swim trunks.

Clara walks over with a mop to clean the water off the marble floor.

"Oh. Let me help you with that," I say, scrambling to help her. She places her hand over mine on the steel mop handle.

Her eyes soften before she says, "Please, eat. He gave me strict instructions that you don't have to lift a finger. He doesn't want you to clean or trouble yourself. He wants you to feel welcomed and relaxed. He said you would be here from now on and I really need this job."

My eyes soften, and I release my grip on the mop, knowing the feeling of needing work and then a feeling of warmth at her soft words.

I give her a nod and she wastes no time cleaning up the water on the kitchen floor.

He wants me here, he made that clear last night.

After eating the most delicious breakfast and fussing with Clara, trying to wash my plate and tidying up the kitchen, she assures me that she can manage. She gives me a wink and tells me to go get changed.

Making my way through the glass hallway, my bare feet pad on the pristine white marble toward the master bedroom.

When I reach the double doors, Jaden is already showered and dressed with black sweats hanging off his hips and a white tank top. He looks clean and deliciously hot. His gaze travels down my body dressed in his clothes.

"I love the way you look in my clothes, but I know you would rather change into your own clothes," he calls me over to him with his finger and I take four steps forward. "I want to show you where your clothes are kept. I'm sorry I left you alone this morning, but Clara was here early to make you breakfast and I couldn't risk putting on a show and her freaking out and leaving."

The thought of Clara seeing Jaden and me having sex causes me to shiver in embarrassment. "I suppose that wouldn't make her feel comfortable working here."

He gives me a smirk. "I needed to cool off so I took a dip in the pool." He slides his fingers through mine and tugs me toward a white wall and a frosted glass door with a flat silver knob. He pushes the flat knob and the door opens to a room that is supposed to be a closet. The lights along rows and rows of shelves and glass drawers turn on, giving every piece of clothing, pair of shoes, and item a glow like it was in an art gallery.

"Wow. This is your closet?"

He nods and walks forward into the room and then to another frosted glass wall. He presses a button and the tinted frost on the glass disappears to reveal a clear glass wall that houses a closet fit for a celebrity. Rows and rows of designer purses, shoes, and clothing is highlighted by bright lights. Some of the items catch my attention because some of them are the same ones I left behind three years ago.

The Chanel outfits with the matching handbag and shoes I wore to a dinner the first night Giselle and I went out with them. The Balenciaga knife boots he gifted me when I mentioned them to Giselle jokingly because of the ridiculous price tag one day when a magazine came in the mail at the gym.

"I moved all your stuff you left behind because I knew I had made a mistake in having you live at the apartment when you should have been living with me. I know you can tell I bought you more items. Everything else besides the items that were in the apartment when we were together is brand new. I had the boutiques ship me the latest trends and Clara organized them. I hope you like them."

My eyes go wide, and I don't know what to say or how to react. Jaden has always been a flashy guy because he said he worked hard and wanted to have everything he never had or always wanted.

"You didn't have—"

"I did, and I wanted you to have a dream closet. Kinda like Barbie."

I give him a grin. "Barbie?"

He shakes his head and chuckles. "Yeah, like a platinum-haired Barbie. I'm glad you like white though, I don't think I could deal with pink everywhere."

I swallow a lump in my throat because when I was little, I never had a Barbie to play with, so I imagined I was her with a dream closet and a jeep. I loved the Barbie jeep but knew I would never have one, ever. It may be silly or trivial, but I never had a birthday party or Christmas. Hell, I never had a Christmas tree. I was lucky I had water to take a shower and clothes that were from donations.

Jaden slides a finger to wipe away tears I hadn't realized were falling down my cheeks. My hands wipe at my face and I sniffle, laughing, trying to play it off. "I'm sorry, I love it. I just never thought… I would have a closet besides the one in an apartment. I was thinking when you said I looked like Barbie."

He looks confused and I continue, "When I was little I used to think I was a Barbie and I would role-play when I was little because I knew I would never get to play with a real doll. I never had a closet or clothes from a store. My clothes were donated by people who didn't want them, or they didn't fit. I never had a Christmas tree or a birthday party like other kids. My mother said those things weren't important or that I didn't deserve them."

Jaden stays quiet and stands next to me while I look at rows upon rows of the most beautiful clothes with their matching shoes and handbags. The smell of the closet reminds me of when he took me to those boutiques to shop. The smell of expensive leather and perfume or when you open a Vogue magazine, the scent of perfume from the samples as you turn the pages.

My eyes wander to a chaise in the middle of the room and I wonder how I would fit into a world that has all the luxuries a woman could ever want. He said last night he loves me but that could have been in the heat of the moment or maybe he thinks it's what I need to hear. Jaden always felt sorry for me because we come from a similar background. We come from nothing.

The last thing I want is for him to think he needs to say words he doesn't feel. He thinks he needs to save me. What is the point of saving me when I'm already lost?

My mind is still reeling at seeing the fairy-tale closet but I had a taste of this type of life with the fancy cars. And in a blink of an eye, it was gone.

They were given to me because he wanted to be with me and when he didn't want me, they became reminders.

Temporary.

Stepping back, I hit the button and the glass turns back to a white frost. "Brie, are you alright?" Jaden asks.

"I-I'm fine. It is just overwhelming."

"What? Brie, did I do something wrong?"

Shaking my head, I say, "No. You have been great. I'm just… confused."

I don't know what to make of it and the voice in my head keeps whispering in my head. It is my mother's voice telling me when I was a teenager, *"Men only want you for your looks and body. You're just a whore and that is all you will ever be. Men will see you as nothing more. You are just a whore. It is all you're good at and when they tire of you, they will kick you out of their lives and replace you. You mean nothing… you're a whore who will end up dancing for money. A stupid whore…. no one will ever see you as nothing but trailer trash. You're a stupid girl with a stupid fantasy… no boy will ever love you. No one can love a whore. Now go lie down and make me money."*

Tears fall and I sniff and grab my stuff. The words echo in my head like a mantra. My mother's words and the guys back home chanting… I'm a whore. I can't even pay for school without dancing for money. "Brie, wait. Where are you going?"

"I-I'm sorry, Jaden, but this is a mistake. I need to go. I need to leave."

"No," he says and grabs me hard without hurting me. My clothes, bag, and phone are scattered on the floor. "You are not leaving. Stop acting like this. Talk to me."

My chest rises and falls and I feel like I can't breathe. My hands tremble and I look up at him, but my eyes are blurry. "What do you want with me? Are you not done with me?"

His grip on my arm loosens and I begin to sniffle as I remove my clothes until I'm naked. He looks at my body and then watches as I lie on the bed.

"Brie? Talk to me. What the fuck was that all about?" he says in a hard tone.

"If you're not done with me, then get it over with so I can go home. I don't need fancy clothes or you to dress me up. Just get what you paid for and I'll leave."

"You think I'm paying for you to be my whore?" His eyes are like stone and the anger is radiating off of him in waves.

He looks at me naked on his bed and he grips my chin with his forefinger and thumb. "Look at me, Briana," he says in a stern tone. When my eyes find his, his soften. "Who told you that you were my whore?"

Sniffling, I look at his handsome face and sharp jaw. "Isn't that what you paid for last night? A whore?"

His face turns into a scowl, and I stiffen because Jaden angry is a force to be reckoned with. "First, I don't pay to be with a woman. Second, I don't need to. There are things you don't know about me, things that I'm part of that grant me access to certain things or allow me to get away with certain things I'm not very proud of, but there are things I have had to do to survive. You are a survivor, Briana. I don't think you are my whore and I never want you to use that term to describe yourself. The last thing you will ever be considered is a whore and whoever uses that term and your name in the same sentence is going to deal with me. Understood?"

I nod but my hands shake because now I'm cold.

He wraps me in his arms and whispers, "I know I have made a lot of mistakes when it comes to you but believe me, I never meant to hurt you. I thought you would like the closet with all the beautiful things you deserve. I want you to feel pretty. It was never meant to insult you or make you think I'm buying you. I said I paid for you last night to get you to stay in the room with me. I am not trying to pay you for sex or a lap dance. I want to have sex with you because I'm in love with you." The warmth of his body is welcoming and his muscles bulge as he holds me. "When I realized I lost you, I had them expand the closet and make room for you because I knew you belonged with me, but I was too much of a coward to find you. Maybe, deep down, I was waiting for you to come back. I know I'm an asshole and I don't deserve you. It will take time for you to trust me, and I get that, but please don't ever think I view you as a whore. Please stay…" He sighs. "I haven't even given you the birthday presents you missed."

My brows pinch and I look up at him. "You don't have to get me birthday presents."

He smiles. "Yes, because I have a feeling not many people have given you birthday presents. I owe you a lifetime of those."

He moves to the closet and finds a fluffy designer robe with matching slippers, and I get dressed.

Clara has already left when he guides me to the garage.

When the doors open, sitting with pink bows are three white cars. A white lifted jeep with big tires, a white Porsche 911 Carrera, and a white Ferrari. All three convertibles.

"Oh, Jaden," I say softly.

He wraps his arms around my waist. "You can't be Barbie without her jeep, Porsche or Ferrari," he says.

My hands are both covering my mouth in disbelief.

When I approach the cars, I look inside and there are Barbie dolls inside from every year since I was born with the dream house and boat.

When I grab one of the dolls with happy tears streaming down my cheeks, I ask, "How did you know that I loved Barbie?"

He slides a strand of my hair behind my ear. "There is this ballerina I know that told me she would lend her best friend her Barbies to play with but you would never take one home with you because of an evil mother that would be upset someone gave you a doll instead of money. She told me you loved Barbies and that you actually looked like one of them." He grabs one and places the box next to my face and I smile. "Yep, but better."

I give him a deep kiss and thank him because I know I

would have been excited about just getting the dolls as gifts but who can deny real-life replicas of cars that Barbie would drive.

I give him a playful grin. "So, does this make you Ken?"

He grimaces and says, "Umm, no. I'm the bad boy that steals Barbie from Ken," he points out.

CHAPTER TWENTY EIGHT

Jaden

I received a text from Nate that he received the information on the two assholes, Ben and Daniel, with their information. I also received a follow-up text from Ethan that says the same thing he promised. I'm not concerned about Ethan because he can never love Briana like I can.

Briana is my responsibility, not his, and I will protect Briana and send a message to her mother to leave her alone or I will have her locked away in a rehab facility.

Walking inside the gym, I head into the office to see Nate.

"Hey brother, you got the message with the info?"

I nod, looking at the pictures of the bastards I'm going to kill. "Yeah," I tell him, studying their profiles and planning on how I'm going to kill them. The rage that I feel for these two assholes who savagely hurt her has me on edge.

He waits until I take a seat in the chair across from the desk. "Are the other details about Briana's birthday all set?"

Nate and Giselle are helping me throw Briana a birthday party, even if it is not her actual birthday, but who cares? I missed it because I was too stupid to realize my girl was struggling and I wasn't there for her. I decided a belated birthday party would be good for her.

"Yep, Giselle is more excited about it than planning our

wedding. She said her dream was for Briana and her both to be married so they could even plan on having their babies close to each other. They wanted their kids to grow up close in age like siblings."

My head snaps up, listening to what Giselle has told Nate. An idea forms in my head and I smile, angling my head toward the picture of all of us. "Then let's give it to them. Let's do it. Are you down for that?"

He raises his brows. "I'm down if you're down, but a lot of things have to happen first."

I sigh. "Yeah, they do. Did you hear from Morales's team about canceling the fight?"

Nate slides his hand over his face. "Yeah, Zavier wants to pull out of his camp and find another team." His eyes find mine. "He is canceling your third fight and wants to train with us in a different weight class with Briana as his physical therapist."

Rolling my shoulder, releasing the tension, my nostrils flare. "Do I have to kick his ass for him to stay away from Briana?"

He chuckles. "Nah, he made sure to tell me they are friends, and it is strictly professional, and he knows you guys are together. He saw your last fight. He wants to switch sides and be part of our team."

"Fine, we'll see what the kid's got, and it would be good for Briana professionally. So one more fight?"

"Yep, you need Brie to help you through this one again before you take some time off. We will handle the other situation before though."

He means we need to kill these bastards before the fight and then we'll have a solid alibi.

"Good, I like it."

CHAPTER TWENTY NINE

Briana

It's been a week since he gifted me the cars, I'm in the closet Jaden had built for me in his home, looking through the rows of shoes that would look good with my outfit.

"Those." Giselle points to the silver heels that would look beautiful with my white minidress.

"You don't think they are too high?"

"Umm-no. I think you would look great in those, and your legs would look like they go on forever in those shoes."

I pull them off the shelf and look at them. "Gianvitto Rossi." I read out loud.

Jaden told me I could have Giselle over to his house, and she cannot believe the impressive home Jaden lives in, hidden away from everyone.

He said he will try to work on inviting certain people he calls family. Nate and Giselle have been our family and so it was a no-brainer for him to agree when I asked if Giselle could come over and get ready for a night out.

The guys are chatting in the living room, waiting for us to emerge from the master bedroom.

"I can't believe he had this built for you. This is amazing,

Brie," she says, looking at the built-in California closet with ultra-high-end modern touches. "He is crazy about you, you know that, right?"

"Do you think I'm dreaming?" I ask.

Tears pool in Giselle's eyes because she knows I'm afraid to be disappointed. "No, Brie, you are living a dream. A dream you deserve."

We both stand watching ourselves in the reflection of the gigantic mirror Jaden had installed so I could look at myself when I dress from all angles. I could literally walk in like I'm on a runway to watch myself and how I would look when walking inside this closet. Turning to the side and looking at the back side of the dress to make sure I'm not revealing more than what I'm willing to let anyone see, I sigh in relief that the dress fits me perfectly.

Giselle is wearing a short minidress in red with gold heels and she looks stunning.

"Come on. We both look hot as fuck."

When we make our way to the living area with our heels clicking against the pristine white marble floors, both Nate and Jaden stop mid-sentence when they spot us approaching. My eyes find Jaden and he is openly staring at me from head to toe, his gaze his caressing every inch of my outfit.

"Does it look okay?" I say, worried.

Jaden clears his throat and looks to Nate as he closes the distance to stand close. He slides his strong hand around my waist. "You look gorgeous," he says in a husky voice.

I smile, relieved that I'm dressed ok and that he thinks I look beautiful.

Nate and Giselle murmur something to each other. Jaden slides his fingers through mine as we make our way outside to Jaden's Zenvo and Nate's Lamborghini. We each head out to the Las Vegas Strip to an exclusive club that they reserved for us.

When we arrive, there are photographers and people in

line waiting to get inside. We can hear the screams of Nate and Jaden's fans as they shout Nate and Jaden's cage names, The Destroyer and The Reaper.

Giselle and I give each other knowing glances as we were prepared, knowing that fans would go haywire when they saw us pull up in flashy cars with pro-MMA celebrity fighters to an exclusive club with a long line of people waiting to be allowed inside.

When we are seated in the club in the VIP section, we toast and drink. Champagne flows. Giselle and I danced and let loose for a couple of hours in the club.

After my third drink, I take a break from dancing, Jaden gets close and whispers in my ear to follow him upstairs to a secluded room.

When we arrive, there is a chair that looks like a throne. I look at him with my brows raised.

"Sit," he demands.

I sit in the chair and when I look around, I see that the room is empty except for the chair and a table with cuffs, a blindfold, and a single feather. He moves to slide curtains that expose a tinted glass window to the club. My eyes widen and he grins.

"You can see them, but they cannot see you. I want you."

"Right now? But… Giselle and Nate."

"They are in another room," he quips.

I bite my bottom lip and watch as he grabs the blindfold. "Do you trust me?"

I swallow and look up into his eyes and shake my head. "Y-yes."

"Don't be nervous. I need you to trust me, remember?"

"Okay. I trust you."

He places the blindfold around my eyes, enveloping me in darkness. I wince because the darkness reminds me of the night terrors but I remind myself that Jaden is here and people are outside the room.

"I want to be your light in the darkness of your mind. When all you see is dark, I want you to remember that I'm here and nothing will happen to you. I want to fuck you with the blindfold on because when you think of the dark, I want you to remember how I made you feel. How my cock fucks that tight cunt I love so much."

My head tilts, I can't see but I can hear him and smell his cologne. My legs open. My breathing becomes frantic when he places my arms and legs in cuffs with the chain tethered. He blows air between my heated core. I'm wet. My nipples hard against the soft white fabric.

"I want you to be a naughty girl with me, Briana. I want you to tell me how you want me to pleasure you."

"Okay," I say breathlessly. I'm so fucking turned on my pussy is throbs against my thin panties. I can feel my clit pulsing and aching. "I want you to slide your tongue on my pussy and see how wet I am for you."

"Fuck, you're so sexy," he says against the skin of my thighs. The feeling of something soft slides between my thighs toward my pussy. I writhe, the cuff and chain stretch with a clank sound as I open my legs wide to feel the soft touch that I now realize is a feather.

"Please," I plead.

He leans between my thighs and I can feel his tongue up my thigh until he gets to my aching clit.

I moan when he swipes his tongue, giving me the first dose of pleasure. "Fuck, yes. Please."

My hands find his hair and I slide my fingers through it, hoping to push his face where I want it between my thighs. His tongue licks my pussy again. I slide my ass to the edge of the chair.

My hands grasp the arms of the chair. I get frustrated and place each leg over the arms of the chair until the chains cuffed to my ankles stretch in protest.

My hands find the edge of my dress near my chest and

release my breasts. I can't see but I can feel the cold air assault my aching nipples. I'm bared to him, spread eagle on the chair, hoping he has mercy on me and gives me my release.

"I see you trust me because you want me to pleasure you. I love to see your tight cunt as it leaks for me, Brie." He grips my thighs and nuzzles his face between my legs and sucks my pussy. My arousal leaks. I can feel the trickle sliding down my ass.

He places kisses on my pussy and rasps against my flesh. "When I come up for air between your thighs. What is the first question that comes to mind?" he asks.

"How'd I taste?"

He snickers. "You taste pure, like fucking heaven."

I smile and my heart constricts like he is bringing it back to life. He is telling me I taste pure, like I'm not damaged or ruined.

He eats my pussy like a man starved. I moan. I gasp. He slides his tongue inside, fucking me savagely. A wave of my orgasm runs through my body.

I explode on his tongue but he doesn't stop sucking until he swallows every last drop of my release.

My legs shake on the armrest of the chair and I can hear him rise and slide my trembling thighs down. I am sitting in the chair feel his tongue licks my nipples and suck, making sure they each get their turn. His tongue runs between my breasts until he reaches my lips in a scorching hot kiss.

I can taste myself as he devours my mouth and he whispers, "I love you."

He removes the blindfold and my eyes squint until they adjust to the light of the room. I can see through the glass window. The clubgoers drinking and dancing. He grabs my hands delicately so I can rise from the chair, my arms and legs still cuffed.

"Walk and lean on the glass. Don't worry, no one can see you."

I swallow. "How do you know?"

He grins and nods to the glass. "Because Nate and I are part owners of this club. It is how we are allowed in this room."

"Oh," I say, my eyes widening.

"Place your breasts against the glass, Brie."

I do as he asks, trusting and following his every instruction. His words are still repeating in my head that he loves me. There are so many things that I don't know about Jaden.

My cheek is on the glass. I can see people dancing, grinding on each other and it is erotic to know that I'm semi naked against the glass and no one can see that I'm here.

Jaden slides my panties off, and they are stretched at my ankles above the chain. He motions for me to spread my legs as far as they can go. I hear him unfastening the button of his jeans. The tip of his cock is between my thighs, he grips my lower belly with one hand.

"Fast or slow, baby? Tell me how you want to have a good time."

"Fast."

I gasp when he slides his cock inside me and I'm jolted forward. He holds me steady so that my head doesn't hit the glass. My hands are tied, abut I can't place them flat without the chain hitting it.

He stops for a minute until he is sure I can take him fully. I'm very petite compared to his massive size. His arms are solid like a block of concrete.

He leans close, his breath ghosting my ear. "You see all those people out there having a good time? If they only knew you are watching them while you're getting fucked. Makes you wonder who is having a better time."

He starts fucking me hard, grunting with each thrust and I fucking love every minute of him inside me. My body feels him everywhere. He pounds into me with forceful thrusts and my orgasm begins to build.

"Yes, Jaden. I want more. Faster, baby, please."

"Fuck, Briana. I love the way your pussy grips my cock. You're so tight. I want to stay inside you."

He grunts as he increases his speed and we both groan as he fucks me. I look down and my dress is bunched up at my waist and my legs and hands are bound. Every muscle in my legs is straining to its limit. He bites my neck and then licks the area with his tongue. My nipples harden on the cold glass. He pounds into me relentlessly until we both come hard.

Flashes of lights explode behind my eyes. "Yes, Jaden! " I cry out. "Fuck… yes."

CHAPTER THIRTY
Briana

After the best two weeks I have had in a long time with Jaden, I'm walking from school to the white jeep Jaden gifted me but I have a sinking feeling in the pit of my stomach. I keep looking over my shoulder to make sure no one is following me. It's dark. The lights in the parking lot bouncing off the shiny white jeep.

Jaden is training light in the gym until the last fight of the year since Zavier backed out of the fight and is moving to another weight class.

I'm about to unlock the car when a voice that has plagued me in my nightmares stops me. "Look at what we have here, Ben. Our nice little pocket pussy is all grown up."

My stomach somersaults at the disgusting name Daniel and Ben would call me when they would rape me. Bile burns the back of my throat. My hands tremble with the key fob, trying to unlock the jeep, but it falls, hitting the black pavement of the parking lot.

My eyes squeeze shut, and I try to ignore his next words. I don't want to look at them but my want is short lived as he pulls my hair back and it feels like it is ripping out of my skull.

"Your cunt of a mother owes us. She told us you were

parading that fine tight pussy of yours around some rich folks. You know why we are here. We want money or you can work it off just like before. I hear you like to twirl on a pole around here and looking at you now, you lookin mighty fine."

"Yeah, look at these sweet wheels. So which one bought it for you? Which one did you have to get on your knees and suck his cock or did you give them a taste of that sweet pink pussy we love to ride?" Ben says.

"Please, let me go. I don't have your money and my mother's debt is not my problem. If she owes you money, then you need to talk to her about it. I haven't seen or heard from her. Now leave me alone."

My phone begins to ring but my head is tilted back painfully by Daniel's grip and I can't see who is calling.

Ben snatches my bag from my hand and retrieves the key from the ground. I squeeze my eyes shut and I scream.

"Help! Help me, please," I yell but a painful blow knocks the wind out of me and everything goes black.

CHAPTER THIRTY ONE

Jaden

Walking into the office after calling Brie's cell phone has me in panic mode. I see Nate looking through some paperwork and he looks at me with a frown.

"What's up, brother?"

"Can you pull up Brie's GPS on her cell phone? I keep calling her, but she doesn't answer. She should have been here from school by now. It was her last day at the center."

Nate quickly pulls up her GPS location on her phone and the most recent pins. When I look at the screen of the system I installed, I see the pin of her cell phone moving in the opposite direction of the gym. My instincts have me on high alert and I know something is wrong. Very wrong.

Brie has officially moved into my house. Our house. It has been two weeks since the night at the club and I have made sure to pay her handsomely for her time at Equinox with me as her VIP.

Today was her last day and we were set to congratulate her. *Fuck.* Something is very wrong. I can feel it

"Don't lose her, Nate. Something doesn't feel right. She

told me she would come straight over. Call Giselle and ask her when was the last time she heard from Brie."

"You got it, brother."

I look outside the office and scan the gym for Nick and Jake. "Yo, Jake. Yo, Nick," I call out, waving them over.

They run up like they have fire on their asses at the sound of my voice.

"What's up?" Nick says.

"Something is wrong with Brie. She isn't picking up." I look at Nate when he hangs up with Giselle and he shakes his head. The fear begins to build in the pit of my stomach. They took her. I know it. "Those motherfuckers took her."

Nate bunches his hands in tight fists and my nostrils flare. "Nate, stay here with Giselle and send me updates on Briana's phone. She took the jeep this morning. Where is it?"

Nate's fingers type fast, entering the code for the white jeep and the map pinpoints it as being parked at the center. Her phone is moving but her car is still there. Fuck.

I glance at Jake and Nick. "You down? I need to get my future wife from some assholes who took her." I lower my voice. "You know the end result."

They both nod in understanding and I rake my hands through my hair. My cell phone vibrates and I answer placing the phone on speaker.

Ethan's voice filters through my ears, "I know I said I would let you handle this but I'm in a black SUV parked outside of your gym. Let's go. We don't have much time."

I hang up and look at the guys. Carter is out front waiting. I don't have time to kick his ass, but I need to get Briana before they hurt or worse.

I slide in the passenger side, Jake, Nick, and Brian slide into the back of the armored blacked-out Escalade.

"Damn, you really are with the Mafia," Brian says as the car lunges forward, peeling out of the parking lot.

Ethan is driving and hands me the coordinates of where

Daniel and Ben are taking her. "They are on their way with her to a drug house they have outside of Nevada. I have a guy at a rendezvous point right outside waiting for us to arrive."

"Good," I tell him, placing my black hoodie over my bullet proof vest and adjust the baklava on my face.

I check the scope and round the chamber of my Glock and place it in its holster. The guys in the back do the same as Ethan floors the SUV leaving dirt in its wake.

"Jake, give me the bag."

He hands it over to me and takes out my cutting knives and what I call my filet-o-fish knife. For those pesky little jobs that require a little extra carnage.

"Are we off the grid?" I ask Ethan. It means the other leaders are not involved and don't know what we are doing.

"My father knows. You have nothing to worry about. He says you have full support. She will soon be your wife and she is considered your immediate family. Castellanos is aware."

I nod. "Thank you. I appreciate you keeping your word. I still want to break your face though."

He scoffs. "I think your fiancé broke more than my face the last time she saw me."

"Good. I'm glad she came to her senses. Now, let's go get my girl."

After an hour, we pull up to the drug house and it is a dusty shit hole.

I turn my head to Nick. "Get me the blanket and blind-fold," I tell him.

Ethan looks at me with a confused expression as to why I would need a blindfold.

"It's for her. I don't want her to see. It is something I have been working on with her. She doesn't need to see this shit," I tell him.

He nods and speaks to a microphone in his hand. "They are in position." He turns to me. " On your move. You call the shots, Cyprus."

I nod. "One, two, three." The doors open and I move with lethal precision toward the back. Nick follows behind me.

When I reach the back window, I can see two figures, but I don't see Briana. I motion Nick to breach the back door. Bam! I bust the door down with my gun raised and aimed at whoever jumps out. Both Daniel and Ben have their heads turned away. They thought the sound was coming from the front door instead of the back. Placing the barrel of the gun against Daniel's head, I say with clenched teeth. "Where is she?"

"I-i-in the back room," he stammers.

Pushing the gun into his skull, I see Nick has Ben in a similar position. "Walk, and if you make a move, I'll blow your fucking head off. Take me to her and so help me God if you have so much as laid a finger on her. I will kill you."

They're already dead in my book but I'm not going to tell them that just yet. I'll keep it to myself a little while longer. He walks me to the back. The smell of burnt meth makes me want to gag. I walk slowly, the floorboards groan. The black-stained walls reminds me of the little house I grew up in I called the pit of hell.

We reach an old wood door and I brace myself when he opens it. She is tied to the bed naked and the rage inside of me boils before erupting.

"Who are you?" she asks, sobbing. "Please, help me," she pleads, her hands are tied together and trembling. She has red marks and handprints on her delicate skin. Then, I remember she can't see me with the mask on. "It's me, baby. I'm here."

Her face is red and her lips are already chapped.

"Oh, thank God. Jaden, please get me out of here. I'll do anything."

My heart breaks listening to her pleading for my help. I promise to love her and protect her and never let her out of my sight again. I hit the fucker on the head with the gun and he passes out from the blow. My hand reaches out and I untie her. She wraps her arms around herself and I grab the blindfold.

"You trust me?" I ask her.

She nods and I inspect her body. "Did they?"

She knows I'm asking her if they violated her, but to my relief, she shakes her head. "No, they pulled my hair and touched me, but they were waiting until dark to rape me and then ransom for money."

"I need you to put this on, baby, because I'm going to do things and I don't want you to see. You think you can place this over your eyes? I promise I am not going to leave you here and no one is ever going to touch you again," I whisper, kissing her on her temple.

"O-okay. I trust you, Jaden, but please get me the fuck out of here," she says in a shaky voice. "I can't be here."

"I know, baby, but I need to take care of these assholes."

I peek my head out because I don't have much time before Daniel wakes up.

"Blanket."

Nick throws it over and I wrap Briana in it, covering her exposed body. She is shivering.

I Place Briana by the exit, her body and eyes covered. Nick and me get to work.

After twenty minutes, Daniel and Ben look down and scream at the top of their lungs. Nick helped me tie them up by their hands and feet, with them spread wide.

"Oh my fucking Christ." Daniel sobs, screaming.

"I wouldn't move if I were you," I warn. "Everything might just… fall out."

"Oh fuck, it hurts," Ben screams in agony. "You mother-fucker." His eyes roll back. He is close to death, but not yet.

I cut both their stomachs open with their intestines hanging out and sliced their cocks off so they'd bleed out slowly.

"You're fucking crazy and sick," Daniel yells on agony. He

grunts and blood is oozing out of his mouth, his life hanging by a thread.

Nick is kneeling, watching, not feeling an inch of remorse for these sick bastards.

"I'm sick?" I mock. "How about the shit you did to my girl? You raped and beat her. An innocent girl. She has nightmares that haunt her."

"It's because she loved our cock when we would take turns, you pathetic piece of shit."

I suck my teeth, getting pissed off at how he talks about what they did to Briana. I grab my filet knife and cut every finger off and stuff a rag into their mouths, taking turns like in the movie *SAW*, slicing their skin and finally shoving a knife in each of their rectums so they can feel the burn. The memory of watching Briana screaming in her sleep that it burned. Every pain, emotion, and torture Briana has suffered was inflicted all at once on these men before ultimately meeting their maker.

I'm sitting in the back with Briana in my lap. My arms are wrapped around her as Ethan drives us to the gym.

"I want to go home. Take me home, please," she says against my chest.

Ethan looks at me through the rearview mirror. He sent a cleanup crew to handle the mess I made, and I sent someone to get her jeep from the center.

"I miss my white bed and the sound of the water from the waterfall in the pool," she says between sobs. "I want to take a shower and need you to scrub their hands off my skin." She sobs with fresh tears. She turns to Nick and says, "Thank you for the headphones."

Thank God Nick was smart enough to place headphones over her ears so she wouldn't listen. She is calling my home, her home. Because, it is our home. She loves the sound of the water hitting the pool. She is seeking peace.

"Anytime, Dr. J," he says.

More like Dr. C for Cyprus if I have anything to do with it.

Epilogue

It has been two months since the incident and Jaden has been patient with me. He took me to meet with a really well-known therapist that told him about BDSM and bondage as a way of therapy for both of us.

It has helped tremendously with trust and intimacy. Jaden takes things slow and listens to how I'm feeling. He tells me he loves me all the time and never forgets my white lilies every morning.

"Everything smells funny, and I hate the smell of eggs," Giselle says, complaining.

I laugh. "I actually like the taste of eggs but only scrambled, if they are fried, I'll upchuck them."

Giselle and I both found out we are pregnant. Nate and Jaden didn't look surprised, so we concluded they planned it. Makes sense considering the constant sex.

I'm dealing with what happened slowly but finding out we are expanding our family has helped. We decided to get married in a civil ceremony. We both wanted a wedding but none of us have parents or any extended family members except the guys at the gym. I'm proud to be Mrs. Cyprus and Giselle is Mrs. Phoenix.

Jaden has postponed his fight until after the baby is born and I am happy with his decision to follow the therapy outlined by myself and another doctor that taught me every-thing I know when attending school.

"Are you ready for your surprise, Dr. Cyprus?"

"Yes, Mr. Cyprus. Where are you taking us?"

"It is a surprise."

My stomach gets butterflies, and I am not sure if it's from excitement or the fact that I have a token of our love growing inside of me.

"Let's go, wife," Nate says to Giselle. She smiles at him with pure adoration.

We drive for four hours into California. I look out the window of the Range Rover in confusion when we reach the docks.

"Why are we here?"

"You'll see," Jaden says as he opens the door to the back seat of the Rover. "Close your eyes and don't open them until I tell you."

"Okay," I say with a smile. "I trust you."

He walks behind me and guides me forward carefully. "Ready?"

"Yes," I say, anticipating one of Jaden's surprises.

"Okay. Open your eyes."

My eyes slowly open and I gasp in surprise.

"Surprise! Happy birthday!"

Everyone from the gym, including Nate and Giselle, are on top of a white boat with pink Barbie accents. Birthday signs are everywhere, and the main sign reads "Welcome to Briana's Birthday Party!"

"Barbie cannot be complete without her yacht. Except this one is not a toy," Jaden says.

My eyes are wide with shock. "I hope this is rented."

"Umm-no. I actually bought you a white yacht and named it Briana. The light at night glows under the yacht and is hot pink but I'll deal with it. It changes colors," he says with a playful smirk.

We board the yacht, a crew greets me and so do our friends from the gym, including Zavier, Jaden, and Nate's newest fighter on their team.

"There is one more surprise I wanted to show you," he says once I'm aboard.

"Jaden, this is amazing. My very own birthday party on a yacht you purchased for me. I am the luckiest woman alive. I couldn't ask for more. I love you more than anything."

He smiles and gives me a peck on the lips and rubs my still flat stomach. "Trust me, this surprise is very different and it is for both you and Giselle."

"Okay."

Giselle looks at me confused and stands next to me when a short woman in her late fifties walks toward us with two children flanked on each side.

"Hi, my name is Cynthia Garland and both of your husbands would like to introduce you both to Caroline and Michael."

"Hi Caroline and Michael. How old are you?" I ask with a smile.

"Hi, you both are very pretty. My name is Caroline and I'm eight years old and this is Michael. He is ten and we need a new mommy and daddy. Ms. Cynthia said you would be my new mommy."

My eyes fill with tears, but I hold them back, not wanting to scare the children. My gaze turns to Giselle and her eyes are glassy, trying to hold back her tears.

My gaze finds Jaden's and he nods toward them, and my heart constricts. The little boy speaks up and my heart breaks when he says, "I come from this ugly place that I call the bad house."

I nod. "I know, baby, I came from a bad house too, and so did your daddy, but your new mommy Giselle is a beautiful ballerina and has a beautiful house that is warm and full of love." My hand reaches out to Caroline. "I would be honored to be your new mommy."

Caroline runs into my arms and Jaden is there to wipe my tears as I ask Caroline, "Do you like Barbies, sweetheart? Because your new daddy bought me a bunch of new dolls."

She jumps up and down and I laugh. "I love Barbies, but I've never really had one of my own," she says in her sweet little voice.

I give her a hug and so does Jaden. We all come together and hug the kids as a family.

When we are alone in the cabin of the yacht with the smell of lilies mixed with new carpet and fresh paint, Jaden hugs me after making sure the kids are comfortable in the spare room. We let the social worker stay to make sure they were comfortable and let her know that we were adopting the children. Jaden and I will adopt Caroline and Nate and Giselle agreed to adopt Michael.

"I love you with all my heart, Jaden. Thank you for making me so happy. Our family is growing."

He caresses my face and says, "I'm the happiest when I'm with you. I'm honored you agreed to my wife and the mother to our children. I love you and I'm sorry for everything I have done that hurt you or caused you pain, but I promise to make it up to you every day."

"I love you, Jaden."

The End.

Acknowledgements

I want to thank my readers who loved Briana and Giselle. I hope you like the dark edition in paperback. I think it is one of my favorites.

I feel books have a life of their own. They change and evolve. I don't think there is a book I have written that doesn't go through a process to make it better. A better cover. A bonus scene. A special edition. If you loved one of them. Hit me up and tell me. I listen. Even if it sucks.

I also want to thank everyone who has supported me through this journey. There are so many things that go into writing a book. I also want to thank my beta readers, editors and all the authors out there have given me insight.

—CR

Carmen Rosales is an author who writes Steamy, Latinx, and Dark Romance. She also writes erotic horror under Delilah Croww.

She loves spending time with her family. When she is not writing, she is reading. She is an Army veteran and is currently completing her Doctorate Degree in Business and has the love and support of her husband and five children. She loves to see a review and interact with her readers.

Join her VIP list and Newsletter- www.carmenrosales.com

Follow her on Social Media and stay up to date with her new releases: